Neptune's Fury

Clay Warrior Stories
Book #10

J. Clifton Slater

Neptune's Fury is a work of fiction. Any resemblance to persons living or dead is purely coincidental. I am not a historian, although I do extensive research. For those who have studied the classical era and those with exceptional knowledge of the times, I apologize in advance for any errors.

The large events in this tale are from history but, the dialogue and action sequences are my inventions. Some of the elements in the story are from reverse engineering techniques and procedures. No matter how many sources I consult, history always has holes between events. Hopefully, you'll see the logic in my methods of filling in the blanks.

I need to thank Hollis Jones who kept the story on track and grammatically correct with her red pen. Without her, the project would have wandered far from my plan. And gratitude to my hard-core readers who are Legion. I'm not sure if it's because you are many or, are spiritual descendants from an ancient Roman army. If so, Salute!

J. Clifton Slater
Email: GalacticCouncilRealm@gmail.com
Website: www.JCliftonSlater.com

Neptune's Fury

Act 1

The abatement of major hostilities in the Etruscan region to the north allowed the Roman Senate to focus on war with the Qart Hadasht Empire. On land, the Legions had trapped a superior force in Agrigento. Plus, even though outnumbered in some cases, the Legionaries delivered victory in every skirmish and clash with the Empire's mercenaries. As a result, cities on Sicilia were signing treaties with Rome. While the heavy infantry dominated land warfare, off the coast was a different story.

The vast Carthaginian Navy ruled the Mediterranean Sea, and the Ionian, Adriatic, and Tyrrhenian Seas that touched the Republic's shoreline. If sufficiently motivated, the Empire could isolate segments of the peninsula and cut the Roman's trade by blockading the Republic's sea lanes.

Fear of losing the shipping routes that connected regions of the Republic brought heated debates. Isolationist, fiscal conservatives, expansionists, and senators seeking peace or war stood and argued their points. One fact became apparent from the discussions. They needed more warships. While Rome could lease transports from maritime neighbors, persuading another country to charter warships to go against the Carthaginians was another matter.

'Destitutus ventis, remos adhibe' translates from Latin to 'If the wind does not serve, take to the oars.' One interpretation of the saying - if other factors do not support you, count on yourself.

To counter the threat of the Qart Hadasht Empire, the Roman Republic needed to count on themselves and build a navy. In order to keep Rome's new warships from being used as an excuse to attack, the senate required a stealth shipyard far from the prying eyes of Empire spies.

Although the Etruscan region was at a stalemate, the area wasn't safe from bandits or friendly to Latians. Thus, it was totally unsuitable for secretly building warships. The Umbria mountain people in the adjacent region, however, were capable of supplying the manpower and the raw materials. If they could be convinced to help.

Welcome to 261 B.C.

Chapter 1 - Been to Volsinii Lately

The stream gurgled over pebbles creating a rhythmic sound. Distorting the musical notes, the horse sucked up water and the mule snorted while munching on the tender shoots growing next to the creek. Alerio Sisera stretched and gazed up through the limbs. A few stars and Luna's glow shone between the high branches. Closing his eyes, he willed his body to relax in hopes of going back to sleep.

Out of tune with the natural sounds, a stick snapped.

The Legion officer rolled from under his blanket, leaving it with an undisturbed appearance. Continuing to roll, he moved beyond the circle of firelight and came up on a knee. While his gladii, shield, and matching swords were across the campsite, he wasn't unarmed. From his lower back, he pulled a dagger and from his hip, a Legion pugio. Both double edged and razor sharp their points already tracking three shapes moving through the moonlit forest.

Alerio sunk deeper into the shadows. When he was well outside the flickering light he rose and vanished into the dark.

***

In any attack, commitment was proven by forward momentum. By their approach, Alerio could tell the three bodies were committed. They applied solid tactics, as well. Two split wide and the third covered their approach by targeting the lane to his bedroll with a notched arrow. Soft footed and intense, the two barbarians closed in on the blanket.

Alerio eased forward. Over the archer's left shoulder, he saw the two, who appeared to be Etruscan tribesmen, stab his blankets. For as long as he'd carried the bedroll, it hadn't been damaged until this morning. And for what? A few packs, a mount, and a mule. Then he realized the spears weren't simply damaging his bedroll. They were meant to kill. Flushed with indignity, Alerio stepped forward and cocked his right leg.

He drove his foot into the side of the bowman's left knee. The joint snapped and the man collapsed, falling to the side. As he crumpled, Alerio hammered the tribesman's right ear with the pommel of his Legion pugio. During the action, the bow string snapped and the arrow released.

Figuring to dispatch one of the two attackers by surprise, he planned to then swing around and take the last one from the side. Alerio hurled the archer and sprinted at the pair of robbers. He was two steps towards the men when he noted the tribesman on the left had folded up around an arrow in his thigh. The barbarian fell.

3

His first target out of the fight, Alerio went for the other. He planted his right foot, crossed and stepped out with the left leg to change direction. But his right foot skated on the dried leaves. Legion officer, Alerio Sisera, fell face first onto the ground.

***

The narrow head of the tribal spear arched over the tribesman's shoulder as he twisted his torso around. At the bottom of the rainbow shaped path, the traveler he intended to rob sprawled, waiting to finally die.

"Vofionus, ancient spear wielder," prayed the barbarian to his God, driving the tip of the Etruscan spear at the undefended back. "guide my weapon through the Latian's heart."

"Quirinus, God of conflict and the spear," Alerio prayed to his Latian God. "stay the steel and spare my flesh."

He had been taught while growing up, elicit the Gods' favor but help them help you by moving your lazy cūlus. Before the plea to the Latian deity ended, Alerio rolled and the spearhead sank into the depression left by Alerio's body. Slamming an arm into the soil, Legion officer Sisera used his forearm to drag his legs under his hips. From the crouch, he sprang at the barbarian.

One blade swiped left, gouged into the spear as it sank into the wooden shaft. Alerio brought the other knife across and slashed the shoulder muscle of the tribesman. That much damage deadened the arm and forced the left hand to release the spear. Holding it in his right, the barbarian stumbled back while attempting to bring the spear tip to bear on the traveler. But the end of the shaft was under the control of the pugio's blade.

"You Etruscans are just as stupid as the last time we fought," Alerio announced. He stabbed out with the Ally of the Golden Valley dagger.

The razor-sharp double-edged blade jerked forward and as the tip reached the Etruscan's neck, Alerio yanked it to the side. A thin line, dripping red, appeared on the man's throat. Before he could cup the wound with a hand, Alerio called on Apollo.

"I'm not sure why? I should simply kill him. But give me the strength from your sport, god of boxing."

Alerio dropped the Legion knife and delivered a powerful uppercut. It lifted the tribesman off his feet and drove him back. The Etruscan bandit ended up peacefully, almost as if sleeping, on the leaves.

"Great. You sleep and I'm up," Alerio complained. After retrieving the pugio, he glanced up and studied the dark sky. Then commented. "Luna has retired and missed my devastating punch."

While he tied and gagged the three bandits, Centurion Sisera chastised himself. This situation would be easier if he just ended their miserable lives and sent a squad from the fort at Orte to retrieve the bodies. But they were down and out and, he was mostly finished binding them.

***

The Legion Private blinked, trying to see better in the light of early dawn. On the road coming from the south, three men staggered into view. As they got closer, he could see two leaning on the middle man for support. It seemed as if they would have sat down but for the mule. Connecting the men with the animal was a rope. Behind

5

the mule a mounted man with a switch snapped the branch at the mule whenever it slowed.

"Sergeant of the Guard," the Legionary cried out. "Main gate."

His call was picked up by the other men on guard duty. Soon, an Optio, Tesserarius, and four armored and shield bearing Legionaries jogged from Fort Orte.

"Report," the Sergeant demanded.

The duty sentry lifted an arm and pointed at the strange caravan.

"Optio. I bet it's a good story," the guard suggested. "but I wouldn't want to unpack that for our Centurion."

The infantrymen peered into the gloom and chuckled.

"Knock it off," the Corporal ordered.

The five Legionaries were silent as the procession worked its way up the road.

***

Under directions from their Sergeant, the infantrymen moved forward and herded the three wounded men off to the side.

"Centurion Alerio Sisera," Alerio reported while slipping off his mount.

"And who are your companions, sir?" the Optio inquired.

"I have no idea. Except my bedroll has two spear holes. It didn't have them before I went to sleep last night," Alerio stated. Then he leaned towards the three men and said. "I'm assuming they are brave, heroic Etruscan tribesmen from Volsinii, out for a moonlit lover's stroll."

The description sent the three captives into a rage. Between their injuries, tied hands, and gags, it wasn't a very dramatic outburst. Even so, to keep them calm, the Legionaries poked the trio with the butt ends of their javelins.

"Have you been to Volsinii, Centurion?" the Sergeant inquired.

"I was with Gurges Legion when the General fell," Alerio told him.

"I heard that was rough," the Optio commented before adding. "The plateau has been deserted since General Flaccus leveled the city and sold the barbarian residents. Lately, the Senate has allowed Etruscan settlers to begin rebuilding. But the name has been changed to Orvieto."

"What does that have to do with me, Optio?" questioned Alerio.

"I assumed you were heading for Orvieto, sir."

"No. I have orders to report to Stifone," Alerio informed the NCO. Then he bent at the waist in the direction of the bandits and asked. "Can you take these worshipers of Mendacius off my hands?"

Based on their situation, considering the trio of Etruscans as being followers of the God of cunning, deception, and treachery was an obvious jest. All five Legionaries laughed and the Corporal let his infantrymen enjoy the moment.

Chapter 2 - An Unfortunate Tribunal

"Centurion Sisera, it would have been easier if you had executed them," Centurion Baccharis explained. "I

7

could have sent a squad and a wagon to collect the bodies."

Alerio sat across the desk from Fort Orte's Senior Centurion. The unembellished office held few pieces of furniture or decorative objects. Several personal awards, some captured swords, and two symbols identifying the fortification as being part of the Northern Legion completed the décor.

"I almost did," Alerio replied. "But they were down and, well, I've had problems with missing Princes before. Lacking knowledge about your situation here, I opted for mercy."

"I won't be that generous. The three brigands will enjoy their last sunset mounted on oak," the senior officer informed Alerio. "Come, we'll breakfast together and you can tell me about Sicilia."

"There's not much to say about a siege," Alerio admitted.

Centurions Baccharis and Sisera stepped out of the office and began strolling while they talked. Ten steps down the colonnade, the duty Optio intercepted them.

"Sir. The prisoners," stammered the Sergeant.

"What about them?" Baccharis urged. "Come on Optio, out with it."

"Sir, they aren't Etruscan," the NCO informed the officer. "They're Umbrian."

"Oh merda, I am abandoned by Sors," Baccharis exclaimed. "First, I get posted at the end of the civilized world just as the majority of the fighting ends. Rather than battle, I'm charged with overseeing a road and chasing bandits. Now I have to deal with the Umbria. If it weren't for bad luck, I wouldn't have any of the God's blessing."

"What's the problem?" Alerio inquired.

"In the mountains north of Orvieto are hostiles," Baccharis replied. "Etruscan tribes begging for a visit from my heavy infantry. Helping them join their ancestors is something I'm trained for. But the Umbrians are a favorite of the Senate. That's not a guess. Just a few weeks ago, a Tribune stopped here on his way to Stifone."

Relief flooded Alerio. Having a staff officer in Stifone meant he was joining a garrison. Or, maybe a diplomatic mission based on the Senior Centurion's observation.

"Why are the prisoners unlucky for you?" Alerio questioned.

"Umbria is close to joining with the Republic," the senior officer answered. "Meaning your attackers are almost citizens. Tribesmen I can crucify. Citizens I can put on trial. But your trio of clowns are somewhere in between. That makes them a diplomatic crisis heading right for my neck. Now, I wish you had killed them."

"What are you going to do?"

"Treat their wounds and give them a military tribunal," Baccharis described. "If they come from prominent families, I'll order a few less lashes from the whip. Just enough to scare them, mind you. Afterward, I have no choice but to release the three pieces of cow dung. I'm sorry it's not justice for you, Centurion Sisera."

"I've been assaulted and I've been hungry," Alerio observed. "One thing I've learned, you can't eat revenge. You mentioned something about feeding me?"

"Optio. Take the prisoners to medical and inform the doctor I expect the very best care for them," Baccharis instructed. Then he turned to Alerio. "A man can work up a powerful thirst dispensing compassion and leniency. Come on, let's go find vino and food."

The two infantry officers continued their stroll down the colonnade. But they didn't talk. Both were too busy thinking.

***

Senior Centurion Baccharis occupied the head of a long table in the large meeting room. The three Umbrians sat along one side. Behind them three Legionaries rested against the wall holding javelins in one hand and supporting infantry shields with the other.

"I encourage you to attack me," the senior officer urged.

Two of the tribesmen glanced over their shoulders at the armored Legionaries. Indoors, even in a large room, the mass of the shields and armored bodies gave the infantrymen and their war gear a dominating presence. With eyes wide open, the two shifted to face the Legion officer.

On the opposite side of the table, Alerio understood Baccharis' desire to kill the three if given provocation. He also acknowledged the wisdom of the three Umbrians for not challenging the Centurion.

The third hadn't taken his eyes off of Baccharis.

"Why are we here?" the Umbrian demanded.

"Name?" Baccharis asked.

"I am Federici Rustia, third son of the Rustia family," he replied. "Member of the Umbria Council where my uncle is chairman. I ask you again, Senior Centurion, why are we here?"

Baccharis blinked and his hands formed fists. The use of his rank and the defiant attitude put the Legion officer on notice that the Umbrian knew his situation; probably better than the Senior Centurion.

"Before dawn this morning, you and your two renegade friends attacked this man's campsite."

"I deny the charge. Whose word will you take? A son of Rustia or an impoverished merchant or is he a day laborer?"

"That's an interesting observation," Baccharis suggested. "How did you come to that conclusion?"

Alerio hadn't changed his travel clothing. The washed-out woolens could very well belong to a down-on-his-luck mechanic or workman. Anyone familiar with the Legion would recognize the well-tended hobnailed boots, the pugio on his hip, the short haircut, and the battle scars as being marks of a Legionary. Apparently, the Umbrian didn't.

"A successful tradesman has his goods in wagons and is accompanied by guards," Federici Rustia stated. "This poor wretch has only a mule for his minimal load of merchandise or the tools of his trade. Come to think of it, the horse he was riding is probably stolen."

Alerio stiffened and began to raise to his feet. The infantry officer was about to apply his trade to the neck of the Umbrian but, Baccharis signaled for him to remain seated. When a Senior Centurion curtly motioned instructions, a smart junior officer followed directions.

"Young Master Rustia have your wounds and those of your companions been treated?" Baccharis inquired.

11

"My throat is minimal," Federici replied while touching the fresh scab. "However, Cutu Baldoni has serious damage to his knee and ear. And Vulca Luciena has suffered an arrow through his thigh."

"Craftsman Sisera, do you possess a bow?" the Senior Centurion questioned.

"I own neither a bow nor arrows," Alerio assured him while ignoring the title.

"If citizen Sisera doesn't have a bow, who shot Vulca Luciena?" Baccharis asked.

"I did," Cutu Baldoni volunteered.

A silence fell over the Umbrians at the table. It lasted until Baccharis leaned against the backrest of his chair and offered.

"Then what we have here is a case of mistaken identity," the senior officer remarked. "I find insufficient evidence of assault against Sisera. And, by his own admission, we know who launched the arrow injuring Vulca. This tribunal is terminated."

Baccharis stood and, followed by the guards, left the room. Before Alerio could challenge Federici, a Sergeant marched in and waved for Alerio to join him. They left the Umbrians alone in the conference room.

"Where are we going, Optio?" Alerio inquired when they started down the colonnade.

"The administration office, sir."

***

A junior Centurion and an Optio staffed desks but neither looked up as the duty NCO guided Alerio to a back room. Inside, they found the Senior Centurion.

12

"That will be all Sergeant," Baccharis informed the NCO. Then he handed a mug of vino to Alerio and suggested. "I suppose you have questions?"

"What happened? I thought you were going to frighten them. It appeared you were more afraid of Federici Rustia?"

"Not him. His uncle. And I did you a favor," Baccharis offered.

Alerio raised his eyebrows and shrugged his shoulders.

"Me, a favor?"

"The unfortunate tribunal, if taken to the planned end, would have made us enemies of the Rustia clan," Baccharis explained. "I have the protection of four Centuries of infantry and my patron in the Senate is a good man. You, on the other hand, are going to Stifone in Umbria territory without protection. It's not a major stronghold so chances are you'll never see Federici Rustia or his idiot companions again. Even so, it's better if they don't have a vendetta against you."

"But there's a Tribune and his staff there," Alerio commented. Then it struck him what the Senior Centurion said about not having protection. "How big a presence does the Legion have in Stifone?"

"Other than the staff officer? An Optio and a Tesserarius are with him," Baccharis answered. "No heavy infantry, Velites, or Legion cavalry. That's why I was worried you'd catch a blade in the back if I pressed charges against the Umbrians."

"Why am I assigned to Stifone?"

"I don't know what the staff Tribunes has in mind," Baccharis replied. "But I do know, you'll be long gone before my doctor releases the wounded Umbrians."

"I appreciate that Senior Centurion," Alerio said honestly. "When do I leave?"

"There's a river patrol boat manned and ready at the dock. They'll land you and your supplies down river on the Nera side. Wait there, one of my scouts will swim your horse and mule over."

"Thank you," Alerio said with a salute.

Senior Centurion Baccharis started to explain that infantry officers don't salute each other. Then he realized it was an expression of gratitude. He returned the salute and walked out of the door.

Chapter 3 - You Are Welcome to It

The ground was level east of the Tiber and along the bank of the Nera River. At about three miles, the land began to elevate and, although not steep, the hills became higher and the valleys narrower. After another night under the stars, Alerio hiked into the hills above the river. Keeping the ribbon of water generally to his left, the Legion officer trekked further into the foothills.

From a peak two valleys away, he caught a glimpse of what he assumed to be the village of Stifone. Stone roofs stood between the limbs of tall trees and a background of high ridges seemed to cradle the building tops.

Being a trained infantryman, Alerio studied the ground and trails. If the duty in Stifone involved chasing rebels or bandits, this was going to be a mean assignment: physically and mentally demanding on him and his Legionaries. Except, he had no infantrymen. Hopefully, the Tribune at Stifone would have answers and a description of his responsibilities.

Late the next day, the path dropped steeply to the river's edge before drifting right and following the Nera River. He led the animals out of the hills and onto a sand bar. The ground beside the river was a solid mix of dirt, sand, and gravel. It crunched under foot and hoof but provided solid footing.

Stifone sat on the hills where the Nera twisted to the northeast. From the sand bar, Alerio noted the village was nothing more than a collection of buildings on four terraces. The upper ones reached into the tree tops. These were the structures he saw from the summit of the adjacent hills.

***

Alerio tied the pack animal and his mount to a tree and started up a path towards a leather goods shop. The craftsman, who worked hide, dealt with everyone. And the proprietor should know where the Legion detachment was quartered.

On the second terrace, a door slammed open, two men burst through the frame. The second one slammed the door closed behind him.

"Then why are we here?" shouted one in a Greek accent.

"Politics. Everywhere I go. It's someone wants and, another person doesn't want," the second man, a Latian, complained.

Alerio smiled. It seemed there were two unhappy people in this peaceful mountain village. He continued on the path when the Latian man added.

"If the Tribune doesn't believe, why waste our days?"

At the mention of a Legion staff officer, Alerio raised his arm and called up to the men.

"Excuse me," he shouted. "Where can I find the Tribune?"

"If Nemesis hasn't visited yet, you'll find his exalted self in the building," the Greek replied while jerking a thumb over his shoulder.

Three things were revealed in the answer. Obviously, the staff officer was egotistical and the Greek expected the Goddess who punishes arrogance to visit the Tribune. Then, based on his straight speech and tone, the Greek was a freeman doing business with the Legion. Lastly, the pair didn't stop to offer additional help as if they wanted to get as far away from the staff officer as possible. Alerio tried not to prejudge the Tribune but, the observations wouldn't leave him.

With trepidation, Alerio changed course and mounted a stone staircase. In most Legion detachments, there were layers of command. A Private could use a Tesserarius as a shield against a crazy Optio or a Centurion could depend on a Senior Centurion to deflect anger from a Tribune. In Stifone, Alerio was a junior infantry officer assigned to a Tribune. No matter the personality of the staff officer, Centurion Sisera was the next stop for all issues.

He opened the door to the Legion offices.

***

16

Alerio walked over the threshold and his mouth fell open. In the front room of the building, he found a Sergeant and a Corporal kneeling on the floor over a game of chance with mugs of vino at their elbows. Three other men, probably locals, leaned in examining the fall of a set of dice.

"I am sure there is an explanation," Alerio barked. It wasn't that he had a problem with gambling. His issue was turning a Legion office into a gaming hall. "But I can't imagine what would excuse this behavior."

The room was mostly bare of furniture except for two desks and four chairs flanking a rear door. Beside each desk was a flag of the Republic and a unit symbol identifying the space as a Legion administration office. It may be in a small village at the base of the mountains in Umbria territory and only a detachment but, the Legion NCOs were subject to discipline and order.

Continuing, Alerio added, "It's a good thing I found you before the Tribune discovered this."

The Optio glanced up, noted the rough workman's clothing, and dismissed the stranger. He failed to notice the Legion boots, dagger, and battle scars.

"You want to see Subausterus, he's in the back," the Sergeant remarked.

Big mistake - NCOs ignored infantry officers at their own peril. In three quick steps, Alerio moved from the doorway to the Optio's undefended side.

"We seem to have gotten off on the wrong foot. Here's the right one," Alerio growled as he planted the flat of the hobnailed boot in the Sergeant's ribs and shoved. The push rolled the Optio across the room. "I am

17

Centurion Alerio Sisera and when I talk, I expect attention."

"What is he going on about?" one of the locals protested. "Can we get on with the game?"

Alerio knotted his eyebrows and stared down at the NCOs.

"The game is over. Get out," the Corporal announced. He jumped to his feet, squared his shoulders, and introduced himself. "Tesserarius Ludovicus Humi, sir."

"And who is that, Corporal Humi?" Alerio inquired by jerking his chin in the Sergeant's direction.

"Optio Adamo Florian. We are the NCOs for the Stifone detachment."

"Is that correct Sergeant?"

Optio Florian hopped up and moved to stand beside Humi.

"Yes, sir. We are here to show the flag, I guess."

"Does that include fleecing the locals out of their wages?"

"No sir. It's just we don't have anything else to do and Tribune Subausterus never comes in here before his morning rub down."

"And when he does, what are his orders?" Alerio inquired. Then he suggested. "Good NCOs anticipate needs and get ahead of the day's duties. Shouldn't you?"

"Centurion Sisera. We would gladly anticipate any orders," Adamo Florian remarked. "But, sir, there are never orders."

"Just us standing around witnessing the Tribune argue with Masters Pous and Monilis," the Corporal commented.

18

"Who are they?"

"The engineer and the builder," Optio Florian offered. "They just left. You might have passed them on your way here."

When the infantry officer didn't respond, the Corporal questioned.

"Orders, sir," Tesserarius Humi inquired.

"Clean this place up," Alerio instructed as he walked to the rear door. "And return the coins to the Umbrians."

Alerio felt as if he had half a story. With a furious builder and equally angry engineer on his mind, Centurion Sisera marched to the doorway. Pushing it open, he hoped to get the rest of the story from the Tribune.

***

He was reclining on one of a pair of sofas. With a platter of food balanced on his knee, the man nibbled on a sliver of meat held between two fingers. On a table beside him sat a porcelain cup of wine. Three servants stood along a wall ready to refill the cup or the platter. The scene could have been transported directly from a villa's sitting room in the Capital.

"Tribune Subausterus. Centurion Alerio Sisera, reporting in," Alerio announced.

"You are who?" the Tribune inquired in a sluggish and bored manner.

"I am a Centurion," Alerio replied. "My name is Sisera."

"I got that part," Subausterus declared. Almost as if he just woke up, the Tribune came alert and demanded. "The reporting in part, enlighten me."

19

"I have been assigned to Stifone. I assumed, I should report to you," Alerio explained.

"You are a Legion officer?" the Tribune whispered.

"I am."

"Teucer. We are going home," Subausterus declared. One of the servants stepped to the center of the room and bowed. "Fix Centurion Sisera a platter and go pack. We leave at dawn."

Seeing Alerio standing at attention in the doorway, Tribune Subausterus waved him to the other couch.

"What are we doing here, Tribune?" Alerio asked. He sat and a platter of meat and cheese was shoved into his hands. "I mean, no one seems to even know we're here."

"We're one of several," Subausterus said before closing his eyes. Then he rambled. "I have horses at my villa. Beautiful animals, strong, sleek and fast. I miss them. As well as my wife."

The Tribune fell silent and Alerio attempted to get a handle on the situation.

"One of several what?" he questioned.

"Sites. This one is so obviously unacceptable," Subausterus stated as if Alerio had knowledge of the topic. "I'll happily leave it to you. The Senate will eventually want a report. If you need help, come see me in the Capital. Or at my summer villa and I'll have Teucer scribe it for us."

"A report on what? Unacceptable for what?" Alerio begged. "I don't know what you are talking about."

"And neither does the Senate," Subausterus offered while bursting out laughing. "Now, if you'll excuse me, I must go and supervise the packing. Best of luck."

20

Before Alerio could place the platter on the table, the Tribune jumped to his feet and practically ran to a set of steps in the rear of the room. He stopped three risers up, turned and bent down to look back into the room.

"The mad idea is all yours, Centurion Sisera," Subausterus declared. "And you are welcome to it."

As he vanished up the steps, Alerio stood and strolled to the exit. He didn't get a complete answer from the Tribune. But he did get enough information to let him know he needed to chase down the builder and the engineer. Hopefully, the revelation would come from them.

Chapter 4 - Isn't that great

Hasty words with Optio Florian and Tesserarius Humi sent the Corporal to tend to his animals and gave Alerio a direction. Outside the doorway, he hooked a left and located the stairs to the next terrace. At the top, Alerio swung to his right and stopped.

From this height, he could see the Nera river pour through a narrow gorge. It traveled in a sweeping path down to where the river broadened as it passed beneath the village. Then, the ribbon of water angled away in a northwest heading before hooking a left and vanishing around a bend in the landscape. The dry gray gravel he walked when he approached Stifone stood out from the green trees on the banks and the clear water.

"What did the Tribune find unacceptable about this place?" he remarked to the river valley. "If I knew that, I'd know why I was ordered here."

Shrugging his shoulders, the Legion officer followed the path to the fourth house on the left. According to Optio Florian, it was the house rented by the engineer and the builder.

***

The Greek opened the door, cocked his head to the side, and started to close the door when he saw the man in the washed-out traveling clothes. Alerio placed a foot on the threshold.

"I've just come from Tribune Subausterus," Alerio announced.

The door slammed into his boot but remained ajar.

"*Non est magnum quod,*" called a voice from inside.

"Isn't what great?" Alerio questioned from the doorway.

"That you carry tidings from Tribune Subausterus," the Latian's voice replied.

"Does he have another word for unsuitable, impossible, or unachievable?" the Greek inquired. "Because even if you are a bard of renown with a magical command of language, we've heard all the negatives."

"And nothing that encourages effort," the Latian added.

The door opened slightly, then slammed shut on his boot.

Alerio's patience snapped. He lifted his left arm and slammed it into the door. As if launched from a ballista, the Greek hurled across the room. Moving fast, the Legion infantry officer came through the door and crossed to the Latian. The man had a knife half drawn. A rough, strong hand stilled the motion.

"You do not want to do that," Alerio threatened. Then softening his tone, he suggested. "Let's all sit down and talk like civilized men."

"How civilized? Civilized like I can't wait to get back to the Capital and my horses," the Greek scolded.

"Or so civilized you can't visualize anything short of a perfect course of bricks or a marble column?" the Latian demanded.

"You two have spent a lot of time arguing with Tribune Subausterus, haven't you?" Alerio guessed.

"Three weeks, give or take a day off from the exasperation," the Latian agreed.

"Excellent," Alerio announced. He walked to a bench where he plopped down as if settling in for the day.

The Greek and Latian exchanged puzzled glances before turning to stare at the young man.

"Who are you?" asked the Latian.

"Centurion Alerio Sisera," he replied. "And come tomorrow morning, or so I've been informed, the officer in charge of the Stifone detachment."

"Subausterus is leaving? And you're in charge?" the Greek questioned.

"And the project?" the Latian inquired. "We can move forward?"

"That's why I'm here," Alerio admitted. "I don't know what the project is."

But neither man was listening. Instead of asking specifics, they launched questions at Alerio.

"And you'll deal with Nardi Cocceia?" the Greek asked. "And…"

"Hold on, both of you. The reason I'm here talking," Alerio corrected. "is I don't know about the project. Or even, what I'm doing here."

The Latian raise both hands over his head, looked up and announced, "*Sicut decora*, just lovely. The Senate sends us a clueless officer."

"Then, how can you be in charge?" the Greek questioned.

"In a melee battle, the first order for a Legionary is to find another and get shoulder to shoulder with him. Then, the two find another and do the same. In those simple moves, a Legion combat line can re-form and a Century can take back control of a fight," Alerio explained. "This is me seeking a shoulder. Let's start with names."

The Greek and Latian frowned trying to decipher the analogy. Finally, the Greek jumped up.

"You are equating our trials to an infantry situation," he offered. "Hoplites, strategies, and campaigns."

"Pretty close. Do you have a name?"

"I am Cata Pous. A builder of warships," the Greek bragged.

"Warships?" Alerio ventured. "The ocean is over a hundred miles from here."

"And I am Pejus Monilis. An engineer and surveyor," the Latian announced. "The ocean may be far but the raw materials for building a ship of war are all around you."

"I've spent a little time on triremes," Alerio remarked. "Beyond the wood and rope, I imagine you'd need space to build one. And the Nara has steep banks."

24

"But you have me," Pejus Monilis boasted. "An exceptional engineer and surveyor. And I have a daring plan to overcome the terrain. *Producat illum efficere.*"

"Bring what on?" Alerio asked.

"The challenge, Centurion Sisera," Cata Pous commented. "if you can get Nardi Cocceia to agree."

"I thought Tribune Subausterus was the hold up?"

"He is only the first step. Next is Nardi, the head of the Cocceia family in this area," Pejus Monilis advised. "We'll need workmen. Lots of labor to turn Stifone into a naval shipyard."

"And Nardi controls the workmen," Cata Pous added. "and the woodlands."

"All right, where do I find him?" questioned Alerio. He stood as if ready to race out of the door and attack the next obstacle.

"Hold on there, Legionary," Pejus Monilis suggested. "A least get an idea of the scope of this campaign before you go charging into battle."

"Fine. Where do we start?"

Cata and Pejus closed their eyes and held their breaths. Either both were visualizing something or praying. Eventually, they opened their eyes, exhaled, and the Latian stood.

"Let's take a walk," Pejus urged while heading for the doorway.

Chapter 5 - Fluid's Flow and Magic

The three men took the steps down to the river bank, dropped off the grassy slope and landed on the gravel sandbar. Alerio peered up at the heavy forest growing on the surrounding mountains. There was no denying the abundance of wood for warships or the lack of flatland for assembling them.

"I can't imagine building on this," Alerio pointed out while adding a stomp to his pace. The pebbles under his foot sank and water filled the depression. "Although I guess given enough labor, we could terrace the land above the river bank."

Neither Cata Pous or Pejus Monilis offered a reply. They continued to hike the sandbar until they reached the trail were Alerio, his horse, and his mule had left the hills. Expecting to take the path up, he angled off the gravel. The engineer and ship builder kept walking.

***

Branches hung down to the top of the water hiding the tree trunks and land at the river's edge.

"You weren't wrong about terracing," Pejus Monilis stated. He pushed aside a low hanging branch, snapped off a dead twig, and used his heel to kick out a trench three feet long. "At this bend in the Nera, soil has built up over rock. We clear the trees and brush and cut the hill back to broaden and level the land. There's all the terracing you'll need to do. It'll give us a thousand feet of work space."

"What's with the trench?" Alerio inquired. He noticed the engineer's foot remained in the bottom of the kicked-out ditch.

"There's the magic of this operation. We cut a trench and build the boats in the cut," Pejus described. He dropped the twig and it fell into the excavated channel. "After the warship is constructed, we float it out to make room for the next build."

"How?" Alerio asked.

The engineer dragged his heel back, plowing the soil away until it reached the river. Water flooded the shallow ditch and the twig floated.

"We take advantage of the flow of fluids with a dam on either end of our channel."

"Just how large a ditch are we contemplating?" Alerio questioned.

"Ten feet deep and fifty feet wide," Cata Pous explained. "That will allow us to build anything from patrol boats to a proper quinquereme warship."

"If the Senate approves this site," Pejus Monilis added.

"If the Senate approves?" Alerio repeated. "I'm an infantryman and we like our orders plain and straight forward. So, break this project down into simple language for me."

"The Senate needs to build a fleet but they don't want the Qart Hadasht to know," Pejus Monilis, the engineer, explained. "And they can't build near the sea because the Empire fleet will row in and destroy the shipyard."

"As experiments, the Fleet Praetor sent out Tribunes and teams of builders and engineers," Cata Pous the ship builder informed Alerio. "Each charged with proving their site is capable of manufacturing warships."

"How do we prove this area is capable of building ships?" Alerio asked.

"We build a quinquereme, Centurion Sisera," Cata Pous answered. "Row it to the Capital, pass sea trials, and collects bags of gold."

"But first, we dig and dam the channel," Pejus Monilis added.

"And before that, you convince Nardi Cocceia to supply the labor and materials," the Greek informed him. "Is that straight forward enough for a Legionary?"

"The objective is clear. Verify Stifone as a viable boat building facility. Even if the battlefield isn't familiar," Alerio admitted. "I can try. How big is our bank for the building of the quinquereme?"

"The Tribunes were selected for their wealth," the Latian engineer advised. "According to you, our financial means will be leaving in the morning."

"Will he loan us the gold?"

"We asked and he laughed at us," Cata Pous, the ship builder, stated. "In Tribune Subausterus' words, throwing coins at this project would be like casting leaves on the Nera. Both would never be seen again."

"Show me the actual site," Alerio urged. "And, where you plan to dig this trench. Come to think of it, how long will it be?"

"Nine hundred feet," engineer Pejus Monilis announced. He shoved into the branches while stepping up on the low bank. As the others followed, he held the limb back and clarified. "Most of the excavation will be through rock."

Centurion Sisera's stomach knotted and he realized this fight wouldn't be won with blade skills or by issuing orders. Even if diplomacy was far from the privy of an infantry officer, he was sent to Stifone to serve. And now that he knew the mission, he would do it to the best of his abilities.

Act 2

Chapter 6 - The Road to Amelia

Alerio and Subausterus had a discussion the night before in the staff officer's quarters. At the conclusion of what could only be described as a failure for Alerio, Tribune Subausterus agreed to give the Centurion a letter of introduction to the Umbria administrator for Stifone.

The next morning, two groups departed the village. The Tribune and his servants headed west, following the Nera, while Alerio and the Sergeant marched to the river in a northwesterly direction. Alerio didn't feel the need to see the Tribune off.

Centurion Sisera and Optio Florian guided their mules down the embankment and into the cold, swiftly flowing water.

"It's only five miles, Centurion," Florian stammered through chattering teeth. He yanked on the line when the animal carrying his gear hesitated. "We could hike it in a morning without these four-legs-of-stubborn holding us back."

"Sergeant. I've found when a march will end in the unknown," Alerio advised. "It's best to be over equipped and rested. Losing a little daylight to have extra gear may be excessive but it may also prove valuable."

"When I made this journey with Tribune Subausterus, he brought four mules and a horse," Florian offered. "That was over prepared."

"What did he accomplish?" Alerio questioned.

29

The water reached their chests and the Legion NCO and infantry officer tightened their jaws against the cold water. Then the river began to recede as they crossed mid channel and splashed to the far bank.

"As far as I could tell, sir, the only thing the Tribune achieved was looking splendid and noble on his mount when he rode into Amelia," Florian replied. This time the mule attempted to charge passed the NCO to escape the icy mountain water. "But I have no real knowledge of their talks. I was never invited to attend his appointments with Administrator Nardi Cocceia."

The Optio hauled back on the line until the mule slowed and fell in behind him. He and his pack animal took a position to the rear of the Centurion and the other mule.

"When we reach the outskirts of Amelia, we will put on our war gear," Alerio informed the Sergeant. "And because we are heavy infantry, we will be both splendid and noble when we march into the Umbria city."

"Tribune Subausterus objected to Corporal Humi and I wearing our armor, helmets, and carrying shields," Adamo Florian remarked. "He said it might insult the Umbrian's pride."

"He wasn't wrong," Alerio commented. "Which is exactly why you will have your shield and I'll put on my rooster. We want them to be aware that the Legion has come calling."

Alerio smiled a toothy grin at his description of the colored horsehair brush on his Centurion's helmet.

"I'm not sure, sir, if two men can project that much power."

"It's not our numbers, Optio," Alerio commented. "It's the threat of having a Legion of heavy infantryman leveling their city."

"Does a Centurion have the authority to order that, sir?" Florian inquired.

"I haven't the slightest notion," Alerio admitted. "I'll probably start with a more diplomatic approach."

"A fine idea, sir," the Sergeant agreed.

***

Alerio and Adamo followed the river bank until they came to a saddle between knolls. On the far side, the topography changed to rolling hills dotted with farms. From the numerous stone walls, Alerio could tell the farmers worked hard at clearing and digging out rocks to prepare the soil.

Farmers, like good commanders, planned every step of their annual campaigns. The process included selecting the ground on which to plant or fight, as the case might be. Then strategizing which crops to plant and how deep to till. It was all based-on prior campaigns and experience.

Thinking about Tribune Subausterus' behavior towards the Legion NCOs and not allowing them to wear armor and helmets in Amelia caused Alerio to reconsider his approach. Like a bad commander, he was about to open a new battle front by emulating a failed strategy. Taking out the introductory letter from Tribune Subausterus, Alerio crumpled it into a ball and placed the parchment in a pack with his fire starter materials. Then, he began to seriously think about how to approach the Umbria administrator.

***

31

"Your first impression?" Alerio asked when they came up a rise and saw the city of Amelia in the distance.

"Can't tell much about the town from here. But the high ridge to the north and east makes for a natural defensive wall," Florian observed. "There's no approach from there. Legion engineers would have to make ladders to climb the terraces. That would prevent Centuries from getting caught on the steep roads while pacifying the upper levels."

"My thoughts exactly," Alerio commented. "Amelia would be a challenge if the Umbrians gathered to defend her."

"Do you think it'll come to that, sir?" Florian inquired. "I mean war with the Umbrians?"

The Sergeant had been disheartened under the command of Tribune Subausterus and his dismissive mannerisms. When Centurion Sisera arrived, the NCO expected to regain a sense of Legion pride. He did but Alerio Sisera lacked diplomacy and reserve. There may only be two of them but, the Centurion acted as if they had Centuries of heavy infantry at their disposal. Subsequently, the infantry officer approached the situation at Stifone and Amelia as if they were part of a military campaign. Right now, Optio Florian wasn't sure which attitude he preferred.

"Two of us couldn't conduct much of a war," Alerio replied to the question. "But our dead bodies may bring the Legion to revenge us and force the Umbria to respect the Republic. But, not to worry, there's little chance our three gladii will start a war."

Sergeant Florian glanced back to see if there was a third Legionary with them. Then he stared at the back of

32

Sisera's head and tried to discern if the Centurion happened to be foolishly overconfident, completely insane, or just had a death wish.

"That farm," Alerio announced.

They had walked by several paths leading off the dirt road. At the end of the trails were collections of buildings surrounded by green fields. The Centurion ignored the prosperous estates and indicated one where the farmer had left three fields uncultivated. Weeds grew almost to the crops in his adjacent plots.

"Are you saving coins by going to a poor farm?" Florian commented. "I would think a successful farm would be more stable. And a better place to leave our mules and extra gear."

"Desperate people can't be trusted," Alerio responded seeming to agree with the Sergeant. Yet he continued to walk towards the compound he selected.

"That one over there or that one," Sergeant Florian declared while pointing to other farming estates. "All of them have an abundance of fields filled with crops."

"Farmers using every square foot of land aren't necessary successful," Alerio suggested. "The landowner ahead is confident enough in his skills that he is resting the soil in those fields."

"And if he is poor and can't afford the workers or seeds to plant the bare fields?"

"Then we'll soon know."

And they did learn when three tall, broad-shouldered Umbrians came from a building and blocked their path. An older man shoved between them.

"You don't look like buyers," he stated. "Best turn around and head back to the main road."

Alerio took off his petasos, ran a sleeve across his forehead, and smiled at the older man and the husky trio. All three resembled the man.

"I'm an only son, myself. On my father's farm, all of the hauling fell to me," Alerio explained as he fingered the brim of his hat. "It wasn't his fault, he married later in life. That didn't help me during the harvest or birth season or the shearing period. At times, I'd have given my left testis for a brother."

The three youths laughed before the youngest remarked, "No you wouldn't. If you had to deal with these two every day of your life."

"That's enough," the farmer scolded his son. He squinted at Alerio and said. "But you aren't a farmer now, are you?"

"No, Master Farmer. My name is Alerio Sisera and I'm a Legionary of the Republic," Alerio replied. He placed the petasos on his head and stared at the father and sons from under the hat's brim. "I have business in Amelia with Administrator Cocceia."

"The city is that way," the farmer directed with a wave of his arm.

"But my associate and I need to appear official," Alerio informed him. "It's hard to look dignified leading pack animals."

The farmer nodded and allowed a grin to crease his weathered face.

"Nardi Cocceia wouldn't understand meeting with a mule handler or someone who works," the farmer stated. "Since his mentor joined the council, he's living in the big villa."

"What else can you tell me about him?" Alerio inquired. "I'm here to convince him to invest in an opportunity in Stifone."

"You're an administrator yourself?"

"No, sir. More of a boots-on-the-ground supervisor," Alerio replied. "Think of it as being in charge of the harvest. If you had to run from one farm to another to accomplish the task."

"I'm Roscini. My youngest, Tite, will show you where to stow your gear and get you a meal," the farmer informed him. "But it'll cost you a few coins and a favor."

"The coins I have," Alerio assured him before asking. "What's the favor?"

"We'll talk later. Right now, go put away your stuff, wash up, and eat."

"Thank you, Master Roscini."

The farmer simply strolled away. Two of his sons followed while Tite indicated the main house with a wave of his arm.

"What's a Legionary?" he asked as the three moved towards the villa.

"Professional soldiers of Rome," Alerio answered. "But if you want to know more, Optio Florian is a Legion NCO. He's a wealth of information."

Florian frowned and knotted his eyebrows. The last thing he wanted to do over a meal was play tour guide like the priests from Temples in the Capital.

Chapter 7 - The Umbria Administrator

The God Erebus waved his hand and his shadows vanished. From the cool shade beside the wall, Alerio found himself in the warmth of the overhead sun.

"Good food and excellent vino," he exclaimed while standing. "Sergeant. We have a diplomatic mission."

Adamo Florian and Tite Roscini were oblivious to the strong midday sun. They were deep in conversation as they had been for the entire meal.

"Gear up, Optio," Alerio instructed.

"Here's an opportunity for you, farm boy. You can see how the armor fits," Florian advised. "You aren't a citizen so you can't be a Legionary. But the equipment is available for an irregular to buy."

The Sergeant pulled on his chainmail shirt, a chest piece, shoulder rig, and belted on an armored skirt. After the armor, he settled a helmet on his head and unpacked a javelin. After considering the weapon, he put the javelin back. Finally, he peeled a cover from his infantry shield.

"All that looks heavy, Optio," Tite declared at the sight of the Sergeant in his war gear.

"A Legionary can hike twenty miles and march into battle without rest while wearing this equipment. Plus, of course, his rations," Florian bragged. "It's only heavy for a little while."

"Then it feels lighter?" Tite asked hopefully.

"No. Of course not," Florian replied while shifting his shoulders to settle the armor. "You just get accustomed to carrying it."

"If you two have finished your love fest, we have a mission," Alerio stated while snugging the Centurion helmet down on his head.

Rather than a pair of weary travelers tugging on willful mules, the two men who left the farm were armed and armored Legionaries of the Roman Republic.

***

From the gentling rolling farmland, the grade on the road became a steady climb. At each level of elevation, the number and size of the structures grew and the building materials changed. At first, the fences were stone and the tradesmen's compounds were wood. When they topped the final rise, the fences were logs and the villas were stone.

As the construction changed, so did the types of people living on the levels. From farmers, to craftsmen and apprentices, the residents of Amelia seemed to evolve. At the highest level, the streets were occupied by businessmen rushing around and young men idling in groups around benches.

"If this was a Legion camp, I'd find work for those slackers," Florian stated.

"What's the matter Sergeant, can't stand to see men relaxing?" Alerio teased.

"Centurion, aimless men do disruptive things to break the boredom," the Optio ventured. "Youthful muscle will flex. Either for good, or for evil without direction."

"They aren't our problem," Alerio asserted. "Where do we find the administrator?"

"The big structure on the hill. That's the government building," Florian offered. "When Humi and I accompanied Tribune Subausterus here, he had us wait. There's a café on the next street over, I'll be there when you're done."

37

"I didn't bring you along to decorate a seat. Or to supply a novelty item to break the monotony of bored Umbria tribesmen," Alerio exclaimed. "If I'm going to die on a cold stone floor because of bad diplomacy, then you're going down with me."

Sergeant Adamo Florian stopped in the middle of the road. His eyes searched the infantry officer's face, trying to detect if he was serious or jesting. No humor or flexibility was reflected in the young officer's features.

"You're willing to die for this mission, sir?" he questioned.

"Earlier this year, I was in Sicilia at Agrigento," Alerio informed the NCO. "The Empire controls the waterways. Because of their navy, getting the Legions across the Messina Strait was a challenge. Keeping them supplied is just as taxing. Until our Republic gets warships, we are at the mercy of the Qart Hadasht Empire. Thus, yes, I am willing to die for this mission. Now get that shield off your back, stiffen your posture, and follow me."

Alerio waited for the Optio to strap the infantry shield to his arm. Then they marched to the government building, up the steps, and through a pair of decorative front doors.

Inside, they crossed the stone floor and approached a pair of scribes.

"Who is in charge of Stifone?" demanded Alerio.

The question puzzled Sergeant Florian and he started to remind the officer that Nardi Cocceia was the administrator for Amelia and Stifone. Before he could intercede, the tone from one of the scribes stiffened his back.

"The administrator does not see anyone without an appointment," one of the clerks sneered. He snapped his wrist and indicated a spot on a corner of his desk. "Leave your gift. I'll check to see if he can fit you in."

Legion Optios were the keepers of discipline in the Centuries. Although he hadn't known Sisera long, Florian felt obliged to remind the scribe that he addressed a Legion officer. Before he could respond...

Alerio swung his arm from behind his leg and slammed his palm into the bottom of the desk. The piece of furniture lifted before crashing back to the floor. It sounded as if four spear butts had been hammered into the stone. In response to the violence visited on his desk, the clerk jumped up and stumbled backward.

"You may not realize it," Alerio said in a calm and even tone. "But I just saved you a lot of pain. You see, my Sergeant is a stickler for regulations. Now, before he comes to my rescue, answer me."

After delivering the assertion, the Legion officer stood staring at the scribe with no expression on his face. Between the assault on his desk, the blank expression, and the piercing eyes, the clerk couldn't remember the question. While that scribe wilted under the gaze of a Legion officer, the other one ran for the doorway.

"Centurion Sisera asked who is in charge of Stifone," Florian reminded the clerk. "Do not keep him waiting."

Ten young men pounded over the threshold and stopped halfway across the floor. They fanned out and leveled their spears at the Legionaries. Behind the robed Umbria warriors, the second scribe poked his head around the doorframe.

"Sergeant Florian, hand me your gladius," Alerio ordered.

Reluctantly, the Optio drew his Legion sword and offered the hilt to the officer.

"If I knew you would unarm me, sir, I'd have brought my javelin," Florian complained.

"But then you would have started killing Umbrians," Alerio remarked. He took the offered gladius with his left hand and pulled his own blade with the right hand.

Optio Adamo Florian wasn't sure what Sisera meant earlier when he talked about dying to complete the mission. Even when the Centurion slapped the clerk's desk, the NCO didn't foresee a duel to the death. And certainty, he didn't anticipate being unarmed in a battle against ten Umbria spearmen. This seemed an odd choice for opening a negotiation. But it did provide proof that the God Furor had touched the young officer, for Centurion Sisera was surely as mad as a rabid dog.

While the Sergeant attempted to sort out his thoughts in order to grasp the situation, the Centurion leaned in his direction and confirmed the mad rage.

"I'll be starting on the left side. Keep the others off of me," the infantry officer whispered before charging at the tip of a spear.

***

It took half a heartbeat before the words and actions registered in Sergeant Florian' mind.

Blessing of Fortūna brought luck for Alerio. The Umbria warriors were young and brash but leaderless and undisciplined. They froze for three heartbeats.

Held loosely in the hands of the Umbrian on the end, the shaft jerked to the side from the impact by Alerio's right blade. The warrior concentrated on trying to bring the tip back to the front. It didn't occur to him that a single man might attack a line of spearmen. He caught a fist and hilt in the face for his mistake and dropped. His spear bounced on the stone floor and rolled away.

The next two spearmen spun while tracking the man with the horse hair comb on his helmet. To them, he was trying to escape and, as if a rabbit triggering the chase instincts in a pair of dogs, they took a step in his direction.

Optio Florian was three paces behind the Centurion. When the first Umbrian dropped, the two beside him twisted away. The Legion NCO bent his knees to lower his center of gravity and angled his shield. Coming up, he plowed the first spearman into the second and powered both of them into the third warrior. The three toppled in a line as if columns shoved off a temple's porch. The Sergeant kicked and stomped the three before racing to where his officer waited by the front door. While running, he decided the Centurion was not right in the mind. Who came to a government building, started a fight, then ran without even attempting to speak with the administrator?

Alerio reached the doorway, skidded to a stop, and grabbed the slow scribe. After pulling the man inside, Alerio kicked the decorative doors closed. By the fourth heartbeat, the six remaining Umbrians realized the Legionaries were at the door and attempting to escape. The fastest man moved ahead of the pack. He was the first to be beat to the floor by the heavy infantry shield.

"Aren't we leaving, sir?" the Sergeant asked. He peered over his shoulder to see Alerio drop the locking beam into the brackets.

"Why, Optio Florian? We just got here," Alerio replied. Propelled by flicks of his wrists, he spun both blades in circles at his sides. "And really, there are only five left."

The Legion officer scurried to the NCO's right. Coming from around the shield, Alerio parried two spears while the Sergeant slammed into two other warriors.

The fifth, an Umbria soldier named Pannacci, hopped back and forth behind the engaged pairs. He couldn't decide which was the safest place to lend his support.

Alerio shoved one spear shaft high with his left gladius, dipped his knees, and slapped the other spearman's ankle with his right blade. The injured man dropped his shaft, grabbed his ankle and crumpled to the stone floor. Batting the shaft of the second man from side to side between his blades while dodging the spear's tip, Alerio glanced over to see how the Legion NCO was coping.

Sergeant Florian bashed both spears and spearmen aside. Stepping into the gap, he pounded one with the shield and kicked back at the other. In the pause while one regained his balance and the other limped back on a badly bruised thigh, the Legion NCO spun and attacked. The bruising showed marks from the tread of a Legion boot and the weak shuffle demonstrated the efficiency of the kick. With a hop and a step, Florian droved the warrior to the floor. Intending to hunt the last of the pair, Florian turned.

There was no target behind him. Centurion Sisera had beat the other spearmen to the ground. Together, the Legionaries pivoted to face the last two Umbrian warriors.

"Stop this," a voice cried from an interior doorway.

Only a single pair of warriors were on their feet. The other eight crawled away or sat nursing bruises or headaches.

"Sergeant, stand down," Alerio ordered. Looking at the man in the richly appointed robe, he inquired. "And who are you?"

Pannacci raced to the inside doorway and away from the Legionaries. Once there, he held his spear as if defending the older Umbrian.

"I am Nardi Cocceia," the man announced as if Alerio should be impressed.

"Good for you," the Legion officer acknowledged before turning to Sergeant Florian. "Round them up. We'll crucify all ten at sundown. If any give you a hard time, kill them."

Florian' mouth fell open but, he wasn't the only one surprised by the orders. Nardi, from the doorway, began breathing rapidly and stammering.

"You. You can't execute Umbria warriors," he finally got out.

"I'm not," Alerio replied.

"That's better, now what…"

But he never finished his sentence.

"They aren't warriors. These are listless youths looking for a brawl," Alerio described. "Not being citizens of the Republic, I can murder them where they lay. Isn't that right, Optio?"

43

"Sir, a Centurion has the power to forgive," Florian stated. "Or the right to punish, up to and including the crucifixion of noncitizens."

"That's ridiculous," Nardi Cocceia proclaimed. "You are in Umbria territory. You have no authority here."

Alerio glanced around the room, paused in his inspection to stare at the barred doorway, then shifted his eyes to the two scribes huddling in a corner.

"I believe my authority has been established," he insisted by lifting both gladii. "But I do have an issue that needs resolving."

The Administrator swept the room, took in the damaged warriors, and decided diplomacy was preferable to fighting. At least for now.

"We can talk in my office," Nardi offered.

"I accept," Alerio responded. Putting away one of the gladii, he said to the NCO while handing over the other. "Come along Sergeant. We have an audience."

Optio Florian placed the tip of his blade at the mouth of the sheath and missed the opening. The Centurion had taken them to Amelia, started a brawl in the government building, somehow avoided seriously injuring ten spearmen, and then was rewarded by an invitation from Administrator Cocceia. When the steel finally lined up with the sheath, the Sergeant slammed the gladius in up to the hilt and glared at the Umbria warrior standing beside the door.

Maybe, just maybe, Centurion Sisera didn't have a death wish. With that thought in mind, the Sergeant followed Alerio through the doorway and into the administrator's office.

Chapter 8 - The Offer and Assumptions

Nardi Cocceia indicated a couch for Alerio while he settled onto a one-man sofa. It didn't escape Alerio's attention that the room's décor was very Roman in design.

"When Tribune Subausterus visited, he brought gifts and observed the pleasantries of civilized negotiations," Nardi informed his guests. "He was a cultured man. You? I don't know what you expected to accomplish by attacking my warriors."

"I expected to get your attention," Alerio replied. He held out both hands, palms up, as if presenting the outcome of the statement. "I expected you to attend to my requests. For I will get results, or…"

The word hung in the air. Between the smile on the Centurion's face and the armored Legionary standing three paces behind the officer, Nardi shivered.

"Or what?"

"Or, I march a Legion on Amelia, subdue the city before taking control of Stifone," Alerio answered. "However, you are sitting on the border of my decision. And mind you, that's the worst possible place to be."

"I am the Umbria administrator for this region," Nardi bragged. "On my word, I can raise an army of ten thousand Umbria warriors. Both the Etruscans and Gauls fear me."

"Did you notice that ten of your fearsome fighters fell to two Legionaries," Alerio pointed out. "Optio Florian. Why didn't you employ your gladius?"

"You took my blade, sir."

"You see Administrator Nardi Cocceia, I took his gladius to prevent him from slaughtering your men," Alerio stated. "So, let's review your situation. Two Legionaries defeated ten of your warriors and one of them didn't have a weapon. In short, I could easily take the area required by the Republic with twenty-five Centuries of heavy infantrymen."

Nardi Cocceia could raise an army but it would take weeks and a meeting with the Umbria council. He wasn't sure the Legion would take that long to arrive. Besides, the talk of war unsettled the Umbria official, so he changed the subject.

"Tribune Subausterus offered an insultingly small amount for manpower and raw materials to build a warship at Stifone," Nardi revealed. "He didn't think the site was suitable and thus the reason for his low offer. What makes you think you can use Stifone?"

"Let's call it faith," Alerio suggested. When the administrator looked puzzled, he added. "I can and will see the ship built. That kind of faith."

"I require a small token of recognition for facilitating the effort," Nardi declared. "And of course, gold for the workers' wages and raw materials. In advance, I might add."

"Optio Florian, take note. This is how diplomats and men of business negotiate," Alerio remarked while twisting around to look back at the NCO. "It's very civilized and nice, wouldn't you agree?"

"Nice and civilized, yes sir," Florian confirmed.

Shifting back to face the administrator, Alerio cocked his head and blinked his eyes as if having trouble focusing on Nardi Cocceia. Then he nodded as if understanding had just come to him.

"Let me explain. The Tribune is a staff officer. Talking is his specialty and passing judgement is his job," Alerio listed. "I am an infantry officer. Killing is my specialty and driving men to achieve the impossible are my jobs."

"Well certainly, Centurion Sisera. You are the man to complete the task," Nardi flattered the Legion officer. "If you'll leave the coins, I will begin gathering the workers and ordering the wood, ropes, and iron."

"Did you miss part of what I said?" Alerio inquired.

"You mean about needing Stifone? Or achieving the impossible?"

"When I look closely, I almost feel like I'm in my patron's Villa in the Capital," Alerio suggested while beaming a smile as he looked around the room. Then the smile dropped and the Legion officer pressed his lips together. "One fate has you up on the boards, dying with a treetop view. And me marching to Stifone and completing my mission."

"But you said we were negotiating," Nardi implored.

"One thing is interesting," Alerio offered. "A citizen of the Republic can't be crucified like that."

"A citizen? Are you offering citizenship?" gushed Nardi. "I could become a citizen of the Republic?"

"It is appealing. Don't you think, Administrator? A citizen can't be tortured or whipped, and a sentence of death can be commuted to voluntary exile," Alerio explained. "Plus, a citizen of the Republic has the right to make legal contracts and to hold property as well as having immunity from some taxes and legal obligations.

47

Oh, and the right to sue in the courts and to appeal a magistrate's or a lower court's decision. You can't say the same for an Umbrian dealing with the Republic."

"Tribune Subausterus never mentioned Roman citizenship," Nardi uttered suspiciously. "How can you?"

"The staff officer was buying a shipyard," Alerio responded. "I'm proposing that we build one warship to prove our capacity. Let me ask you. When the Republic depends on one administrator to manage the building of their warships, how important is that man?"

"You would think, important enough to make him a citizen. And to shower him with gold," Nardi ventured. Then off handedly, he asked. "What part of what you said did I miss?"

Alerio hesitated while thinking. He had one thing in mind but changed it.

"That I kill people," Alerio finally answered. He stood and saluted the administrator. "I'll expect five hundred men in Stifone over the next few days. We have a lot of work to do."

But Nardi Cocceia simply waved the Legion officer away. He was lost in the fantasy of being an important and wealthy citizen of the Republic. The two scribes rushed in when Sergeant Florian opened the door. The administrator ignored them.

Pannacci's eyes followed the Legionaries as they walked from the office. If hate was arrows, both would be dead before taking another step. The spearman wasn't a brave man but he had a knack for influencing other men, and a streak of pride. A nasty combination of traits that screamed for revenge.

***

Once through the doorway, Alerio ordered, "Draw."

Both Legionaries jerked their gladii from the sheaths. Holding them against their thighs where the blades were naked and visible, Centurion Sisera and Optio Florian marched directly to the ornate doors. On either side of the room, Umbria warriors followed them with hate filled glares and spear tips. More waited on the stairs outside. But, like the ones inside, they didn't interfere with the Legionaries' progress.

Streets from the government building, Alerio put away his gladius and signaled for Florian to do the same.

"Centurion Sisera, my head is spinning and, while I collect my thoughts, can you answer a question?"

"What is it, Optio?" Alerio inquired.

"I know you can't call out a Legion but, can you really make the administrator a citizen?"

"No. But I never said I would. Nardi Cocceia brought it up and I merely advised him of the benefits of being a citizen of the Republic," Alerio informed the NCO. "What made him susceptible was the fear of dying and the safety and benefits of being a citizen."

"You hesitated when you challenged him to remember what you said," Florian remarked. "What were you going to say?"

"Optio, I was faking the entire thing," Alerio confessed. "But at the end, I settled on the infantry slogan. Win at all cost. We began with violence. I thought it fitting to end with a threat of more. It worked out better than if I said have faith in my ability to get the warship built."

"My first Optio always said, those who dare carve their own path," Florian offered. "I think fear of you overrode Nardi Cocceia's greed."

"Maybe faith would have been closer to the truth."

***

They left the streets and densely packed yards and walls behind. Dropping down the many levels, they eventually reached the cultivated fields. After a steady hike, the Legionaries arrived at the turn off for the Roscini farm. A quarter of a mile along the path, the farmer and his three sons stopped flipping over shovels of soil, leaned on the handles, and watched the armored men approach.

"We thought you'd spend the night in luxury," the farmer teased. Then he spit into the dirt and questioned. "Couldn't reach an agreement with the old phony? I guess we can make room for you tonight."

"Master Roscini, I must say your attitude towards Administrator Nardi Cocceia is rather harsh," Alerio suggested. "But rest assured, it's not the reason for denying your offer of hospitality. Let's just say, we reached an accord and it's advisable for us to leave right away."

"You reached an agreement but aren't staying for a feast?" Roscini inquired. "That's not Nardi's style. What's going on, Centurion?"

"Your farm is too close to Amelia," Alerio remarked hoping to skip a long explanation so he could get on the road. "Sometime after dark, over a hundred inebriated and outraged Umbria warriors will come looking for Optio Florian and me."

50

"How can you negotiate a successful deal yet bring the ire of our military down on you?"

"It's a gift from the God Sors," Alerio answered. "Purely luck."

"Excuse me, sir," Florian interjected. "I was there and would suggest the Goddess Discordia was deeply involved."

"Growing success from chaos is what farmers do," Roscini observed.

"As do Legion officers," Florian added. "It's getting late, sir, we should be going."

"Tite will help you load the mules," Roscini stated. "He is already packed."

"Packed for what?" Alerio asked.

"Tite is coming with us," Florian replied. "It's the other half of the payment for storing our animals and gear."

"What are you going to do with a farm boy?" Alerio inquired.

"There's only Tesserarius Humi and I for sentry duty," Sergeant Florian informed Alerio. "Until now, we've been enough. But you'll need a militia force to guard the equipment and keep order in the camp. Tite Roscini is going to be a Lieutenant in the Sisera Detachment at Stifone."

"Sisera Detachment?"

"Yes, sir. We don't have a Legion, we don't have a staff officer, but we sure in Hades have an infantry officer who is in command."

"Lieutenant Roscini reporting for orders, Centurion," Tite announced.

"He gets paid, doesn't he," the farmer inquired.

51

Alerio looked at the Sergeant for the answer.

"Yes, sir. We have funds for pay purposes," Florian informed the farmer and the officer. "Now we really need to vacate the area."

"Lieutenant Roscini, load us up," Alerio instructed. "Let's get Sisera Detachment on the march."

"Yes, sir."

Chapter 9 - Rock and Limbs

Two Legionaries and a young man accustomed to working in the fields all day had no problem hiking throughout the night. Except for a break while waiting for moonrise, they force marched to the north bank of the Nera river. Long before sunrise, they waded across, climbed to Stifone, unloaded the mules, and curled up in blankets. That night, the insulted Umbria warriors never got close to the Legion officer.

When most of the residents of Stifone threw off their covers to begin their day, Alerio Sisera stood at the bend in the river a half mile downstream from the village. Scanning the river as it flowed away and wrapped around the outcrop of land, he began to sketch. After noting the height of the bank on a piece of parchment, he stepped up and paced off where the flatland reached the hills that climbed out of the river valley. High above, a terrace was visible.

Moving into the trees, he paced off distances and noted features. Slowly, the Legion officer filled in details on the map as if planning an assault. Nine hundred feet from where he entered the thin forest, Alerio emerged on the river bank to see the Nera flow back around the knob of land.

"You aren't what I expected," a voice said from behind Alerio.

Pejus Monilis stepped from between the trees and walked up to stand beside the Legion officer.

"What did you expect?" Alerio inquired.

"A political appointee looking to make a name for himself," the engineer replied.

"What makes you think I'm not?"

"I spoke with Optio Florian this morning," Pejus stated. "Tribune Subausterus gave you a letter of introduction. You didn't use it. Instead, you started a war, negotiated a deal, and declared peace."

"That sounds political to me," Alerio offered.

"That my, young Centurion, is far from diplomatic," Engineer Monilis observed. "It isn't what I would expect from a Legion staff officer on a mission."

"Heavy infantry," Alerio corrected. "Over the next few days, a work force will arrive. I need us to build a warship, fast. Let's just say, we need to finish the first one before the administrator realizes the truth."

"And what is the truth?" questioned the engineer.

"That Nardi Cocceia is paying for a warship and may never get reimbursed in coins or in status."

"So, you didn't get peace. You just delayed the first battle of the war," Pejus suggested. He pointed to the map and instructed. "Show me what you have there."

"Tell me the minimum of what you and the master ship builder need," Alerio requested while handing the map to the engineer. "Once this operation starts, like a Century in combat, there will be no rest or retreat."

"Until you declare victory?" Pejus Monilis inquired.

"No, Master Engineer, not me," Alerio responded while stomping a foot on the thin layer of soil covering the rock of the river bank. "Until Fleet Praetor Sudoris accepts the product of our labors. Oh, and authorizes funds to expand the shipyard and pay for more warships."

"Expand the shipyard?"

"That's correct. For the first one, we are working short and fast," Alerio informed him. With the side of his boot, he scraped away the dirt to expose the underlaying granite. "Unfortunately, here the Goddess Tellus' earth is rock. It's as hard as this campaign."

"Then within Tellus' rock, we will build a Republic warship," the engineer promised. "And may Pluto bless us."

"Because all things fall back into the earth," Alerio recited a saying about the god who watches over the riches of the earth. "and also arise from inside the earth."

"That's close, but I plan on removing rock not mining ore," Pejus advised. "In order to allow Neptune's domain to flow."

**

It wasn't the next day or the day after when the first group of workers crossed the Nera and climbed to Stifone. Centurion Sisera didn't see them. He was in a building, arguing the need for sleeping quarters for the work force.

"We'll need to clear the ground up slope at this level area," Alerio suggested while running his fingers across a ridge on the map. "We'll create a terrace for their quarters. Between that soil and the dirt from the slope, we'll have plenty to level the boat building area."

"Which is more important, Centurion Sisera?" questioned Pejus Monilis. "The housing level, the width of the work area, or the boat trench?"

"The boat channel," Cata Pous insisted. "I need it to construct the warship quickly. Afterward, we'll flood the channel and float the completed ship right out the other side."

"Your productivity will suffer if you don't take care of your work force," Alerio insisted. "The housing area is just as important."

"I can see a Legion officer wanting to think about the men," Pejus Monilis added. "But from what I know of manufacturing sites, you'll need a flat expanse on either side of the canal for the process."

The officer, the boat builder, and the engineer pointed to Alerio's map and insisted which area they felt needed to be constructed first. Although the men pressed their points, it was a friendly competition. They had a day or two before setting the schedule.

"Sir, there are Umbrians approaching," Corporal Humi informed them when he stepped into the building.

Cata Pous, the Boat Builder, glanced at Pejus Monilis, and the engineer in turn gazed at Centurion Sisera.

"Are they armed?" Alerio asked the Corporal while ignoring the craftsmen.

"No sir. They're toting bags and carrying tools," the Tesserarius responded.

"Then let's go see who is the first to answer Nardi Cocceia's call," Alerio suggested. "Humi. You and

Florian grab bows and take positions behind me. I don't know about the farmer."

"Tite says he's a hunter," the NCO replied.

"Arm him, but make sure he doesn't shoot me in the back," Alerio advised as he crossed to the threshold.

Outside, the Legion officer blinked against the afternoon sun before peering down to the steps. From the river bank, a barrel-chested man walked ahead of fifty others carrying identical leather bags. Some had long handled hammers resting on their shoulders while others had sharp edged pickaxes.

"Thoughts, Master Monilis?" Alerio asked the engineer.

"Those are miners," Pejus replied.

The big man reached Alerio, stopped and inhaled, expanding his chest even further.

"Mezzasoma, master rock miner," he announced. "Who is in charge?"

Cata Pous, the boat builder, started to point at Alerio. Before he could speak, Centurion Sisera placed a hand on Pejus' arms and pulled the engineer to the front.

"Master Monilis is our engineer," Alerio offered.

"You have us for three days, then we have to get back to our mine," Mezzasoma warned. "Make them count."

"Let's go look at the construction site," Pejus suggested. He turned to Alerio and assured the Legion officer. "Miners are exactly what I need and I will make the days count."

Monilis and Mezzasoma took the steps downward and the miners followed.

"What do you need, Master Pous?" Alerio inquired.

"Warships are made of wood," Cata remarked. "I need carpenters and woodsmen. But right now, I need to go supervise the miners. Especially when they clear young fir trees."

"Why the fir trees?" Alerio inquired.

"Because Centurion Sisera, each trunk of those young trees is an oar," Cata Pous replied.

The boat builder fell in line behind the miners leaving Alerio standing alone on the terrace. Lifting an arm, the Legion officer waved it over his head.

"Stand down," he called out.

"Standing down," Optio Florian reported. "Corporal Humi and Lieutenant Roscini stand down."

The three loosened their bow strings, slipped their arrows into pouches, and took ladders from the roofs to their officer's level. They moved to stand in front of him.

"If the miners can get to Stifone that fast," Alerio reflected. "their soldiers can be here just as quickly."

"We'll maintain a guard overnight, sir," Florian explained. "We may be few but, we won't get caught unaware."

"That's all I can ask," Alerio acknowledged. He spun, walked through the doorway and into the building. There had to be a compromise, he pondered the argument of what was most important on the construction site. Then he remembered the boat builder's comment about constructing warships quickly.

***

Trees fell and the Greek boat builder rushed from downed trunk to downed trunk. At each, he directed the miners to haul the logs to specific stacks.

"Are you finding your fir trees?" Alerio inquired when he caught up with Cata Pous.

"Some, but we'll need more to create one hundred and eighty oars for a quinquereme," Cata proclaimed. "The pine and cedar will make excellent rowing seats and internal struts. But we'll need a lot more of them as well."

"What about the frame?" Alerio questioned.

"There's no oak here. Wood for the hull and keel will come from deeper in the mountains," Cata observed.

"Tell me the minimum area you need to build our warship."

"The channel must be over one hundred and forty-eight feet long to fit the length. With a draft of ten feet, the channel needs to be at least that deep to float the finished ship. And at twenty-four feet wide, we'll need double that width to give us space for assembly."

"What if you built a trireme?" Alerio inquired.

"I thought the Republic wanted warships," Cata Pous complained. "A trireme is good for chasing and sinking pirates. But, if your senate wants to do battle with the Qart Hadasht Navy, they'll need quinqueremes. Ships that can do more than ram and carry dispatches. Of course, a quinquereme can ram but, the 'five' is a stable platform for bolt throwers and archers. And it has room for one hundred and thirty Hoplites."

"Legionaries," Alerio corrected. "You meant a quinquereme can carry one hundred and thirty Legionaries."

"Whatever Centurion. A heavy infantryman is a heavy infantryman," the Greek boatwright stated. "I'm a builder not a military man."

"That's obvious. What are the requirements to build a trireme?"

"It can only haul ten Legionaries, in good weather. And support maybe four archers," Cata Pous sneered. "The trireme is barely a warship."

"Alright, how about a Legion patrol boat?"

"Why not a fishing boat?" shot back Cata.

"Or a sturdy raft?" Alerio barked. "Lash a few tree trunks together and I'll row it to Ostia. Maybe I can convince Fleet Praetor Sudoris to support Stifone based on the quality of the wood and not the shape."

Cata pointed to a pair of miners who stood over a fallen tree.

"You two, place it with the other fir trees," he instructed. Then he dropped his eyes to the ground and mumbled. "Five feet."

"Five what?" Alerio questioned.

"The draft on a trireme is five feet," the Greek answered. "We only need a five-foot-deep channel for the one hundred and thirty feet of ship. The width is about the same because the 'three' is twenty feet wide."

"Five feet less rock to dig," Alerio uttered. "Where is Master Monilis."

"He's up on the slope with the rock miner boss," Cata Pous told him. Then he added. "I suppose I am going to build a trireme."

"We, Master Pous, we are going to build a trireme," Alerio corrected.

He walked away while Cata ran to inspect another fallen tree.

At the bottom of the hill, Alerio found a tall pine tree pressed into the slope. The limbs on the front and back had been trimmed away leaving branches on two sides to act as rungs. Alerio scurried up the natural ladder to find Mezzasoma, the rock miner, and Pejus Monilis standing on the edge of the ledge.

"Centurion Sisera. We were just admiring the view from the sleeping quarter's level," the engineer suggested. "Come, see for yourself."

"Sorry to change the mission," Alerio offered. "But we're going to compress our vision."

"How so?" Mezzasoma demanded.

"You are going to cut a shallower trench and chop the end of this slope," Alerio replied. He pointed downward and motioned with his hand as if squaring off the bottom of the hill. "We'll quarter the workers on the work level. It's not ideal but it'll give us what we need."

"You have three days," Mezzasoma reminded Alerio and Pejus. "Our focus is on the channel?"

"It is," Alerio assure him.

The big miner waved his arms and shortly, all of his crewmembers were looking up at their boss. He made a series of hand signals. When he finished, some went back to cutting trees. Others picked up their tool bags and carried their gear to the stakes marking the end of the channel. And a third walked to the Nera River and began hiking along the bank.

"Where are they going?" Alerio asked.

"Those are my journeymen," Mezzasoma answered. "I don't need them to cut trees, or even do rough cuts. Instead of having them standing around, they're collecting driftwood from the river bank."

"For your campfires tonight?" Alerio guessed.

"No, Centurion. For the rock," the master miner responded.

***

In the spring when the Nera ran high, the water deposited broken branches and tree limbs on the river banks. Stripped of bark by the rocks during the voyage from the mountains, the naked wood rested above the water's surface and baked in the summer sun.

The journeymen miners collected and piled the dried-out wood on either side of engineer' channel markers. Inside the markers, teams of master rock miners chiseled straight lines along the boundary. Behind them, teams of apprentices hacked deep, jagged fissures two feet from the straight edges.

"What are they doing?" Alerio asked when the craftsmen pulled knives and began cutting long, thick wedges from the pieces of driftwood. Then he observed. "The slices are too large to be kindling for campfires."

"You are about to witness a secret of rock mining," Mezzasoma informed him. "The metal ores we mine reside in spaces between the granite. Usually, we removed rock to expose the ore. For the channel, removing the overburden is the purpose of the dig. However, there are two differences."

"What are they?" Alerio asked. "And what is the secret."

"We have fresh air and the mountain isn't going to fall on us. Now watch."

The journeymen miners took their carved wedges to the fissures, inserted the narrow ends, and proceeded to hammer the dried wood into the rough cuts. With each whack, the wood curled, splintered, and filled the gaps.

"The wood is too soft to split the rock," Alerio exclaimed.

"Is it now?" questioned the master rock miner.

While the fissures were being jammed full of wood, the apprentices took leather buckets to the river, filled them and returned to the work area.

"Wet them down," Mezzasoma instructed. "Slow, let Neptune's spit sink in."

Almost dribbling the water from the buckets, the apprentices poured along the lines of wood. To Alerio's surprise, the dried wood absorbed the water leaving no overflow on the surface. After two passes the buckets were empty and the rock surface remained dry.

"Where did the water go?" Alerio inquired.

"Remember you said the wood was too soft to split the rock?" Mezzasoma commented.

"It is," Alerio assured the miner.

"Pickaxes, show the Legion officer what the soft wood did to the hard rock."

Where they had to use steel chisels to cut the fissures, the picks hooked and pulled out pieces of rock.

"The granite is broken," Alerio gushed. "How?"

"The soft wood expanded from the water and the pressure cracked the rock making it easier to dig out," Mezzasoma explained. "In a wall of rock, we can use fire to heat the granite. Splash on cold water and the face cracks. But here, the flat surface wouldn't dry enough between fires so, we used wedges."

"Can your crew finish the channel in three days?"

"Not only can we dig out your trench," Mezzasoma assured him while pointing from the edge of the channel to the toe of the hill. "We'll cut back the rock slope. I spoke to Cata Pous and he needs a lot more space for the carpenters."

"Thank you," Alerio offered.

"Don't thank me," Mezzasoma suggested. "Thank administrator Nardi Cocceia. He's paying my team."

"I am all too aware of that," Alerio confessed, under his breath, while he walked away.

Chapter 10 - Keel Notches

Three days later, Alerio walked between miner, carpenter, and laborer camps in the thin forest. On the far side, he entered the clearing that stretched from the end of the tree line to the Nera river. Alerio had spent the day and most of the night before in Amelia with the Umbri administrator. During his absence, the boat building channel and yard had changed. Load upon load of rocks had been removed from the trench. Now hard and flat surfaced, the yard benefited from large pieces hammered into smaller stones and spread over the ground. And the building channel had square sides and a rough but near flat bottom.

In spots around the yard, logs rested on supports and men sawed and chopped boards from the tree trunks. Other crews hauled in more logs and stacked them out of the way until the carpenters were ready for them. With all the hacking and forming of lumber, Alerio expected to see wood in the channel or stacked on the sides. There was none. Instead, a long building with smoke rising from the seams occupied a large area.

"Master Pous, is the wood coming in satisfactorily?" Alerio inquired as he approached the boat builder.

"We have the oak beams for the center of the keel, the bow, the ram support section, and the stern," Cata Pous remarked.

Looking over the five-foot-deep and fifty-foot-wide trench, Alerio noted a few rock miners chipping away, smoothing out the bottom. "I don't see any beams in the channel."

"They're in the hot lodge," Cata explained while indicating the long building. "The wood needs to dry before we can begin joining the pieces."

"On my father's farm, it took months to dry wood before we could use it for building," Alerio moaned. "I don't suppose you can build a warship with fresh wood. Then again, the boat will get wet when we float it, won't it?"

"Wood dries from the outside inward," Cata described. "If we carve the nubs and notches in fresh wood, when the sections dry, they'll shrink and the seams will be sloppy and the joints loose. Think of a broken shield flopping around on your arm. Then imagine the sides and keel of a warship doing the same."

"That's frightening," Alerio offered. "How long to dry the beams? We don't have all summer. Hades, we may not have another month."

"Is Nardi Cocceia getting worried about his investment?"

"He took great pains to show me his ledgers and to explain the costs in manpower and materials," Alerio reported. "I drank his wine and cooed over his generosity. And I dodged every question about when an official would arrive from Rome to pay him back and bestow citizenship on him."

64

"We have fires burning in the lodge all day and all night," the builder said steering the conversation away from politics. "Another day to be sure the inside is dry and we can begin joining the beams."

"Build us a solid warship and prove Stifone is a viable ship building location," Alerio encouraged the boat builder.

"That, Centurion Sisera, is the point of all this," Cata remarked. "Although, the speed you require is worrisome."

"Having Nardi Cocceia march an army over the Nera to butcher us because we fail to meet his expectations is more troublesome," Alerio warned. "I'll give you what weeks and protection I can."

"How do you plan to do that?" the builder challenged. "You don't even have a phalanx here."

"A Century, master builder, but you are correct," Alerio advised. "If it goes bad, you and I will be sneaking out of Stifone in the middle of the night."

"I'd rather build a ship," Cata remarked to the Legion officer. "We have a lot of work to do."

"And not many weeks to do it in," Alerio confirmed.

***

On the fourth morning, Alerio dodged the line of rock miners. Their job done, they headed up river to the crossing point. Even with their camps gone, the way through the sleeping areas of the remaining workers required zigzagging. Where the trees ended, the Legion officer stopped to scan the work yard.

Six long beams rested end to end on the lip of the channel. Conversely, the wood drying lodge had been reduced in size. There was an obvious connection. Cata

Pous moved between beams, giving directions to carpenters. All the craftsmen had saws, hammers, boring tools, and chisels laid out waiting for the boat builder to finish his detailed instructions.

"Centurion Sisera. The day has arrived," Pejus Monilis said while striding over to join Alerio. "Cata is starting the keel sections."

The master boat builder shouted and the tradesmen placed angled boards on the beams, made marks, and began cutting. In a short time, one end of each beam sprouted a long nub while the opposite end was hollowed out to fit another nub.

"Put your beams in the channel," the builder announced.

Some laborers jumped into the trench while the rest lined up on the other side of the beams. Lifting the wood, they carried the sections to those waiting in the canal.

Alerio and Pejus moved to the edge and peered down at the carpenters and the beams. Cata Pous stepped on the forward section that would eventually hold the ram.

"Join the fore sections," he ordered.

The end nub pushed into the hole and a tradesman bored a hole in the side. Once the drill passed through the nub and out the far side of the beam, a dowel was driven into the hole. When done, the extra lengths were cut flush with the beam.

"We have a good joint," Cata Pous declared after jumping up and down and savagely kicking where the two beams met. "Slide the next one up and pin it."

When eight lengths of thick rafters were joined, there was a seamless oak beam over one hundred and forty-five feet long in the bottom of the trench.

"That's your keel and the beam for your ram," the boat builder announced while walking up a ramp from the canal.

"It's flat," Alerio remarked.

"The curved beams for the fore and aft will be joined later," the boat builder explained. "We'll start the bottom course of the hull first."

"Why not complete the keel?"

"Because once we add the raised sections, we'll need to install the hypozomata," Cata replied.

"The what?" questioned Alerio.

"A rope looping from the front beam to the rear beam of a warship. It's wound tightly to hold tension, keeping the keel beams from being pushed out by the weight of the hull boards," Cata Pous described. "There's no sense in installing the rope too soon. During construction, we'll keep it tight and the original hypozomata will stretch and fray."

"If the rope is so important, we should have an extra," Alerio offered.

"The hypozomata is so critical," Cata assured the Legion officer. "Every warship carries at least one spare. But the extreme length of the line is difficult to construct. It takes over a month to weave the fibers."

Alerio peered around as if looking for something specific. In truth, he wasn't seeking anything. He was trying to find something that needed his attention. Combat Legionaries trained and worked on projects between campaigns. Infantry officers oversaw the endeavors and dealt with personal issues. Between the ship builder, Cata Pous, the engineer, Pejus Monilis, and Optio Florian, Centurion Sisera had nothing that required his attention.

"I didn't see any tar in the area," Alerio remarked. "Do I need to send out a detachment on a search mission?"

"We don't need tar. We have plenty of birch bark," Cata answered. "We'll grind it up and burn it near a wall of the trench. Once the residue is scraped off and collected, we'll have birch-pitch. Reheating it will create our caulking compound."

"Add hemp or other fibers to the mixture and you have all the ship sealant you require," Pejus added. "Sorry, Centurion Sisera, but we have everything under control. You can go take a nap or write a report. Whatever Legion officers do between wars."

If Alerio had a Century of eighty Legionaries, he would be busy. With only Optio Florian and Tesserarius Humi, there weren't enough personnel to occupy his day. He thought about going to inspect Lieutenant Tite Roscini and his seven-man Umbrian security force. But Sergeant Florian was still organizing them. A visit from a Legion officer wouldn't help the training at this point.

With nothing to do and feeling useless, Alerio located the pine tree ladder on the hillside and climbed to the high ledge. In the future, if there was a future boatyard, the terrace would house workers. At the moment, it was a good place to watch the process and stay out of the way.

***

From where he sat on the hill overlooking the channel and work yard, Alerio peered down at the construction activity. Apprentices carried oak boards from the hot lodge. At stations, carpenters measured and carved furrows into the edges, two at the top, on the bottom, and on the sides. Then the boards were passed down to carpenters in the trench.

Another team of carpenters held them edge to edge against other oak planks. Between the planks, flat pieces of oak resembling thin barley cakes were tapped into the furrows. Then the boards were lined up and hammered together. The flat pieces of oak interlocked and held the boards in place.

Holes were bored into the planks, though the flat biscuits and, out the other side. Next, dowels were hammered into the holes locking the two adjacent boards together. As more boards were joined, sections of a wall grew from the center of the keel beam. When the center reached chest high, the carpenters divided to allow separate crews to work the hull from opposite sides.

Late in the afternoon the wall of joined boards reached the aft and the process stopped. Cata Pous and a carpenter measured, chopped, and chiseled on the end of the keel beam. Once they had a square hole, a curved section of oak beam was carried over and the nub inserted. After boring and pinning, the keel of the trireme rose into the air.

Ladders were placed and another curved section was lifted up and set in position. Sticks braced against the walls of the canal held the tail section upright. Soon, other sticks were employed to support the growing height of the hull.

It was beginning to resemble a warship, Alerio thought while gathering his legs under his hips and pushing off the ground.

Partially to a standing position, Centurion Sisera's body jerked to the side then jolted to a stop against the ground. Grass smashed into the side of his face and he sucked in the smell just before something struck him in the back driving the air from his lungs. The sense of not being able to catch his breath ended when the something cracked against his skull.

Act 3

Chapter 11 - Sisera Militia

The sun's rays filtered through the trees to the west. Based on its position, the day passed while Alerio was unconscious. Twisting his neck sent a bolt of pain through one side of Alerio's head. The headache helped him ignore the agony in his wrists. It didn't matter that the pain forced his eyes closed. He couldn't see his wrists. They were bound behind his back. Both hurt and, when hands jerked him to his feet, one shoulder throbbed from the rough treatment.

"Not so tough now, are you?" a voice announced from behind him.

Opening his eyes, Alerio turned his face to the speaker.

"Do I know you?" he inquired.

"Pannacci. War leader," the man bragged while stepping forward. "It was me standing in the administrator's doorway, stopping you and your Legionaries from reaching Nardi Cocceia."

It wasn't how Alerio remembered the confrontation in the government building. Only he and Optio Florian had been involved and they hadn't attacked Nardi. Then it occurred to Alerio, the war leader was talking louder than necessary when speaking a hands width from an ear.

Glancing around, Alerio saw the real audience for Pannacci's words. Three young warriors holding spears. The tips were aimed at the Legion officer's chest.

"Let me guess, you are new to the war leader job," Alerio informed him.

"It doesn't matter how long I have held the position," Pannacci informed Alerio and the three tribesmen. "You slighted the Umbria people and now you will suffer our revenge."

Shuffling back half-a-step as if intimidated by the sharp points, Alerio inquired, "Does the administrator know you're here?"

"Nardi Cocceia is a busy man," Pannacci replied. "I do what I must to avenge the honor of my people."

"And what must you do?" Alerio questioned while looking from spear tip to spear tip. "Besides killing a Legion Centurion?"

Shaking his head as if trying to deny the reality of being a captive, Alerio moved back and away from the spearmen. When all four Umbrians were to his front, he began to twist his wrists.

"Afterward, I will run my knife blade between your ribs," Pannacci said while glancing at his warriors as if to confirm the plan. "And then, I'll throw your dying body off the terrace."

Although it hurt, Alerio could feel the leather bindings stretching and loosening. His limited manipulations weren't enough to unwind the strips from around his wrists. But the pulling and rotating created give and allowed separation between his hands.

"After what?" Alerio questioned.

Pannacci whipped out his knife and the three warriors tensed.

"After we burn that abomination of a boat," Pannacci threatened. Using the knife, he pointed down at the keel

72

and developing hull in the channel. "Once the flames have purified the Umbria dignity, the Republic's desire for Stifone will cool with the ashes."

"Can I ask you something?" Alerio inquired.

"A dead man should be granted a final request."

"What will Nardi Cocceia say when you tell him, the coins he spent on this project have gone up in smoke?"

"The administrator is wealthy and can survive the loss," Pannacci assured the Legion officer. "In time, he will accept the fact that Umbria's future does not lay with the Republic."

Alerio had assumed this attack was purely revenge. But the addition of a political message changed his understanding of the situation.

***

On the boatyard level, carpenters and apprentices stowed tools. Some climbed ramps up and out of the work canal while others walked directly to their camps. In the thin forest, fires flared to life at campsites. Happy at the end of the work day, some of the apprentices began to sing.

To the triad of Umbrian deities
Patre, Marte, and Vofione
Every prayer from every station
Enough to bless
Everyone in the Umbria nation

Alerio's mouth began moving but he didn't allow any sound to escape. When Pannacci turned from looking over the edge, he noted the moving lips.

"What are you saying?" he demanded.

"Let each give to their means, to the priest to buy the beasts and," Alerio mumbled so low that the

73

inexperienced war leader leaned forward. *"the duty of the slaughter."*

Alerio's head racked back then shot forward. Not expecting to be assaulted by a man bound and guarded, Pannacci's neck wobbled like a loose rope, snapping his head from side to side. The unexpected violence from Alerio's headbutt wiped Pannacci's mind and the war leader went comatose.

From below, the apprentices sang as they cleaned up after another hard day.

Every man must offer
And in return receive
As the gods perceive
Their just needs

The three Umbria warriors were singing to each other and not looking at their hostage. But the noise from their leader crashing to the ground snapped them out of the song.

"Three red boars, at the small fountains will be cut," Alerio sang while he dropped to his backside. Once on the ground, he rolled onto the small of his back, jerked his arms with the loose binding from under his butt, and brought them to his chest. *"Upon the ground, spills their blood and guts."*

The Umbria warriors hesitated while determining who was more important, their leader or the prisoner. They decided when one dropped to check on Pannacci and the other two raised their spears, hunched their shoulders, and stalked towards the man sitting in the grass.

Accept our offerings Patre
Everyone beseeches you

74

For a slice of sacrificial meat, creativity
And unique to each, prosperity

Alerio rolled forward onto his knees and lifted his arms. The two spears drew close as if to intimidate the helpless man.

To the nobleman prosperity means
coins of gold
To the Craftsman it lays in parity
To the Freeman finding a betrothed
To the Servant helpings of casserole
And to the lowly Apprentice
Our journeymen are so stern
We strive to survive by uniformity
It's the extent of our prosperity
May the God Patre take pity

Twisting to face the closest spear, Alerio held his hands up and out while he sang.

"Let each give to their means, to the priest to buy the beasts and," he swung both arms out allowing them to fall on either side of the spear's head. *"the duty of the slaughter. Every man must offer."*

The bindings were sliced by the blades of the spear freeing their captive's arms. Stabbing forward and through the target as they had been taught, the Umbrians went for the kill. But their hostage, instead of falling backward, tucked his shoulders and rolled forward. The man's body and the spear tips passed each other by the width of a few fingers.

"And in return receive, as the gods perceive," Alerio crooned while leaping from the ground and onto one of the spearmen. *"their just needs."*

He raised an elbow and hammered the warrior in the back of his neck. Although not a killing blow, the strike caused a spasm to roll down the man's spine.

"Three black cows, at the Tesenaca gate will be cut," Alerio sang. He planted his feet, rotated his hips, and pulled. The spearman arched back, slid over Alerio's hip, flipped, and sprawled on the grass. After executing a quick Legion stomp, the infantry officer snatched the spear from the grass and stepped back three paces. Resetting his feet, he brought the shaft to a guard position. *"Upon the ground, spills their blood and guts."*

With one down and unarmed, the kneeling spearman beside Pannacci rose and raced to join the other warrior. Where they had held a prisoner at spear tips, they now faced off against him.

"You'll not make it off this terrace alive," one of the Umbria warriors threatened.

"Do you see me running?" Alerio asked before resuming the song. *"Accept our offerings Marte. Everyone beseeches you."*

For a slice of sacrificial meat, position
And unique to each, ambition

Below, shouting rose from the tree line when five men bearing torches ran onto the shipyard. They hoisted the burning limbs, drew back, and flung them at the partially constructed trireme. Flipping and snapping flames as they flew across the distance, the torches were an exact match to the activities of Alerio's panicking stomach. It overturned and burned as well.

"To the nobleman ambition means a victorious stand. To the Craftsman recognition," Alerio mumbled when the five burning torches vanished inside the oak walls of the hull.

76

All his bravado and chancy strategies had come to nothing. In frustration, he began to twirl the spear shaft. *"To the Freeman some farmland. To the Servant a dry divan."*

The Legion infantry officer rushed forward. He smashed one warrior's spear shaft off line, bent at the knees, and allowed the rotation of his shaft to carry the oak wood into the other man's spear. Not just the spear but into the man's forward hand. Three fingers broke under the impact and the rotation stopped.

"And to the lowly Apprentice, our daily goals are given," Alerio warbled while reversing the pull and thrusting the butt of his spear into the other Umbrian's head. *"We just want to go fish-in. It's the extent of our ambition. May the Goddess Marte take pity."*

With one warrior out cold, their war leader sitting crossed legged on the ground staring off into space, and another nursing broken fingers, Alerio could have called for the final spearmen to surrender.

He could have but, behind the Centurion's eyes, visions of his mission going up in flames burned and the fire flowed from his mind, down both arms, to the shaft gripped tightly in his hands.

"Let each give to their means. To the priest to buy the beasts and," Alerio stepped forward. With the shaft extended, it appeared as if he offered to duel with the last Umbrian. *"the duty of the slaughter."*

Every man must offer
And in return receive
As the gods perceive
Their just needs

It wasn't a duel or even a fair fight.

77

"*Three white faced oxen, at the Vehiia gate will be cut,*" Alerio crooned. While the words came out no rougher than before, the side to side strikes of his spear were harder and firmer. The Umbrian held on, unable to attack, only to defend against the angry onslaught. "*Upon the ground, spills their blood and guts.*"

Alerio had enough. He pulled the spear tip across the side of the spearman's neck. "*Accept our offerings Vofione.*"

The artery spewed a river of blood but Alerio missed the red deluge. His anger hotter and a deeper red than the blood.

"*Everyone beseeches you, for a slice of sacrificial meat, deflection,*" he sang while stabbing the man with the broken fingers. Then, the Legion officer ran the shaft through the chest of the unconscious Umbria warrior. "*And unique to each, protection.*"

Drawing the Golden Valley dagger from the small of his back, Alerio walked to Pannacci. Reaching down, he hooked the man's arm, and jerked him to his feet. Then he shook the Umbria war leader to get him focused.

"You are new at this and not very good at leadership," Alerio offered while using the tip of the dagger to point out the three dead men. Then, he began to sing while staring into Pannacci's eyes. "*To the nobleman protection means, an oaken spear. To the Craftsman perfection. To the Freeman a good year. To the Servant nothing to fear.*"

At that line, Alerio rested the dagger's blade along the ridge of Pannacci's nose.

"*And to the lowly Apprentice, our daily goals are directions,*" he sang. "*We just want to pass inspection. It's the extent of our protection. May the God Vofione take pity.*"

78

"I am going to blind you before throwing you off the terrace," Alerio warned. "If the fall doesn't kill you, you'll have a few moments to ponder that your future does not lay…Oh wait. You don't have a future. Because when I climb down, I'll finish the job."

"At least we burned the traitor's boat," Pannacci whined. "You'll not have Stifone."

Alerio turned away from the war leader and glanced down to the burning warship. Except there was no bright flame coming from the channel. In the closing darkness, he could make out seven men battling five shapes. There was little doubt the cohesion of the seven was from Legion training.

"Fortūna smiles on you, War Leader," Alerio informed him.

"What?" Pannacci asked.

But he didn't receive an answer. Alerio lifted the knife then kicked Pannacci over the cliff.

"To the triad of Umbrian deities, Patre, Marte, and Vofione," Alerio sang as he walked to the pine tree ladder. *"Every prayer from every station. Enough to bless, everyone in the Umbria nation."*

Chapter 12 - It's Our Trade, but Still Murder

"We had men stationed as fire watchers, with buckets of water in the construction trench," Cata Pous explained. "They put the torches out almost as soon as they landed in the hull."

"A militia patrol spotted the five strangers walking through the workmen's camps," Sergeant Adamo Florian added. "Tite had the patrol follow them and sent one man back to collect me and Corporal Humi."

"Their take down was efficient," Alerio complimented while nodding to Lieutenant Roscini and Tesserarius Humi. His gesture acknowledged their leadership and the skill of the militia when attacking the arsonists. Then the Centurion focused on Florian. "Almost Legion tactics."

"The militia are learning," the Optio replied. He puffed up a little at the recognition of his part in teaching the Umbrians how to fight in a line.

Alerio extended a leg and, with the toe of his boot, nudged Pannacci. The body, crumbled at the base of the cliff, moved as if it was a sack of grain. Lifting briefly on the Centurion's boot, the body settled back into the relaxed pose when the toe was removed.

"And that is a Legion tactic, as well," Alerio commented. The infantry officer referred to the blood stain at Pannacci's groin. "One crisp, targeted thrust. Your work?"

"It's the prescribed ninth strike of spear drills. And smartly delivered," Florian confirmed. "But none of the militiamen have owned up to the killing."

"You don't think it was over exuberance?" Alerio questioned.

"You mean like one of the militiamen got carried away and practiced on a comatose body?" Florian answered. "No sir. The defensive wounds on the hands tell a different tale."

Alerio bent a knee, gripped both of Pannacci's wrists, and twisted them until dead man's palms were visible.

"Deep cuts, both ways, along the length of the hands," Alerio described. He stood and gestured at the dead scattered on the ground. "Pannacci didn't have a chance to release the spear head before he died. It was a quick, in and out, thrust. Your men did good work, Optio."

"Thank you, sir."

The seven militiamen and Tite Roscini glanced at each other. Centurion Sisera's impersonal analysis of the deaths was harsh. Tite and his seven men were relieved to have survived the fighting. But having the Legion officer lump Pannacci's death into the battle and equate an intentional killing to quality spear work, sat uncomfortably with the farmer.

"I'll open an investigation into the murder, sir," Corporal Humi volunteered. "I'll get you answers, Centurion."

"That won't be necessary, Tesserarius Humi. Lieutenant Roscini, have your men bury the bodies and mark the graves. Then set your guard and release the rest of your men," Alerio instructed. "Optio Florian, walk with me."

***

The Legion officer and NCO strolled away from the base of the hill. Once through the sparse forest and the workmen's camps, they jumped down to the sand bar.

"Do you think someone wanted to keep Pannacci quiet, sir?" Florian offered.

Their boots crunched on the gravel and stone. Instinctively, they fell into a marching pace and matched steps.

"I don't know," Alerio replied. "I'm confident it wasn't suicide."

"I know Legionaries who are more beast than men, sir," Florian added. "Not one of them is crazy enough to stab themselves through their cōleī to reach their guts."

"But somebody did kill Pannacci," Alerio pointed out. "And as much as I appreciate your quality spear training and Humi's offer to investigate, I can't allow any disruption in the operation to find out why."

"You might have been right in the first place, sir," Florian said.

"Right. How?"

"Over exuberance. Maybe one of the militiamen saw Pannacci move and stabbed him," Florian suggested. "He might be embarrassed to admit it."

"Or, Pannacci knew about other threats and needed to be silenced," Alerio commented. "I need to hold a surprise inspection."

They reached the end of the sand bar and climbed the river bank. At the first tier of Stifone, Alerio went to the militiamen's quarters while Sergeant Florian took the stairs to the second level to keep watch.

***

A cursory inspection of the barracks left Alerio with an appreciation for Tite Roscini. Tite had selected his seven militiamen from widespread clans. There was little chance of the militia bonding around old family feuds against any of the work crews. The selection also showed him Optio Florian' worth as an NCO for appointing the farm boy as the unit's Lieutenant.

Centurion Sisera finished looking over the tribesmen's gear and headed for the door. Only one

82

family had two members in the militia. Considering the make-up of the unit, it puzzled Alerio why those two. He made a mental note to ask Tite about it later.

Outside, Alerio signaled the Optio to join him. Before the Sergeant reached the stairs, a laborer jogging along the sand bar waved his arms to get the Centurion's attention. He reached the river bank below the town and scrambled up.

"Centurion Sisera, Master Pous needs you at the boatyard," the young man said. "Right away."

Alerio waved Optio Florian off and headed down to the sandbar.

***

"I decided not to install the primary hypozomata," Cata Pous informed Alerio. "And it's a good thing I didn't."

Jutting above the boat trench, two segments of the keel bent inward and curved towards midship as they rose into the air. Being one hundred and thirty feet apart, there was no chance the graceful arches would meet over the trireme.

"The hypozomata is the rope that maintains tension between the fore keel and the stern," Alerio reported. Then he assured the ship builder. "I paid attention when you told me about it."

Cata didn't reply. He silently handed Alerio a three-foot length of cord. It was as thick as a woman's wrist and composed of twisted fibers. The boat builder, Tesserarius Humi, and two militiamen stood looking at the Legion officer as he studied the section of hypozomata cable.

"That is an impressive piece of rope. But it looks like someone used a hammer and an anvil to work on your primary hypozomata," Alerio observed. One end of the line had been neatly cut by a sharp blade while the other end showed signs of abuse by a blunt tool. He studied the hacked, pulled, and smashed fibers. "Did you have a metal worker separate this section?"

"Centurion, the piece you're holding is not our primary rope," Cata answered. "I wanted to save the primary so I had the laborers unpack the secondary hypozomata. And that is what they found."

"A piece of rope?" Alerio questioned.

"Pieces of rope," the boat builder corrected. "Someone pounded the line with a hammer. They created several ruined areas like the one on that piece. After we cut away the smashed and frayed parts, we won't have enough fibers left to reweave the lines into a single rope. At least not one long enough to serve as a hypozomata."

"But you have the primary?" Alerio questioned.

"We do and it's fine," Cata assured him. "And in a few weeks, we can make a second cable. But someone didn't want us to have a spare. If we get much further in the building process and something happens to the primary hypozomata, we'd need to stop construction."

"Pannacci and his men wanted the warship destroyed," Alerio suggested. "Who wants us delayed?"

"I don't know, Centurion," admitted the ship builder. "That's the reason I sent for you."

"Sir, we can begin interrogating the work crews," Corporal Humi suggested. The Legion NCO smacked a fist into his open palm creating a sound resembling meat being tenderized. "I'll find out who did the damage."

"Of that, I have no doubt, Corporal," Alerio assured Humi. "But I'd rather not break the workers' spirit over a rope. We'll find a different way to uncover the culprit."

Not long ago, Alerio Sisera, with no tasks requiring his attention, grasped for something that needed his direction. He now had a purpose at the Stifone shipyard.

"Who had access to the storage shed?" Alerio asked the ship builder.

"Everyone in the boatyard," Cata replied.

"That narrows it down," Alerio announced with a laugh.

"How do you figure?"

"We know the saboteur is an Umbrian," Alerio announced as he walked away.

Cata Pous didn't understand the smile on the face of the young Legion officer, or the man's good humor at the discovery of a vandal in their midst.

It wasn't levity putting the spring in Alerio's steps. It was the focus required and the thrill of a hunt.

***

"Lieutenant Roscini, why do you want to delay the building of the trireme?" Alerio snapped at Tite.

The young farmer rocked back on his heels from the force of the accusation.

"I don't Centurion Sisera," he assured the Legion officer. Tite pointed at the Sergeant. "Ask Optio Florian. He'll prove I am working as hard as anyone for the success of Stifone."

Alerio raised his eye brows and glared at the NCO.

"Sergeant. Place it on my desk, please," Alerio instructed.

When the Optio hesitated, Tite asked, "Place what on your desk, sir?"

"The proof. You said he could prove your loyalty," Alerio replied. "Let me see it."

Corporal Ludovicus Humi slapped a hand over his mouth. The hand hid his grin and prevented any mouth sounds of amusement from escaping. The humor of the situation flew away when the Centurion shifted his eyes in the direction of the Tesserarius.

"When did the militia last do a mountain run, Corporal?" Alerio inquired. "Maybe you should lead one to show the Umbrians how the Legion does it."

"I'll work that into the training schedule, sir," Humi promised. All traces of humor vanished with the Centurion's mention of a run through the mountains.

"See that you do," Alerio commented before refocusing on Tite. "Lieutenant Roscini, someone planned for us to be caught by surprise with a ruined hypozomata. Optio Florian doesn't like surprises. I don't like surprises. No one in the Legion like surprises."

"Yes, sir," Tite said.

"You have two men from the same family in the militia," Alerio reported. "Is there any reason they would want to delay the construction of the warship?"

"Not that I know of, Centurion," he answered. "They came recommended by area Administrator Nardi Cocceia. And I don't believe he wants any delay."

Alerio looked down at a growing pile of parchment. Each sheet listed manpower and materials used for building the trireme. All were paid by Nardi Cocceia with the expectation the Administrator would be reimbursed once the warship was delivered. As well as a reward by the Senate for his service.

"I do not think the administrator wants to foot the bills for any more days than necessary," Alerio observed. "Set your militia watches so we have overlapping guards on the shipyard and the camps. Let's see if we can prevent any further sabotage. Dismissed."

Lieutenant Tite Roscini saluted, turned, and marched out of the room.

"Thoughts?" Alerio questioned his two Legion NCOs.

"Centurion, Tite is solid. If he trusts his militiamen, I have to think our trouble is coming from elsewhere," Florian remarked.

"We could roust the laborers', carpenters', and craftsmen's camps, sir," Corporal Humi suggested. "A little physical encouragement and I bet we could uncover the culprit."

"What makes you think it's one person?" questioned Sergeant Florian.

"Well, I just thought. That if. Ah well, one person could sneak around and do damage unseen," the Tesserarius finally got out. "Give me the word Centurion and I'll start questioning the Umbrians."

"Let's hold off on beating and angering the work force for now," Alerio stated. "That would slow us down worse than having to assemble a new rope."

"If that's want you want, sir," Humi said.

"Orders?" Florian asked.

"There's nothing we can do short of penning the Umbrians up like slaves," Alerio described. "And we don't have Centuries to accomplish that. For now, all three of us need to be vigilant and visible. Maybe our presence will discourage anymore wreckage."

Chapter 13 - Progress Reports

For three weeks, as the hull rose on either side of the trireme and expanded to close in on the fore and aft beams, nothing out of the ordinary happened. Metal workers sharpened and repaired steel and iron tools. Carpenters notched boards, carved biscuits, and bored holes for the dowels. Craftsmen, laborers, and apprentices scurried around doing the one thousand and one things necessary to build a ship-of-war.

Growing up on a farm, Alerio learned to enjoyed sunrise and the dark, still hours before. It was why he picked the third watch. Plus, at dawn, the work started and he was there to answer questions when the laborers arrived.

Cata Pous, the boat builder, and Pejus Monilis, the engineer, would arrive to supervise. When they did, Centurion Sisera made a habit, to their annoyance, of cheerfully greeting them.

***

This morning was no different. The pair of masters, huddled in robes against the early morning chill of the mountain air, came out of the thin forest groggy and sleepy eyed.

"Good day, master builder and master engineer," Alerio roared. "While you rested in the arms of Hypnos and acted in Morpheus' plays, the Legion was standing watch."

"I neither slept well nor dreamed," Pejus Monilis complained. "I was worried about flooding."

Alerio looked up at the morning sky and searched for clouds.

"I see no sign of Tempestas," he declared. "Perhaps you dreamed of rain and a storm?"

"The dry of summer has passed," Pejus said as if explaining something to a child. "Until the first frost, rain in the mountains will rush down and raise the Nera. A surge of a couple of feet and the river will wash over the sandbar and flood our building channel."

"And the worker's camps," Cata Pous added.

"In your sleeplessness, Master Monilis, did you arrive at a solution?" Alerio asked.

"Yes, Centurion. We move the camps out of the work area," Pejus responded. "And we build an earthen berm between this area and the river."

Alerio peered off into the distance as if he could see through the trees. Slowing pivoting, he rotated, visualizing the bend in the river. Once facing westward where he could see the Nera beyond the partially constructed trireme, Alerio stopped and frowned.

"How far?" he whispered without taking his eyes off the river.

"We'll need to construct a third of a mile of soil and rock barrier," the engineer replied. "Plus, it would be best if we relocated the workers' camps, just in case the dam fails. That means building steps to the higher elevation."

"And what do you have to say about this development, Master Pous," Alerio inquired.

"Diverting all our labor will delay the ship building," Cata answered.

"Pejus. Did you destroy our secondary hypozomata?" Alerio questioned without looking at the engineer.

"Excuse me, Centurion Sisera. Why would you ask that?" Pejus questioned.

"Because the berm is a delay and anyone helping to delay our project is a suspect?"

"Are you accusing me of being the saboteur?"

"Not really. My mind is occupied," Alerio admitted. "I need to go and write a couple of letters."

"Letters? You're thinking of missives while we discuss shifting our efforts?" Cata inquired.

Alerio lifted an arm and indicated the river bank downstream.

"I spotted a Century guide pole between the hills," Alerio offered. "A patrol from Fort Orte can carry letters back to the fort and from there, they can be shipped to the Capital. So, yes, letters. Two to be exact."

In a few heartbeats, the pole with a small battle flag appeared briefly before vanishing behind a hill.

"Letters, yes," Pejus stated. "I need to write my family."

He and Alerio walked away, leaving the Greek standing alone.

"I'll get the carpenters started on the steps," Cata advised.

Alerio lifted an arm and waved back, "You do that, master builder."

***

In his office, Alerio settled behind his desk. With his hand hovering over a piece of parchment, he hesitated. The easy part was who should he write to. It was the exact message that gave him pause.

Even though absent, Tribune Subausterus was next in Alerio's chain of command. Obviously, he deserved a progress report. But, should the staff officer also be warned about Nardi Cocceia's expectations? If dashed by a negative reply from the Tribune, the Administrator would pull his support and end the warship's construction. Alerio settled for a general description of the situation.

"Let's see if you can read between the lines, Tribune Subausterus," Alerio challenged while setting the first document to the side.

Sliding another piece of paper off a stack, Centurion Sisera stopped. This time it wasn't a pause, it was a full halt to the enterprise. He and Fleet Praetor Zelare Sudoris did not get along. Then, two bad thoughts occurred to Alerio.

He could simply not write a letter to the Fleet Praetor. That would solve the problem. But it would leave the Republic's Navy unaware of the new trireme. Besides, Alerio's ego wanted to brag, even if just a little. The second bad thought was to deny Tribune Subausterus any credit in the letter. While it was tempting, Alerio knew the Senate had chosen the Tribune to head the Stifone project. They expected to see him mentioned in all reports.

"Dear Praetor Zelare Sudoris. I, Centurion Alerio Sisera, am a master negotiator and a manager without peer. And possibly, the greatest thing to ever happen to the Republic's Navy," Alerio stated. "And maybe to the Legion in a hundred years."

He didn't write that. Instead, he listed the progress made on building the ship and added a request for funds to enlarge the trench and start work on a quinquereme. One thing occurred to him when he finished. Grabbing another piece of parchment, he started a letter to his mentor, former General and current Senator, Spurius Carvilius Maximus.

In politics, as in a war, you wanted someone you could trust at your back. And he couldn't think of anyone better than Senator Maximus standing with him if this turned into a political battle.

After sealing the three letters, Alerio walked outside to wait for the Legion patrol to arrive. Pejus appeared and displayed a letter of his own. After a walk down to the river, the engineer made his way along the sandbar towards the work site.

***

Centurion Decalcavi allowed First and Second Squads to form a loose line on the upper portion of Stifone. The other two squads he sent down to the sandbar to wait for him.

"Centurion Sisera. Compliments of Senior Centurion Baccharis," the infantry officer said while extending a wineskin. "We received a shipment from the Capital and he thought you might enjoy one of the comforts of the officer's mess."

Alerio started to inform the other Centurion that he hadn't been an officer long enough to miss the comforts of dining with fellow officers. But he had been a Legion NCO and understood good fortune and excellent vino.

"Please thank the Senior Centurion for me," he said while taking the wineskin. "I have letters, if you have an assigned courier."

"Pass the word, I need acting Tesserarius Ippazio," Decalcavi called to the line of marching Legionaries. One broke from the column and jogged back up the hill. Then to Alerio, the infantry officer added. "The rest of my Century are on a reinforced patrol heading north with Baccharis. My Sergeant and Corporal are with him. I'm using the route through Umbria as an opportunity to evaluate the NCO potential of my First and Second squad leaders."

"Are you expecting trouble?" Alerio inquired.

"Nope. We'll touch on Amelia then head northwest from the town looking for signs of an Etruscan force trying to flank the main patrol," Decalcavi explained. "We walk this patrol once a month. It's mostly to show Republic strength. But you never know. Maybe the local toughs will decide to give us a go."

"I doubt that," Alerio ventured. "Optio Florian and I slapped a few around when I arrived. And, I've put most of the area's idle hands to work."

"My scout reported construction activity along the river bank. But I never had a good look at it."

A Lance Corporal marched to the officers, saluted, and inquired, "Sir. You called for me?"

"Decanus Ippazio. Centurion Sisera has reports for the Capital," Decalcavi instructed. "Take charge of them. And, see that the letters catch a courier's chariot when we return to Orte."

Alerio handed the letters to the Lance Corporal along with two silver coins.

93

"These are as safe as a new born lamb in a barn, sir," Ippazio declared while stuffing the missives into a pouch. Then to his officer, the acting Corporal inquired. "I don't see Florian or Humi. Or the engineer, Monilis. They may have letters."

"You'll find them down near the river around the bend," Alerio announced.

"Thank you, sirs," Ippazio said while snapping up a salute before walking away.

"Centurion Decalcavi. I'll make a deal with you," Alerio offered.

"And what would that be Centurion Sisera?"

"I'll show you some good engineering and a warship under construction," Alerio replied. "Then you stay and dine with me tonight."

"I really should keep this patrol moving."

"I seem to have come into some excellent vino," Alerio offered while patting the wineskin. "And I could use some help drinking it."

A smile crept over the infantry officer's face and he nodded his approval.

"It's a worthy task," Decalcavi announced. "Let me tell my squad leaders to set up their tents and we'll go see this mountain craft of yours."

"It's a trireme and it's not mine," Alerio stated. "It's the newest warship in the Republic's Navy."

"If it floats and can make it downriver to the Capital in one piece," Decalcavi challenged.

"It'll do both," Alerio assured the other officer.

**

Lance Corporal Ippazio knew Sergeant Florian, Corporal Humi, and Master Monilis. He knew them by

94

name and on sight. Until this visit, finding them in the village of Stifone had been easy. But the work area he walked through was divided into three general zones and each swarmed with workmen.

The side with the hill behind the partially built staircase had tool sheds. Plus, longer buildings with smoke drifting through holes in the roof. Then there were the metalworkers' fires, their grinding wheels and, raw lumber being sawed into boards.

Another zone was the odd trench cut into the rock. In that zone, a ship was taking form, and workers were visible only on one side of the hull. But the men working inside the ship and on the other side of the channel were out of sight. To add to the confusion, crews of apprentices raced across planks from the ship to solid ground and back.

The final zone on the far side of the ditch had groups of young boys and teens drawing blades up long pieces of board. They rounded the edges until poles about as big around as a thumb were created. Others sliced and shaped wood to make stacks of oak flats. Each flat resembled a biscuit a little bigger than a human hand.

It appeared to be organized chaos and the Lance Corporal crunched his face, baffled as to where to look first. Relief washed away the worry when the two infantry officers strolled out of the trees. He could follow the Centurions and find the other Republic citizens. Then he would collect their mail and get back to his squad.

"You seem at a loss," Decalcavi suggested. "Land navigation failing you, is it?"

"Yes, sir. Ah, no sir," Ippazio stammered. "It's just, this resembles the docks at the Capital when the grain ships come in. Too many people scurrying around to find anyone."

"Tell you what Decanus, as we find them, I'll tell Florian, Humi, and Master Monilis to come to you with their mail," Alerio promised. "I see this every day and forget how confusing it must appear."

"Thank you, Centurion Sisera, thank you," Ippazio said. He saluted and marched into the trees.

On the far side of the worker's camps, he left the trees, jumped down to the sandbar, and hiked the gravel and sand to Stifone.

***

Late at night, the duty Legionary at Second Squad's tent and camp wakened Ippazio.

"Decanus. There's a man asking for you," the sentry informed him.

"Who?" Ippazio asked while he threw back his field blanket. "Is it one of the Centurions?"

If it was an officer, he'd need to strap on his armor, his gladius, and take his helmet.

"I don't think so," the Private replied. "He's standing away from the fire so his face is hidden. I don't know any officer who wouldn't want to be recognized and saluted."

"Do not ever say that out loud again, Private," Ippazio scolded. Although the squad leader didn't disagree, he worried his young infantryman would be charged with insubordination and punished for voicing the opinion. "Get back to your post. I'll be there shortly."

Settling for a tunic, his red cloak and Legion dagger, Lance Corporal Ippazio laced up his hobnailed boots, brushed aside the flaps, and emerged from the tent.

Immediately, he spotted the visitor on the far side of the campfire. And just as the guard had described, the man stood far enough out of the firelight to hide his face. Plus, a heavy wrap disguised his size and the shape of his body. As Ippazio circled the fire, he regretted leaving his gladius in the tent.

"Can I help you?" he inquired.

"There comes a time when loyal men are called upon to aid the Republic," the stranger whispered in what was noticeably a false voice. "Take this."

A leather pouch came from the folds of the man's wrap, flew the distance between them, and landed at Ippazio's feet.

"What's this?" the Legion squad leader questioned.

"Your chance to help the Republic," the man replied. "Put all the mail from Stifone in that pouch. Inside, you'll find a note with an address in the Capital. Send the mail there."

"Letters from field commands are considered progress reports," Ippazio informed the man. He nudged the leather bag away with the toe of his boot. "I will not tamper with Legion dispatches."

"You'll also find several gold coins in the pouch. The coins are yours, as a reward for doing your duty."

"You think I'll take a bribe to betray the Legion?" Ippazio said raising his voice.

"Keep it down," the man in the shadows instructed. "This is Legion staff officer business."

"Trouble, Lance Corporal?" the duty Legionary asked.

"No. Remain on your post," Ippazio ordered. "What is staff officer business?"

"Centurion Sisera has gone rogue," the man explained. "You saw the building sight. Who do you think is paying for all of that? The Umbrian, that's who. And what promises has he made to get their help? And who is going to claim the warship when it's completed?"

"Look man, I'm a Decanus of heavy infantry," Ippazio pleaded. "I don't know anything about warships, commerce or staff officer business."

"Exactly. And that's why you'll take the coins and have the pouch delivered to the address in Rome," the man insisted. "And squad leader Ippazio, you will tell no one about our meeting."

The Lance Corporal bent and snatched the pouch from the ground. As he straightened, he looked for the stranger but the man was gone.

Chapter 14 - Trade Negotiations

Alerio was tired, a little thick headed from last night's vino but, otherwise in good spirits. Centurion Decalcavi turned out to be a great story teller and the two stayed up late trading tales. With just a short nap to refresh himself before relieving Corporal Humi, Alerio could add sleepy to his maladies. Despite the urge to lay down and take a nap, he cheered up when Cata Pous and Pejus Monilis appeared from the trees.

"Good day, master builder and master engineer," Alerio bellowed. "While you rested in the arms of Hypnos and acted in Morpheus' plays, the Legion stood watch."

"Must you be of such a pleasant nature each morning?" Pejus growled. "I've got to stake out a third of a mile for the dam, fighting heavy brush to place each marker. This will be a hard day."

"In the heavy infantry, Master Monilis, if you aren't having a hard day, you are dead," Alerio informed the engineer. "And what about you, master ship builder, are you anticipating a heavy day?"

"No Centurion. With almost my entire work force commandeered to dig dirt and rocks, I'll be sunning my face and sipping cheap Umbria beer all day."

For a heartbeat, Alerio contemplated giving the boat builder the half full wineskin of good vino. Before he could offer it, one of the master carpenters ran towards them.

"The bores are gone," he announced from fifteen feet away.

"All of them?" Cata demanded.

The carpenter slid to a stop, puffed out a few breaths, and replied, "All but three. They were with the metalworkers for sharpening."

"What does that mean for us?" Alerio inquired.

"Each oak biscuit needs two holes. It's how we connect the hull boards," the boat builder explained. "Without the drills, no holes, without the holes no pegs. Without the pegs, well, in short, we'll be delayed for months."

Alerio squatted and placed one fist on the ground to steady his stance. Then, his head fell forward and hung in defeat.

"What are the alternatives?" he questioned. "Can our metalworkers make new drills?"

"Their forges are small and mostly used for repairs. They can hammer out the bodies for a few tools but they'll require good steel for the boring part," Pejus Monilis offered. "It'll be quicker to buy replacement drills."

"That means going to Administrator Nardi Cocceia for more credit," Alerio whined before warning. "I am way beyond my authority with him as it is."

"How is that possible?" Cata Pous inquired. "You've done an astonishing job of getting Stifone prepared. And look at the progress we've made on the trireme."

"In my talks with Administrator Cocceia, I've led him to believe I have the authority to sanction his expenditures," Alerio confessed. "I'm not sure of the details in the Republic's treaty with the Umbria nation. But I can assume, the treaty does not have a clause permitting a junior infantry officer to conduct trade negotiations."

"I have found, Centurion, that politicians will forgive much if they receive more," Pejus Monilis offered. "And I dare say, a warship for the Republic's Navy qualifies."

Optio Florian and Tesserarius Humi appeared from the trees. Sprinting, they crossed the boatyard to Alerio.

"A militiaman woke us," the NCOs explained. "What's the crisis, sir?"

"Most of our drills are gone," Alerio answered. He looked from one Legionary to the other. When neither spoke, he queried Humi. "What? No offer to torture the workers to uncover the culprit, Tesserarius?"

"Sir. The saboteur has done an adequate job of doing damage and covering his tracks," Humi suggested. "I don't think he'll confess under any circumstance."

"I don't either," Alerio admitted. "Someone, please, tell me how this happened?"

100

Alerio expected to hear an excuse from his Corporal. The NCO had the second watch and the tools must have been taken in the dark. But a master carpenter spoke first.

"We left our saws, mallets, hatchets, and drills at our work stations," he explained. "The tools are our livelihood and our responsibility. They should have been put away at the end of the day."

"But how did all the drills vanish?" Alerio insisted. "I don't believe Vulcan suddenly had a burning need for used boring tools. Awakened last night and decided to visit Stifone and carry our drills back to his godly forge. Yet, someone took them."

"It doesn't matter," the carpenter stated. "They're our responsibility. My apprentice and I will travel to Amelia and speak with Nardi Cocceia about replacements."

"There you go, Centurion Sisera," Cata Pous said. "The carpenter will speak with Administrator Cocceia for you."

Alerio lifted his face to meet the five pairs of eyes staring down at him. In those faces, he read the need for leadership. Realizing his posture was submissive and not relaying confidence, the Legion officer straightened his legs and rose to his full height.

"We have a berm to construct and stairs to finish," he pointed out. "Once the upper area is accessible, have the laborers rotate off the dam detail to move their belongings. Master Pous, you will not be sunning today. I need you to supervise the relocation of the camps to the upper level."

"Orders for us, sir," Optio Florian asked.

"Go rest. I need you two to be alert in case our disparager attempts another delaying tactic," Alerio replied. Then to the carpenter, he advised. "Help with the stairs. Once they're done, move your things to the new site, then head for Amelia."

"Very good, Centurion," the woodworker agreed.

The Carpenter, boat builder, and the Legion NCOs walked away leaving Alerio alone with a grinning master engineer.

"You seem to have revived," Pejus Monilis observed.

"If you have such a hard day of placing markers ahead of you," Alerio stated. "Don't you think you should get started?"

"Yes, sir," the engineer acknowledged, before saluting and strolling to his surveying equipment.

Alerio closed his eyes and offered a prayer to the Goddess Pietas. Hopefully, the letters he sent to Tribune Subausterus and Fleet Praetor Sudoris would bring instructions and authorization. With a sanction from either of them, he could honor the goddess and continue building the warship. But, any delay in the ship's progress gave an opportunity for Nardi Cocceia or any other powerful Umbrian to realize Alerio Sisera was only a junior Centurion, acting on his own.

"Pietas, I am trying," he whispered to the goddess of duty.

***

The aroma of stew drifted through the window and Alerio involuntarily rolled in the direction of the delicious smell.

"If you are cooking under my window, there better be enough to share," he warned while swinging his legs off the bed. "And what is that?"

"Rabbit stew, Centurion," Corporal Humi called up from the yard. "And there is plenty. I went hunting because I was sick of Umbria salted pork and wanted fresh meat."

After slipping on a tunic, strapping on his boots, and belting on his pugio, Centurion Sisera followed the smoke to a table with two chairs located beside the Legion house. Nearby, a large iron pot hung over a low cooking fire.

Humi poured a mug of vino when Alerio approached and offered it to the officer.

"Have a seat, sir. I'll get you a bowl of stew."

The afternoon sunlight filtered through the trees on the mountains. The angle let Alerio know the lateness of the day.

"Did the carpenter make it off alright?" Alerio asked before sitting.

"I'm assuming he left for Amelia shortly after the Optio relieved you, sir," Humi ventured. "I took a nap and woke up hungry. Grabbed a bow and headed into the mountains. Found three fat hares and here they are, gracing our pot."

"They're delicious," Alerio admitted after chewing and swallowing a piece of tender meat. "Where were you stationed before Stifone, Tesserarius?"

Humi stirred the pot then dropped to his knees and, using a stick, stoked the flames. After silently attending to the fire, he stood.

"Did you hear me?" Alerio inquired.

103

"Oh, sorry sir. I was thinking about my time at the Legion transfer station," the NCO said. "I forgot to say it."

"Which station?"

"The northern transfer station at the Capital," Humi answered after a long pause.

"You must know Tesserarius Gratian," Alerio offered. Then as a tease, he added. "Too bad the man hates gambling so much."

Humi's reply surprised Alerio.

"Some NCOs don't understand a man requires distraction from the routine of garrison duty," the Corporal declared. "Yes, sir, he's a fanatic against wagering, that one is."

There could be a number of reasons Humi mischaracterized Corporal Gratian. The most obvious was a Legionary protecting an NCO's reputation from an officer. Alerio could have told Humi he knew Gratian when he was Recruit Sisera. And that Gratian was renowned for his gambling but, he didn't. Then, Humi stepped away from the cooking fire.

"I'm going to relieve Optio Florian, sir," the Corporal announced. "I'll see you later, sir."

Humi marched away and Alerio realized the flames were blazing high up the sides of the iron pot. To prevent the stew from burning on the bottom, Alerio took the ladle and swirled the stew. Bones, bare from where the meat had cooked off, rose to the surface. Except, connective tissue still held some of the bones together. In a stew that had been cooking all afternoon, the bones should be loose.

But stirring released more of the smell and the aroma heightened Alerio's hunger. He forgot about the bones as he dipped the ladle. With a full bowl, Alerio sat and ate more of the delicious rabbit stew.

***

Shortly after the moon passed the top of the sky, Alerio relieved Corporal Humi.

"I have the watch, Tesserarius."

"Yes, sir. You have two militiamen walking counter routes around the warship," Humi reported. "And another stationed at the steps leading up to the worker's camp."

"Is there a problem?"

"Not that I'm aware of," the NCO admitted. "It was Lieutenant Roscini's idea. He mentioned something about wanting to know when someone entered the boatyard."

"An excellent idea," Alerio acknowledged. "You are dismissed."

"Good night, sir."

Alerio walked the circuit and met both patrolling militiamen before cutting across the yard. At the set of new wooden steps, he was challenged.

"Who are you?" a voice inquired.

"Centurion Alerio Sisera," Alerio answered.

He stepped out of the dark and into lantern light.

"Is there much traffic during the night?" Alerio asked the sentry.

"Fire tenders, Centurion," the Umbrian replied. "Apprentices come down to check the fires in the drying houses."

"Anyone else?"

105

"No, Centurion," the militiaman reported. "Sane people are sleeping."

"I can't argue with that," Alerio admitted.

He walked back into the dark to check on the two roving guards.

***

Smoke from cookfires drifted down to the boatyard letting Alerio and the men on guard duty know the laborers were waking. By the time sunlight shoved back the night, men were walking the stairs from the heights.

"Spare us the talk, Centurion Sisera," Cata Pous and Pejus Monilis said at the same time. "We're glad the Legion is here to protect us."

"Couldn't have said it better myself," Alerio responded.

Rather than converging on the trireme, the work force headed into the thin forest where they had recently made camp. On the bank of the Nera, they formed a long line and began sending scoops of dirt, and large rocks to a marked line at the top of the bank.

"We have another crew in the water pulling up river stones," Pejus advised. "They're tossing them onto the opposite side of the berm."

"Will it hold if the river reaches that height?" Alerio inquired.

"If it's a steady rise, yes," the engineer answered. "But, a full-on rushing flood? No. That would sweep everything away, no matter how well we build the dam."

Alerio walked with Pejus as the earthen works grew taller and elongated. They had reached beyond the bend in the river when a cry rose from far behind them. The

106

Legion officer and the engineer raced to the boatyard to investigate.

The woodsmen were charged with cutting and bringing in logs and hunting for food. A large group of them circled objects laying on the ground.

"What have you got?" Alerio questioned while shoving woodsmen aside.

When he finally saw the bodies, the Legion officer stiffened and stepped back. He'd seen corpses before. Some long dead and rotting and others so fresh steam still rose from the flesh. The reaction had nothing to do with death but for the deceased themselves. It was the master carpenter and his young apprentice. They never made it to Amelia.

According to the tale being told by the woodsmen, the bodies had been found off to the side of the trail about a quarter of a mile across the Nara River. Although the woodsmen had broken off the shafts, the arrow wounds were obvious for anyone who knew weapons.

"What about our drills?" Cata Pous asked when Alerio backed up to stand beside him.

"I'll go see Nardi Cocceia, myself," Alerio volunteered.

"It could be dangerous?" Cata offered with a nod at the bodies. "The saboteur is still out there."

"I'm a farm boy and at home in the woods," Alerio growled. "And I'm a Legion heavy infantryman. This trip, the archer will not be dealing with a carpenter and a child. He'll have to deal with a different type of craftsman."

"Different type of craftsman?" the boat builder inquired.

"A craftsman of war," Alerio informed him.

He marched away from Cata and towards where Pejus and where the crews were building up the river bank. His jaw set and both fists curled tight making his knuckles white. Centurion Sisera was looking forward to confronting the saboteur. He would be disappointed.

Act 4

Chapter 15 - Cūlī and Elbows

Arrowheads weren't deadly to an infantryman holding a heavy Legion shield. While a shaft guided by Fortūna might slip between the top of the iron band and the brim of a helmet, armor protected the Legionary. For the trip to Amelia, Alerio wouldn't have personal barriers between his body and the murderous archer. But he planned to hunt in concentric circles through the woods, stay off trails and, away from open ground. Hopefully, through doubling back, tracking, and concealment, he would get within a blade's length of the saboteur before catching an arrow.

"Sir. I have to protest," Humi stated. "Armor and a shield are called for when facing an unknown aggressor."

"I have never hunted game in a helmet or shoulder rig," Alerio replied as he wrapped a length of black silk around his waist. "But I have fought undergrowth trying to work a shield through thick woods. I prefer not to do it again."

"Then at least take Optio Florian or me with you to watch your back," the Tesserarius advised. He pointed at the soft material wrapped around Alerio. "That thin layer of silk will not stop a bee's sting let alone a hunting arrow."

Alerio smiled and ran his palm over a section of the silk.

"You'd be surprised how much damage can be controlled by a length of silk," he described. "No company. I want the saboteur to feel comfortable enough to come in close."

"Bowmen reach out and touch their victims from a distance, sir," Humi warned. "They don't have to get close to kill you."

"Corporal, where's your confidence in your Centurion?" Alerio teased while dropping a soft woolen shirt over his head.

"Oh, I'm confident, sir. And pretty sure this is suicide," Humi declared. "As sure as there are two dead carpenters being buried this afternoon."

"Correction, Tesserarius. A carpenter and an apprentice," Alerio said.

He reached into a travel pack and lifted out a dual gladius rig. While the harness swung onto Alerio's back someone knocked on the door. The NCO hurried across the room and opened it.

"Centurion Sisera, Master Pous wants you at the boatyard," a militiaman said from the doorway.

"What's wrong now?" Humi questioned.

"Nothing Tesserarius. They found the boring tools."

***

The earthen berm protected the shipyard from upstream surges but did not completely seal the entire area. Rising backwater from downstream, where there was no raised dike, would not have the destructive power of waves pouring through the gap from high in the mountains.

'An extensive soaking would dry. But, demolition by flooding involved picking up pieces of broken warship,

110

rebuilding support structures, and mucking silt out the channel,' Alerio thought. 'Redirecting work from the warship to build the earthwork was a worthy diversion of labor.'

He and Corporal Humi climbed the bank of dirt, jogged through the woods, then quickly walked the length of the trireme. Ahead, they spotted Cata Pous, Pejus Monilis, and a file of laborers. The workmen created a line extending from the flatland, over the bank, and down into the river.

The earthen berm followed the curvature of the river but ended before the dike reached the boat channel. There, it tapered down and blended with the riverbank. A few feet away the boat trench cut through the bank until the vertical sides merged with the river. Only a water barrier at the end of the boat trench prevented the river from backing up and flooding the incomplete warship. Both the engineer and the boat builder stood above the cofferdam.

"The need for your perilous journey has been eradicated," Pejus Monilis boasted when he noticed Centurion Sisera and the NCO.

"How do you figure?" Alerio questioned.

"The missing drills have been located," Cata Pous declared. "They were not taken. Rather, our vandal concealed them in the river. One of the crew, while setting river stones, fell in and floated downstream. If not for that happy accident, we would never have discovered them."

"The poor lad cut his foot when he finally righted himself," Pejus described. "He reached down to investigate the sharp object and lifted out a boring tool."

111

"A Legionary who short cuts an assignment, isn't always a slacker," Alerio muttered so low it was as if he was speaking to himself.

"Excuse me?" Cata asked in confusion. "What do you mean?"

"An Optio taught me the lesson when I was a lad on my father's farm. Doing an incomplete job isn't always a sign of laziness or a lack of motivation," Alerio replied. "If not slothfulness, our saboteur might be assuring the work will continue later. Or they had somewhere better to be."

"Which is this?" Pejus inquired. "Someone wanting to get out of work or is there a grand scheme in play?"

"I wish I knew, master engineer," Alerio admitted. "One thing is clear. Our vandal doesn't want to end the trireme or he would have burned it. His aim seems to be a slowing of the process. Master Pous, how long before the carpenters can get back to work?"

"The metalworkers are cleaning and honing the tools as they're fished out," the boat builder explained. "We should be back to full strength by morning."

"Another lesson from my youth. You can work men hard for short periods or longer at an easy pace," Alerio reported. "Here's what we'll do. Split your labor force in two parts. One group starts work at daybreak but ends their shift in midafternoon. The other section starts at midday morning and works until dark."

"What's the advantage of that?" Pejus inquired.

"Beyond a leisurely breakfast and a relaxing dinner for some carpenters?" Alerio offered. "Pacing. Starting tomorrow, I want to see cūlī and elbows."

"Again, I don't mean to be thick headed," Cata pleaded. "but what does that mean?"

"It means, Master Pous, Centurion Sisera does not want to see anyone standing around or resting," Corporal Humi informed the boat builder. "Sir, set the pace?"

Alerio began clapping his hands. Shortly after, a tempo became apparent. Above a resting heartrate but below one experienced during a hard run, the pace could be maintained for long periods by groups working together to complete a task: hauling in a fishing net; rowing in unison; harvesting a field of grain; constructing a brick structure; or building a ship-of-war, the relentless pace always driving the workers forward.

"That's a novel approach," Pejus commented. "I approve."

"Master Monilis, you might not be as pleased by the end of the week," Alerio warned while his hands continued to beat out the rhythm. "This ship will be built as soon as humanly possible."

"I see no problem with the method," Pejus bristled.

"There will be two shifts of woodworkers, metalworkers, and laborers," Cata Pous pointed out. "But only one of me for design and one of you for plotting and layout."

A shadow fell across the engineer's face and his eyes became unfocused for a heartbeat.

"When do we rest?" Pejus demanded.

"Cūlī and elbows, Master Engineer," Alerio stated while walking away.

As he retraced his steps alongside the trireme, the Legion officer's palms beat together in the steady tempo.

Light streaked across the sky, broken in areas by low hanging clouds. As dawn approached, so did the eight militiamen, and both Legion NCOs.

"Where do you want us, sir," Optio Florian inquired.

"For now, line them up at the base of the cliff," Alerio directed. "If they don't move, we'll go up and kick them awake."

In the dark, Tite Roscini and his men formed a rank with Florian and Humi. Alerio stepped behind the line.

"I'll lead us off. You join me on the second round," he instructed.

"Centurion, why don't we simply go up there and wake them?" Tite inquired.

"Because, Lieutenant Roscini, men respond better to chanting than to challenges," Alerio informed him. "Enter a tent and half the men will come at you for bothering them. The other half will pull their blankets over their heads and go back to sleep."

"I have a brother like that," Tite ventured.

"Which type?" Humi asked.

"Both," responded the militia officer. "One likes to sleep and the other likes to fight. Father always called them from the other side of the villa."

"If we are all agreed that chanting works, can I begin?" Alerio inquired.

"Yes, sir," all ten men said.

Alerio elevated his head and scanned the edge of the high ledge. There were no lights or movement. He began to chant.

"Put an end to your nasty sleep
Kick life into your merda and leap

Into the adventure of the fray
Fling off your blanket
As Nyx absconds with the night
And Luna abandons the sky
Stand on your feet
Prepare to die
As Hypnos lefts the veil
Our eyes use the light
To build, to fight
Awaken, be public
For a new day dawns
And there's killing that needs done."

"Ah, sir. You're waking carpenters and laborers, not Legionaries," Sergeant Florian suggested. "Maybe soften the wording?"

"Good idea Optio. Let me try again."

Low, so only those on either side of the militiaman could hear, one whispered, "Just his voice alone would wake the dead. I think the carpenters will get up purely out of self-defense."

"Pay attention," Alerio warned. "You'll be chanting with me later."

"Can we all agree to do it loudly?" the same militiaman added.

Centurion Sisera feeling confident began again.
"Put an end to your private sleep
shake life into your hands and leap
Into the adventure of the day
We ask you Janus
make today a good beginning
And Zelos grant our bodies zest

To hug puppies
To our breasts
The gift of Pietas
Duty gives us the right
To build, to excite
Awaken, be public
For a new day dawns
And there are friends to be won"

"How was that Optio?" Alerio questioned.

"Not totally the proper wording, sir," the Sergeant ventured. "There is no doubt they'll wake but again we're waking carpenters, not shop owners."

"I guess that was a little off," Alerio acknowledged. "Let me try it again."

"Oh, please and let me poke my ears out," the militiaman begged.

Alerio didn't hear the remark, as he had begun chanting.

"Put an end to your private sleep
Kick life into your limbs and leap
Into the adventure of the day
Sol Indiges gives light
By hurling the sun across the sky
And the rays bring Spes potential
Her hope
Is essential
Blessed by the Goddess Bia
For men need might
To build, to fight
Awaken, be public
For a new day dawns

And there are deeds to be done"

A few voices shouted from the camps followed by several items pitched over the cliff.

"I believe they are rousing," Alerio observed. "Let's give them another rendition to be sure the first crew is up."

Before, Alerio could lead, the ten-man line began chanting.

"Put an end to your private sleep
Shake life into your hands and leap
Into the adventure of the day
We ask you Janus
make today a good beginning
And Zelos grant our bodies zest
To hug puppies
To our breasts
The gift of Pietas
Duty gives us the right
To build, to excite
Awaken, be public
For a new day dawns
And there are friends to be won"

By the end of the verse, curses and solid items rained down on the NCOs and militiamen.

"Detail, dismissed," Alerio shouted as he jogged away from the base of the cliff.

His men dispersed rapidly in separate directions. Alerio sighted the master engineer and ship builder and he angled towards them.

"Is that a Legion fighting formation?" Cata Pous inquired seeing the militiamen scatter.

"No, Master Pous. That is the reward for a job well done," Alerio replied. "I believe your work force will be down shortly."

"And if they don't come down?"

"Then I'll go up there and throw one off the cliff," Alerio advised.

"Only one, Centurion Sisera?"

"Usually, that's all it takes for men to realize the seriousness of a situation," Alerio explained.

"Would you deem this situation serious?" Pejus Monilis inquired.

"We have a benefactor who can close us down with the pull of a purse string. An absent Tribune with the authority to endorse our method of operating but can't be reached," Alerio listed. "And an unknown agent who would prefer we relax and take long naps. So indeed, Master Monilis, I would say our situation is critical."

"We should get to work," Cata suggested.

He pointed at the steps. Lines of craftsmen and apprentices filled the treads.

"It seems you won't be launching anyone this morning," Pejus remarked.

"We'll see how the rest of it goes," Alerio warned as he began clapping his hands together in the work rhythm.

"We know, Centurion Sisera," Cata commented. "Cūlī and Elbows."

Chapter 16 - Fire and Prometheus

Four days of extraordinary production saw the hull connect with the fore and aft keel risers. Enclosed in the oak hull, Cata Pous and Pejus Monilis measured the interior. Beginning on one end, they placed markers and etched marks for ribs, beams, posts, and the location of rowers' benches. While the layout appeared roomy in the empty hull, once the rowers were seated, the unitarian positions would be claustrophobic. For now, the trireme appeared to be a wooden replica of a splayed whale carcass.

On the grounds of the shipyard, carpenters shifted from carving hard oak boards to working lighter and softer pine, spruce, and fir lumber. Studs and posts to support the hull and top decks were cut from cedar. The aromatic wood inundated the area with a fresh aroma.

"This will be the best smelling warship in the world," Pejus observed.

"Don't get ahead of yourself," Cata cautioned. "After a few months of oarsmen sweating and relieving themselves, this ship will stink like all the others."

"Although, not presently, master ship builder," Pejus said while carving adjoining lines into the keel beam. "It's as fresh as a new latrine and, an example of why I prefer working on new construction."

They measured and moved to another section. After positioning the angle tool, Pejus notched another set of lines on the oak beam. At the front of the trireme, apprentices lowered planks over the hull where they were untied by journeymen carpenters. Once fitted to the engineer's marks on the keel, holes were drilled and the carpenters pounded in dowels. Then, they reached for the next plank hanging over the side.

Away from the trench and trireme, Optio Florian patrolled between tool storage and wood drying sheds.

"You two," the Sergeant barked at a pair of lounging apprentices. "You are moving with purpose or you are climbing to the camps to take a nap. Which is it? Because standing around comparing the size of your mentulae won't help them grow. Move along."

The two jerked away from the wall of the shed and faced the Legion NCO.

"We are assigned to watch the drying sheds," one reported.

"I can't imagine anything more thrilling than watching wood dry," Florian remarked. "Lets' examine the duty. Is there no part of watching boards dry that requires activity?"

"Keeping the embers buried under ash to prevent the flames from flaring up and starting a fire," the other apprentice answered.

"There you go, a mission," the Optio said with enthusiasm. "Why don't you start with the shed you were holding up?"

"Holding up?" the first inquired.

"With intellect like yours, you could be Veles," the NCO of heavy infantry offered. "Check the shed you were leaning on. Then every shed between the cliff and the channel."

"This shed is for oar drying," the second apprentice offered. "There is almost no heat because the doors are never opened."

"And why is that?" the Sergeant inquired.

"Once they harvested two hundred young fir trees, they sealed the shed," the apprentice explained. "We only check it three times a week."

"What day is this?"

"Tuesday, I guess."

"Imagine that, the exact day you check the shed," the Sergeant instructed. "Movement people, the Centurion wants movement."

Both apprentices rushed for the entrance. They lifted the locking bar, opened the door, and vanished into the drying shed. Optio Florian nodded approvingly at the hustle displayed by the two young men before he continued his patrol of the boatyard.

***

Cold rain soaked their cloaks and water dripped from their helmets and splattered off their cheeks and noses.

"There is something invigorating about being cold and wet on a black night," Alerio lied while lifting his hands to the covered lantern. Almost no heat radiated from the small flame.

"Yes, sir. As the saying goes, misery and third shift go hand-in-hand. And the only time a third shift sentry is happy is when he is relieved of duty," Tesserarius Humi remarked. "I imagine you'll be happy later this morning. Me, I am about to get very warm and happy."

"Dismissed, Corporal," Alerio said relieving the NCO. "Go drink some vino for me."

"Gladly, sir," Humi promised.

The NCO's form blurred into the dark rain and Alerio turned to another spot of light. Using it as a guide, the Legion officer marched from the light next to the

121

construction channel in the direction of the stairs at the base of the cliff.

When he got close, Alerio laughed at the ingenuity of the militiamen. A goatskin wrap hung under the risers of the stairs providing shelter from the rain. A small fire offered heat.

"Can you see who comes down or approaches the steps?" Alerio inquired.

"Yes, Centurion. Both ways and it's dry under here," the man replied. "There's room for two, if you want to come in."

"No. We have roving patrols and if they're walking in the weather, so am I," Alerio responded.

"Stay alert, sir," warned the Umbrian. "Only bad things will come out on a night like this."

"Did you hear something I should know about?"

"No, Centurion Sisera. We're mountain folk and the mountains are full of threats," the militiamen stated. "And nights like this are an invitation for things that hunt after dark to prowl."

"I'll keep that in mind," Alerio remarked before marching away.

Twenty paces from the stairs, Alerio noticed a horizontal bar of flickering light. The odd shape baffled him. Between the light brightening and fading, and the rain acting as a filter, he couldn't understand it. Then his mind sorted the images and he understood.

"Fire," Alerio shouted before a weight slammed into the back of his head.

The strike sent him stumbling forward. After several uncoordinated steps, Alerio fell face first into the mud. Confused as to how he ended up on the wet ground, his instincts wanted him to lay still until his senses returned. When his mind failed to act, his training took control.

'Never be where your enemy expects you. Never take the blow. Never go on defense when attacked.'

The words and lessons to a young Alerio from an experienced Centurion shot through his mind. From the flash of memory, his reflexes sent impulses through his limbs. He tucked, curled, and rolled.

A thick oak board smacked into the ground a hand's width from his head. Feeling the mud splash on his face brought awareness back to the Legionary. He extended his legs and scissor kicked. One foot connected with his attacker's leg.

The man fell forward and his arm shot out to prevent a fall. His hand sank into the mud.

The momentary touch to stabilize the assailant lasted an instant before the man righted himself and ran off into the dark. Alerio rolled to his butt, put his hands on the ground, and pushed off. He drew his gladius and the pugio, dropped into a defensive stand, and waited with both blades extended for another attack.

***

Being soaked from the rain, the roof steamed at first. But the intense fire consumed the walls after burning everything inside the shed. Almost as if tipping a hat in greeting to the dawn, the roof tilted, paused, then collapsed into the flames.

"What was in that shed?" Alerio asked when the engineer and boat builder ran up.

"Those were our one hundred and seventy oars, Centurion Sisera. Plus, thirty or more extra," Cata reported. "It will take a while to harvest that many young fir trees."

"Plus, the weeks needed to dry and carve the oars," Pejus advised. "It seems the saboteur has visited another unpleasant deed on us."

"I sensed desperation in this act," Alerio suggested. He rubbed the back of his head and winced when his palm ran over the knot.

"Because he burned the shed during your watch?" Pejus inquired.

"No. Because for a brief moment, he collected his manhood and came at me," Alerio responded. He pointed to the handprint in the mud. "I want that fenced in."

"The handprint?" Cata questioned.

Alerio spit at the depression. A glob smashed into the imprint of one finger.

"Yes, and I want a sign posted," the Legion officer ordered. "Have it spell this, *by the Goddess Algea, I will break each of those fingers. Until that day, everyone is invited to spit on the handprint of a coward.*"

"You would have us blaspheme the goddess of pain for a public jest," Pejus asked in horror.

"Master engineer, it's better than if I invoke my personal goddess," Alerio informed him.

"And who is that, sir?" Optio Florian inquired.

The NCOs stepped forward to confront their Centurion about a bad decision. They had arrived before daylight and worked with the militia to guard the rest of the sheds. The Legionaries were exhausted from tension and lack of sleep.

Alerio spit on the handprint again and started to march off.

"Sir. I asked you a question?" Florian insisted taking a step as if to chase down the Centurion. "Who do you pray to in the darkest of times, Sisera?"

Alerio stopped and turned to face the group of laborers, his staff, and the construction masters.

"The blessed Nenia is my personal goddess. In my heart when all is lost, I demand that the goddess of death make a choice. Take me or take my enemies," he spoke the words slowly so they sank in. "Fence and sign, now. And gentlemen, do not question me again about oaths of vengeance."

At the words from the young infantry officer, a chill ran down the spine of everyone in the crowd. In addition, one of the witnesses to Alerio's revelation began to sweat.

***

Late in the afternoon, Alerio woke and stretched. Along with a slight headache, his body felt stiff. It was an odd sensation for the extremely fit weapon's instructor. Fearing the job of being the officer-in-charge of Stifone was making him soft, he tossed on his woolen work clothes, strapped on his gladius, took a spear from the weapons rack, and left the house in search of a training partner.

Luckily, as soon as he stepped out of the front door, he spotted five partners.

"I'd like to apologize to you," Alerio declared when he reached the bottom tier of Stifone. The five militiamen stopped their sword drills and stared at the Centurion. "I've been so busy, I've neglected you."

The five stepped away from the Centurion as if a strong wind blew them back.

"What's the problem?" Alerio inquired.

They hesitated before one took a half step forward.

"We do not want your goddess to decide our fate," the militiaman stammered.

Alerio glanced from face to face. Believing it was a sin to let a good myth pass by unreinforced, he agreed.

"I, of all people, understand that sentiment," Alerio said in a low serious voice. The five nodded in appreciation of his dilemma. Having a relationship, so close to a goddess that you demand she take you or your enemy during a fight, was too severe for the Umbrians. Then he eased their tension. "This is not a fight unless you make it one. Nenia Dea has no interest in spear drills. Sheath your swords, stack your shields, and collect your spears."

When faced with the top military authority in the mountain town, the five had no choice but to follow orders.

"Spear drills. First position," Alerio instructed.

He ran them through the nine positions, had them do each in triplicate, then formed the five into a single file.

"Come at me hard. Run through the drills, and move to the back of the line," Alerio told them. "First up. Fight."

The spears swung left and right at eye level. Then repeated the movement at waist level and again at knee height. Every slash found spears clashing as the weapon's instructor easily blocked the militiaman. At seven, the spears ripped upward followed by the downward cut of the eight count. Finally, the shafts shot out directly at the opponents' chests.

"Nine! Good balance and focus," Alerio complimented the man. "Move to the back of the line. Next up. Fight."

On the third rotation, Optio Florian arrived. He found a log and sat to watch the drills. As proficient as any weapon's instructor the Sergeant had ever seen, Centurion Sisera shifted smoothly and efficiently blocking and countering. It was obvious the infantry officer was expending little energy while the militiamen sweated and huffed trying to bash aside Sisera's spear.

"I hate to break up this happy party, sir," Florian finally called out. "But three of your striking donkeys have to go on watch."

"Good drill, militia. I thank you for the workout," Alerio announced. "Dismissed."

He walked to the Optio and made a show of wiping his forehead on the sleeve of his shirt.

"Nice try, sir. But nobody is buying that you worked up a sweat from drilling these Umbrians," Florian told him. "I noticed you didn't have them use their shields."

"And I noticed Sergeant, they didn't miss their shields. You haven't taught them how to combine the two weapons, have you?"

"Or how to attack in unison," Florian remarked. "Some of our Legion's secrets should not be shared with barbarians."

"Does Tesserarius Humi agree with your selective training methods?" Alerio asked.

"Unfortunately, while Corporal Humi is an excellent book and diary keeper," Florian explained. "But he is lacking in infantry experience."

"He's a sea going Legionary?" Alerio guessed.

"No, sir. Humi is a scribe," Florian informed the officer. "A few months ago, I reported to the transit station in the Capital looking for a position. The next thing I know, I'm guiding a baggage train up the Tiber with Tribune Subausterus, his Etruscan slave Teucer, a couple more servants, and Tesserarius Humi."

"Humi knew the Tribune before this assignment?" Alerio questioned.

"I never heard them speak of shared experiences," Florian replied. "But Teucer always deferred to Humi in discussions. I assumed it was mutual appreciation between bookish types. If you'll excuse me Centurion, I need to get some food."

"And I need to bathe," Alerio said while stripping off his shirt. "Despite the fact I didn't sweat much during the drills. Then I'm going to check on the progress of the ship."

***

In the initial phase of the build, the ramps angled downward to the bottom of the channel. It's where the keel was laid and the oak boards were pegged together. With the exterior hull complete, the ramps were moved. They now bridged the distance from land to the top boards of the hull. Inside the empty trireme, the drop was thirteen feet to the keel and the bilge.

"What are you going to do, Master Pous?" Alerio quizzed the ship builder. "Toss the lumber down and try not to hit one of the carpenters? Or, have the laborers balance the supplies on their shoulders and carry them down ladders?"

Alerio stood at the top of one ramp and Cata occupied the adjacent ramp.

"Neither, Centurion. We'll build a landing around the inside perimeter of the ship," Cata replied. "A second platform will step down reducing the drop to the lowest level of construction."

"It does smell fresh," Alerio commented.

"It's the cedar," Cata replied. "But don't get accustomed to the aroma."

On surrounding ramps, apprentices carried planks up to the edge of the hull.

"I see laborers standing around," Alerio observed when he noted some waiting for him and Cata to clear the ramps. "Let's give them room. The sooner we complete this project, the sooner we can get the senate involved."

Even with five feet of warship tucked inside the trench, the men still had to walk the ramps down to the ground. As soon as they were off, laborers hauling planks rushed up the incline to the top of the hull some eight feet above the boatyard.

"It's a beautiful ship," Pejus Monilis offered when he joined them. "One hundred and thirty feet of Republic justice. Wouldn't you agree?"

"I'll withhold my opinion until the day we row it onto the beach at Ostia," Alerio remarked. "and I hand the trireme and Nardi Cocceia's bills over to Fleet Praetor Sudoris."

"If you can't bring yourself to appreciate the work we've accomplished," Cata Pous urged. "At least give us your thoughts on this gorgeous warship."

"Despite the fear that I will call Nemesis down on me," Alerio replied. "I feel akin to Prometheus. I have given the world fire in the form of a ship-of-war. Until it's delivered, I could be chained to a rock and have my liver eaten by an eagle. However, unlike the Titan, I am mortal so, at least, the punishment will be finite."

"I don't see that as arrogance requiring punishment by Nemesis," Pejus offered. "And as far as being penalized for your work here, the senate should reward you."

"How do you relate to Prometheus?" Cata questioned.

"Because the ship represents a cost of over one million eighty-eight thousand silver coins," Alerio said. "and my name is on every promissory note. When I look at the ship, I see a rock and my signature on each piece of parchment as another link in my chain."

"And the eagle?" Pejus inquired.

"My own knife. If we fail to deliver this ship, I might as well cut out my own liver."

Chapter 17 - Retribution Revisited

Lugging a shield and spear around was not convenient. At least not when you needed a free hand to keep your cloak closed against the early morning chill. Ever since the assault and arson attack, Centurion Sisera brought both to his shift while on guard duty. But the cumbersome tools of war were stacked below the lantern near the trireme, while the infantry officer stood across the boatyard next to the steps.

"What about tonight?" Alerio asked the sentry. He extended his hands towards the small fire. "anything hunting in the dark?"

"Night predators pass silently," the militiaman suggested. "or else they wouldn't survive to maturity. You'll only know of their presence when the claws dig in."

"You are a cheery fellow," Alerio mentioned. "I really enjoy our talks, I think."

The Legion officer turned from the steps and the sentry. Before he had gone two paces, the militiaman spoke adding to the lore.

"Most people don't think of shadows after sun down," he offered. "but a blacker shade of night may conceal a hunter."

Alerio didn't acknowledge the observation. However, based on his previous experience with the guard's mountain wisdom, he began searching the deeper shadows for signs of movement. Halfway to the channel, a charcoal line at the end of a dusky bush rose from the black mass.

If he was in the woods, it might be a limb moving with a breeze or shaking from an animal jumping from branch to branch. In the center of the boatyard, dotted with defined geometrical shapes, there were no trees or few bushes. The silhouette was the shadow of a man, drawing back his arm, preparing to throw a spear.

Alerio sprang ahead as far as the quick flex of his legs allowed. While dropping from the short flight, he tucked his head and rolled on his shoulders. The ground hammered his upper back but he remained tucked. Resembling a ball, the Legion officer rotated twice before leaping to his feet. The thud of a spearhead burying itself in dirt and stone rang from behind Alerio. He ignored the near miss and sprinted for his shield.

In Legion training the instructors took great pride in locating undefended backs. A punch or kick soon taught the trainees to fear having their backs exposed. As a result, even when frightened, Legionaries never turned their backs on the enemy. Many times, this face forward attitude had turned hopeless situations into victory.

Alerio wasn't as panicked as he was surprised. He pondered if the fenced-in handprint and globs of mucus partially covering the imprint of the digits were the reasons for this assault. He really didn't care. The thought process was to keep his mind off the feeling that, in the next step, a spear would penetrate his back and slam him to the ground.

Rather than charge directly at his weapons and light, Alerio diverged off to the side. Not too far off line, just enough so his body wasn't highlighted by the lantern light for his enemy.

The training drove and guided him all the way to the edge of the trench. As he came abreast of the lantern, Alerio lunged sideways and slammed the shield with his arm. The barrier and the Legionary continued tumbling from under the light and out into the dark.

***

When he rose to his feet, the shield protected his body and the bare blade of his gladius hovered at his side. Rays from the rising sun peeked over the eastern horizon. They provided a little light for this small battle.

132

"Come face me," Alerio shouted. "I promise not to kill you before I break your fingers."

To his surprise, four shapes peeled away from the darkness and approached him. When the men got closer, the Centurion identified two individuals.

"I see the Baldoni clan is well represented," Alerio stated. The pair were from his militia. "I thought it was odd when Tite selected two from the same family."

"Our cousin limps, and his hearing is bad in one ear," one of the militiamen sneered. "For that you will die."

"Your cousin? Who is he?" Alerio questioned.

"You should know. You cowardly Latians ambushed him and two friends," the other stated. "When they were camped on the road to Orte."

For a moment, Alerio thought about correcting the narrative. It was the Umbrians who assaulted him and not the other way around. Then he realized the futility of explaining.

"Wait. Cutu Baldoni? The inept archer and his two stone footed playmates?" Alerio questioned. Then he inhaled and glanced up at the sky as if searching for something. Two heartbeats later, he shouted. "Nenia Dea! Again, I offer you a choice. Choose…"

The militiamen held spears while the second pair of tribesmen brandished knives. An aware Legionary with a shield didn't feared the short blades. It was the ability of the long shafts to reach over or under the personal barrier that made the spears a priority.

***

"Nenia Dea! Again, I offer you a choice. Choose…"

Alerio sprinted at a spear tip. When he reached the steel point, he nudged it aside with his shield and

133

whirled, allowing his gladius to whip around with his body. The blade sank into the spearmen's neck. The Legionary yanked it free while stepping into the face of a knifeman.

The man leaped to the side. His attempt to reach around the armored screen with his arm failed when the sharp steel of Alerio's gladius ripped upward. Dropping the knife, the man gripped his nearly severed forearm. Sinking to his knees, he tried to hold the sections together and stem the flow of blood.

A shield snapping back and forth had the power of a mule's kick. The second knifemen's hand crunched from contact with the wooden face and the return hammering of the shield knocked him on his butt.

For a heartbeat, the man embraced the pain in his wrist because it took him out of the fight. Images of running off to tend the broken bones flashed through his mind. Then the bottom of a hobnailed boot blocked his vision and crushed his face as the Legion heavy infantryman stomped him to the ground. He died when Alerio stuttered stepped to position his other foot over the tribesmen's throat and stomped again.

The final spearman retreated. In what seemed the blink of an eye, his three companions were down and still or bleeding onto the dirt and rocks.

"I owe you an oath," Alerio advised the Umbrian.

"What are you…?"

The flat of the gladius' blade cracked across the hand holding the shaft. Without support from the forward hand, the spear dipped.

"Close enough," Alerio said as he stepped forward and lunged with the gladius.

Once it entered the tribesman's gut, he twisted the blade expanding the wound. A string of bowels, resembling sausage links, spilled onto the ground. Where the blade sliced the membrane, merda splashed on the soil.

"Cata was right," Alerio commented to the dying man while cleaning his blade on the tribesmen's tunic. "The clean smell didn't last."

***

By the time the sun was a bright ball in the sky, a crowd had gathered around the sight of the small battle. Men whispered about Centurion Sisera's Goddess having made her choices.

"You could have left one alive," Pejus scolded while circling and studying the four bodies. "Now, we don't have an answer."

"Master Pous, have the fence removed and dirt kicked over that handprint," Alerio directed the boat builder while ignoring the engineer. "And get your crews back to work."

"In the grand scheme of things, although you have decidedly dispatched an enemy," Pejus offered. "there remains a quandary."

"What are you going on about, master engineer?" Alerio inquired.

"Why did the assassins, who were bent on revenge," Pejus questioned. "wait to attack you until the hull was complete? But also sabotaged the ship building process to delay the construction of the hull?"

"You are as baffling as the Sphinx," Cata suggested.

"Why is a Goddess bewildering?" Pejus inquired.

135

"Before any traveler was allowed to enter Thebes," Cata, the Greek boat builder, informed them. "The Goddess Sphinx demanded they attempt to answer a riddle."

"Are you saying Master Monilis reminds you of a Greek Goddess?" Alerio questioned. "Because if you are, I don't see it."

"Not in looks but in delivering a riddle," Cata replied.

"I thought the riddle of the Sphinx was unanswerable," Alerio remarked. "Just as the answer to Pejus' quandary is unresolvable."

"All riddles have an answer," Cata advised. "or else there is no purpose to asking. For example, the riddle of the Sphinx: what goes on four legs at dawn, two legs at noon, and three legs in the evening?"

"Unknowable," Pejus declared. "It isn't a logical quiz. Thus, it's an arcane question requiring an inscrutable answer, fit only for philosophical discussions."

"As is your quandary," Alerio said. "At least the unknown part."

"But the riddle of the Sphinx has an answer," Cata explained. "Man, who as a baby crawls on four legs, then walks on two legs as an adult, and in old age walks with a cane as his third leg."

"Babies and old men?" Pejus exploded. "I knew it, an answer for philosophers."

"That doesn't get us closer to the solution for the riddle of Pejus." Alerio scoffed.

"Because, Centurion Sisera, you killed the men who had the answer," Pejus responded. "I've had enough of this. I'm going to check the measurements on the ship's ribs."

"You do that master engineer," Alerio said. "And I'm going to see about a burial detail."

The two masters went to check on the progress of the crews, and Alerio waited for the laborers on the early shift to go. He would pick the gravediggers from the ones who started work later in the day. As he waited, the riddle of Pejus gnawed at the back of his mind.

Act 5

Chapter 18 - Absence of Collateral

Two days after the assault, Alerio walked proudly between carpenter stations. At each, craftsmen cut and shaped benches and posts with angled cuts at both ends. One journeyman held a bench and demonstrated to his apprentice how the posts fit below the seat to support an oarsman. Other carpenters cut long cedar posts and shaped spruce planks for the decking.

Not everything was available in the town of Stifone or the surrounding area. Most of the material for weaving rope had been used to construct additional hypozomatas. The locals would only give up so much of the fiber and, the need for the stabilizing lines shorted the trireme. Also unavailable were large sections of cloth for the two sails. However, both the rigging and sails were available at the Republic's naval base at Ostia. And oddly enough, the territory was deficient in another element.

Copper from numerous mines was a major export for Umbria. While rich in copper, the area did not have tin mines. As a result, Pejus and Cata could not cast the bronze battering ram. The main weapon for the warship would be supplied and fitted by the navy.

On one hand, it hurt Alerio's pride. On the other, it was a relief to avoid the extra days required for the process. Then he heard his name and turned from the work stations to watch a militiaman sprint towards him.

138

"Centurion Sisera. I was sent to ask you to join Optio Florian at the Legion office," the man announced. "They said it was urgent."

"I'll be right along and…," the Legion officer started to reply. Then, his training as a weapon's instructor interrupted his thought. "Where is your sword, spear, and shield?"

It was a foolish question. The militiaman probably dropped the heavy weaponry so he could run faster. Or, he was off duty and 'volunteered' by the Sergeant for the mission. Yet even unarmed, he wore the leather armor of the Stifone militia.

"Sir, Tesserarius Humi said we didn't need the war gear," the Umbrian related. "on account that the militia has been disbanded."

"You mean, Optio Florian said that?" Alerio ventured.

"No sir. It was the Corporal."

"The Centurion is always the last to know," Alerio said before breaking into a jog.

Something was very wrong with his chain of command. And it left a sour taste in his mouth, along with a twisting in his gut and a sense of foreboding.

***

The premonition solidified into an ugly scenario while he raced across the sand bar. Pairs of Legion heavy infantrymen occupied each level of Stifone. Also, a pair stood on either side of his office door. In total, they looked to number about eighty, meaning a Century had come to visit.

Having a Legion unit at Stifone and another infantry officer for company should be a good thing. Except, the armor and helmets matched as if purchased yesterday from an armorer. Combined with the orders issued by his Corporal, someone was paying out a lot of coins to outfit a Century so they matched and resembled toy soldiers. Plus, there was a lack of a standard identifying them as a unit from the Northern Legion. Altogether, the items plucked at Alerio's instincts. His stomach continued to revolt as he stepped up on the riverbank.

Jogging up the steps to the first tier, he approached a squad leader.

"What's your Century's designation, Lance Corporal?" Alerio asked the Decanus.

The NCO seemed surprised that Alerio spoke to him. He recovered and replied, "First Century Subausterus."

Rich associates had the opportunity to invest in arming and training Centuries. Usually, the units were sent to join a Legion. However, before the unit reported in, the Century was nothing more than a mercenary company doing the bidding of its benefactor. The title, First Century Subausterus, did nothing to ease Alerio's anxieties.

"Dear Goddess Orbona," Alerio offered. "Don't you salute infantry officers in your Century, Lance Corporal?"

"Sir, we do," the squad leader assured him. Then he saluted.

Alerio rubbed his forehead as he climbed the next set of steps. His reference to the Goddess who granted children to childless couples just slipped out. But Tribune Subausterus with a Century under his command was exactly like an inept father with eighty toddlers. Given what he knew about the Tribune's dismissal of Florian and Humi earlier, Alerio couldn't imagine the staff officer being able to manage eight squads of heavy infantrymen. Alerio hoped Subausterus' Centurion and his NCOs were very good at their jobs.

***

He reached the building designated the Legion office in Stifone and stopped.

"Are you blind or stupid?" Alerio demanded of the two sentries at the doorway.

"Ah, no sir," one answered.

"No sir, what?" Alerio questioned. "Maybe one of each? Which one is stupid and which one is blind?"

"Sir, I don't understand," the other guard informed Alerio.

"Is there any mistaking my officer's helmet or the markings on my armor?"

"No, sir," they both replied.

"Then it's decided because I don't see a salute or the door opened for me," Alerio scolded the Legionaries. "Be sure to make a sacrifice to your God Coalemus to thank him for the gift of stupid."

One leaned across and opened the door while the other saluted. Alerio marched over the threshold and the sentry pulled the door closed. In truth the two guards were selected for door duty for their size and not for their sharp intellect.

"Mars spare us," their squad leader declared when he rushed up. "Do you know who that was?"

"Lance Corporal Italus, why all the questions this morning?" one of the Legionaries complained. "You said this would be easy duty."

141

"He was a typical officer," the other door guard observed. "Pushy and demanding, what else?"

"That, my thick-headed squad mates, is Death Caller," Hallus Italus informed them. "He's a Legion weapons' instructor with the Goddess Nenia looking over his shoulder. And sometimes, she takes control and guides his gladius arm."

"You served with him, didn't you?"

"In Sicilia, but he wasn't an officer then," Italus commented. "He was my Tesserarius."

"What's he doing here?" one asked.

"I don't know why a hero of the Republic," the squad leader admitted. "would be stationed in a backwater village like Stifone."

***

The door closed behind Alerio and it took a heartbeat for his eyes to adjust. His desk and a Centurion sitting in his chair came into view.

"Are you comfortable?" Alerio inquired. "Would you like some refreshments? But maybe you should be asking me what I want. You seem to have made yourself at home in my office."

"Over one million six hundred thousand silver," the officer commented. He indicated the stacks of promissory notes cluttering the desktop. "Is that correct?"

Alerio started to answer but was interrupted. Corporal Humi and Tribune Subausterus' servant Teucer, stepped forward.

"One million eighty-eight thousand, Centurion," Humi advised the infantry officer.

"Plus, one hundred seventy-three silver coins, to be precise," Teucer added. "All unsecured and fraudulently procured."

"Hold!" Alerio barked. "Would someone care to explain what, in the name of Discordia, is going on here?"

"I, Centurion Lucius Trioboli, arrest you Alerio Sisera for the following. You are charged with using the name of the Senate to extract coins and goods from an ally of the Republic," the Centurion explained. "Further, you are accused of creating a false organization in order to enrich your estate. And, by such actions, you have endangered the peace between the Umbria people and the Republic."

The words rocked Alerio and anger boiled up in his chest. A quick glance around showed him there were at least four Legionaries in the shadows, including the servant and his Corporal, standing around the room. Forcing down his need to strike out, Alerio allowed the tension to drain from his chest and arms.

"Teucer said unsecured," Alerio prompted everyone in the room. "We have a trireme, fully hulled and ready for the final phase of interior installation. That is where the coins and goods went."

Lucius Trioboli cocked his head and pursed his lips as if impatient for an answer he knew was coming. He added the curling of his fingers in a bring-it-on motion.

"Tribune Subausterus has declared the trireme a mockup," Teucer proclaimed. "An unusable model that would sink and break apart when launched. It was designed only to fool casual observers and never intended to be a ship-of-war for the Republic."

143

"That is insane," Alerio shouted. "Where is the Tribune? I would have words with him."

"Tribune Subausterus is delayed in the Capital," Teucer replied. "But his decree is confirmed. The mockup is to be burned and you, Centurion Alerio Sisera, returned to the senate in chains for trial."

"Subausterus hasn't been here for any of the construction," Alerio informed the infantry officer. "How could he have reached such an obviously wrong conclusion?"

Centurion Trioboli shifted his gaze from Alerio to Humi.

"I have kept the Tribune informed of your treachery," the Corporal stated.

Alerio was jolted by the declaration. The trust between a Centurion and a Tesserarius went beyond an officer's reliance on an NCO. The Corporal of a Century was in charge of the accounting books and the coins for pay and burial funds. Humi's betrayal cut deep and Alerio couldn't bring himself to look at the Corporal.

"You, my Tesserarius, lying about our progress?" Alerio stammered with his eyes downcast to the floor boards. At the mention of progress, the word flipped in his mind, and Alerio thought delays and vandalism and his eyes shot up to stare at the Tesserarius. "You. You are the saboteur."

"I prefer to think of myself as an agent for good," Humi responded. "And now that you know, I resign my Tesserarius rank and, reclaim my position as head scribe to the Subausterus family."

Disgusted with Humi, Alerio turned his face to the seated infantry officer.

"You can't burn the trireme," Alerio told Centurion Trioboli. "I sent letters to Fleet Praetor Sudoris and Senator Spurius Maximus, informing them of our progress."

Teucer lifted a pouch that hung at his side and upended it over the desk. Alerio's letters spilled out, as well as Pejus Monilis' letter to his family.

"To prevent you from poisoning others or eliciting them to join in your charade, Master Humi acted," Centurion Lucius Trioboli revealed. "Optio. Is there a suitable cell in this village?"

Alerio's heart sank. Bracing himself, he peered around to see who was being addressed by Lucius Trioboli. A sigh of relief escaped Alerio when an unknown Sergeant stepped forward and not Optio Florian.

"It's been a long night," Alerio declared. "There's a root cellar at the top tier. Take me there, give me vino, cheese and bread, and let me get some sleep."

The abrupt end to his defense and declaration of wanting to sleep rather than challenge the charges struck Humi, Trioboli, and Teucer as strange. But, their part of the play was done and if the victim wanted to end his protests, they would oblige.

"Optio. Take the Centurion's gladius and pugio," Trioboli ordered. "and escort him to the root cellar. We leave tomorrow after the laborers are dismissed. Be sure you have guards posted until then."

His blades were removed and a pair of Legionaries led Alerio out of the room. On the street, the familiar voice of Hallus Italus instructed a half squad to surround Centurion Sisera.

When the Century's Optio stepped to the front of the formation, Lance Corporal Italus eased in next to Alerio.

"Sisera, what's going on?" he whispered.

"I've been arrested," Alerio replied.

"I can see that," Italus said. "Is there anything I can do for you?"

"Get word to Optio Florian that they plan to burn the trireme and erase all signs of it," Alerio replied.

"Decanus Italus, it there a problem?" the Optio asked from the front of the formation.

"No Sergeant, just warning the detail about spacing," Italus lied.

Alerio had more, a lot more he wanted to say to Centurion Trioboli. But, when Pejus Monilis' letter fell from the pouch, he realized the danger. Tribune Subausterus would go to extraordinary lengths in eliminating Stifone as a shipbuilding facility.

Putting Alerio on trial was necessary to make the case for the abandonment of Stifone. Why discard the town and its resources, he wasn't sure? But, simply burning the warship and removing the collateral for the bills of lading, wouldn't erase the witnesses. Sometime that night, assassins would kill Optio Florian, Cata Pous, and Pejus Monilis. It was the only logical course of action. If Subausterus really wanted to place all the blame on a dishonest junior Centurion gone rogue, the others associated with building the ship had to be removed.

It's why Alerio stopped protesting. Hopefully, Centurion Trioboli wouldn't think of rounding up and arresting Florian, Pous, and Monilis. A slaughter in a holding cell in front of Legionaries would be harder to hide than covertly cutting the throats of the NCO, engineer, and boat builder in the dead of night. Nevertheless, Alerio didn't want to force the arrests by emphasizing his colleagues. He needed them free.

The formation climbed the steps and Alerio yawned. It had been a long night and a trying morning. Besides hungry, he was sleepy but, more importantly, he was furious.

Chapter 19 - There is Nothing in Between

Adamo Florian and Tite Roscini forced their way between thick tree branches. Neither man noticed the slope hidden by the boughs. Florian tripped on a root, went to his knees and, slid down the embankment. Roscini, on the back end of the carrying pole, got yanked over the edge. Together they careened down the slope.

The Legion Optio, the carcass of a large deer, and the militia Lieutenant came to a stop in a jumble of bows, arrows, fur, antlers, arms and, legs. Laughing, they untangled, repositioned the pole on their shoulders, balanced the deer, and started downhill again.

"I told you, Latian, I should be in the lead," Tite Roscini warned. "I am Umbria and we are mountain people. You are from the flatland and I take my life into my hands by following you."

"If you are so good in the mountains, Tite," Florian inquired. "Why was it my arrow that brought down the buck?"

"Perhaps I drove the noble animal into your kill zone," Lieutenant Tite Roscini offered.

"I assumed you were lost in the woods until I called for you," Sergeant Florian teased.

"Umbrians are never lost in the woods," Roscini boasted.

Before dawn they had crossed the Nera and climbed into the mountains. In the weak light of the rising sun, they followed a game trail until spotting the buck. Silent stalking and skilled hunting techniques allowed them to get close to the animal.

They split apart and, shortly after losing sight of each other, the deer broke in Adamo Florian' direction. He brought it down with an arrow through the animal's heart. The hoofs were tied over a long pole and the two hunters took the trail down from the higher elevation.

"I have to relieve Centurion Sisera," Optio Florian remarked. "You boasted of your roasting skills. Here's your chance to prove it."

"The Roscini are famous far and wide for our mastery of cooking wild venison," Tite boasted.

"I thought your family were farmers?" Florian questioned.

They came to a chute with steep sides. Hopping from rock to rock to stay out of the fast running creek and off the slick stones, the men worked their way down to the edge of the Nera.

"Hold the pole tight, Sergeant," Tite warned. "If either of us releases our end of the pole in the river, this fine buck will float away. And rather than a feast for us, it'll be fish food."

"Don't you worry, I have my end," Florian replied. "You just take care of your end."

"Hold," Tite snapped.

"I heard you the first time," Florian bristled.

"No Optio, stop and look," Tite pointed down the riverbank at a running figure. "He's one of our militia."

The man's feet ground the grass and left deep prints in dirt patches. His heavy gait and driving legs left no doubt he carried important news. When he spotted them, the runner increased his kick and closed in on his Lieutenant and the Optio's location.

"Report," Florian ordered.

"Early this morning, armed Legionaries fell upon Stifone," the man described while pulling off a woolen cap. "We started to form a defensive line but Tesserarius Humi ordered us to lay down our swords and shields."

"He probably saved your lives," Florian suggested. "The militia is trained for handling civilians. The Legion is trained to kill armed men. Has Centurion Sisera joined them?"

The Sergeant felt a trace of guilt. While his officer needed him at the Legion office, he was off hunting. Then, the Umbrian answered.

"Centurion Sisera has been arrested," the man announced. He wiped sweat from his forehead then added. "They escorted him to the village root cellar, locked him in, and placed a sentry to watch the doors."

"Did they arrest Corporal Humi?" Florian questioned.

"No, Optio. After he had us lay down our arms, the Tesserarius said the militia was disbanded," the runner replied. "Then he and another man, his name is Teucer, followed a Centurion to your office. After Centurion Sisera was taken away, I ran to find you."

"You did good," Florian acknowledged while reaching out and taking the cap. "It sounds as if there's a

Century occupying Stifone. Go collect the militiamen and have them hide among the craftsmen."

"What will you do, Sergeant?" Tite Roscini inquired.

"You and I, Tite, are going to take our kill to town," Florian informed the Militia Lieutenant. He pulled the cap over his short hair. "Let's go see if anyone wants to buy some meat from a couple of hunters."

***

The Legion contubernium on the lowest tier watched as two men struggled in midstream of the river. One slipped below the surface but came up with the pole still in his hand while spitting water. His heroically saving the deer tied to the pole brought cheering from the Legionaries.

Finally, Adamo Florian and Tite Roscini sloshed their way out of the river. As if they were entertainers, Roscini bowed to the onlookers. Then he had to rush to catch up when the pole was almost jerked out of his hand. This elicited another round of cheering from the squad.

"I'd like to speak to your Tesserarius," Florian explained to a Lance Corporal. "We took the deer and thought we could sell it to the Century. It looks to be one, is it?"

"Yes, we are First Century Subausterus," the Decanus stated. "You'll find Corporal Maurilius in his tent on the top tier."

"Thank you," Florian said. "We'll go speak with him."

The two hunters had trudged up a couple of levels when another squad leader stepped in front of Florian.

"Where are you going?" Hallus Italus challenged.

"We're taking the deer to Tesserarius Maurilius," Florian answered. "He might buy it for your men."

"I imagine he might," Hallus commented. Then he looked down and asked. "You wouldn't happen to know where I could find Optio Florian would you?"

"No idea," Florian assured the Decanus. He glanced back and indicated Tite. "We've been in the mountains hunting for the last week."

"I'm sure you were," Lance Corporal Italus remarked. Lifting his face, he looked into the hunter's eyes and suggested. "If you see the Sergeant, Centurion Sisera wants him to know my Centurion plans to burn the trireme and erase all signs of it."

The two Legion NCOs, one on duty and one supposedly disguised, stared at each other for a moment before Florian broke away.

"If I see the Optio," Florian assured him. "I'll pass the word."

As Adamo Florian and Tite Roscini started up the next step, Hallus Italus added.

"I served with Sisera in Sicilia. One thing the weapon's instructor taught was to study a stranger's equipment. You are to be congratulated, bowman. I don't know anyone who goes hunting for a week but takes time each day to polish his hobnailed boots. Move along."

***

Tesserarius Maurilius was happy to buy the hunter's excess meat.

"It's perfect for the celebration tonight," the Corporal explained. "My Centurion wants to host a feast for a

151

scribe from an important family and celebrate the Century's first mission."

"Are they celebrating making it to Stifone?" Tite inquired. "It's a mountain village. Amelia is a much more impressive town. And it's only five miles west of here."

"It's not the journey," Maurilius assured him. "Master Humi has been waiting in Stifone for us. We were delayed, and due to the quick march and fast turnaround, we haven't had an opportunity to hunt. Plus, we'll be back on the trail after a sacrifice tomorrow."

"Enjoy the venison," Florian said.

He and Tite walked along the rear edge of Stifone. When they passed the guard at the entrance to the root cellar, neither man looked at the double oak doors embedded in the hillside. At the last building of the village, Tite selected a path and guided them into the hills.

"We are perfututum," the Sergeant swore when they stopped at the top of a ridge.

He sat down heavily and buried his face in the palms of his hands.

"They have eighty heavy infantrymen, but only one guarding the root cellar," Tite offered. "How bad is that?"

"Worse than you think, Lieutenant Roscini. They're going to burn the trireme in the morning and kill me, Master Pous, and Master Monilis," Florian informed him. "Administrator Nardi Cocceia will be out the coins he invested, the Republic will blame Centurion Sisera, and your favorite Optio will be in hades."

"How do you know all that?" Tite questioned.

152

"The message states they plan to burn the trireme," Florian said. "that erases all signs of the warship. Meaning no witnesses can be left, when they take Sisera back for his trial."

"Did Centurion Sisera do something wrong?" Tite inquired.

"He pushed the boundaries," Florian offered. "When a Legionary pushes, he draws a crowd. One to watch him collect a medal for his armor or a group to watch him collect lashes on a punishment post."

"Is there nothing in between?" Tite asked.

"Rarely, Lieutenant."

"You could take Masters Pous and Monilis to Fort Orte," Tite suggested. "The Corporal said the Century was leaving in the morning. Stay there until they're gone."

"That would be the smart thing to do," the Sergeant agreed. "and maybe what Centurion Sisera wanted. But, is it what he needs?"

"What does he need?" Tite questioned.

"An action as bold as the one he took to start this process," Optio Florian informed the Umbrian. "Only this time, no one will take my gladius."

They talked for a long while before Florian stood and stretched his back.

"Have you got all that?" he asked Tite.

"Don't forget the food," the militia Lieutenant reminded him.

Adamo Florian smiled at the young Umbrian and started to walk away.

"You are my favorite Optio," Tite called after him. "Also, you are the only Optio I know."

Adamo Florian was a rare NCO. During his seven years in the Legion, the Sergeant had not been involved in any major campaigns. All of his combat experience involved chasing bandits. He was good with a shield and gladius and a master at throwing and fighting with the javelin. While he practiced and taught young Legionaries how to fight, he hadn't experienced anything larger than a squad level action. War experience aside, Optio Adamo Florian was a great organizer. He knew men and he knew how to get the most out of them.

A quarter of a mile from where he left Tite, Florian dropped onto the main wagon trail heading out of Stifone. Three steps after his feet touched the relatively flat surface, the Sergeant fell into a Legion shuffle. Two miles later, he followed the road as it dipped into a shallow valley.

Up to this point, the road had run south and away from Stifone and the Nera River. In the lowest part of the valley, the road began a gentle curve as it wrapped up and around a large foothill. When it straightened, the road ran west while the Nera, a mile and a half away, flowed southwest. They would converge six miles downstream from Stifone. There the hills that dipped steeply down to the river would flatten to form a proper embankment along the Nera.

Optio Florian did not stay on the road. After locating a game trail, he left the cleared surface. Trekking around the backside of the large foothill, he descended towards the river. Before the trees closed in overhead, he noted the sun has passed midday. He still had to hike about two miles of steep twisting game trail to reach the river

154

and sandbar. Then, he would pass through the thin forest before the hard part of the mission began.

To accomplish the task, he set out for himself, Optio Adamo Florian had a lot of begging and pleading ahead of him. But the Legion NCO, while not an experienced warrior, was a great organizer.

Chapter 20 - Work Your Plan

The absence of Legionaries in the shipyard should have surprised Florian. But he realized Subausterus' Century already planned to burn the trireme in the morning. Guarding an eventual bonfire was a waste of manpower. Even without sentries, the Sergeant walked in a controlled fashion to prevent alerting any spies. He hadn't realized Tesserarius Humi's situation and wouldn't put it past the scribe to have paid off Umbrian craftsmen to keep an eye on things.

He walked a ramp's incline to the edge of the hull. After a quick scan, the Optio located the engineer.

"Master Monilis, I'd like a word with you," Florian called to the engineer. "It is rather important, sir."

With aggravation on his face, Pejus peered up from a groma. Three of the five plum bobs rested evenly over the keel beam. The final two strings swung as the engineer attempted to level the center stick holding up the cross pieces. At the sound of his name, the survey device that resembled sticks used to control a marionette tilted until only one of the plum bobs hung straight down from the simple frame.

"Optio Florian. It is difficult enough using a tool designed for road work, inside the hull of a warship,"

155

Pejus complained. "But having my attention stolen in the middle of leveling the groma, is beyond my tolerance."

"Master engineer, I wouldn't ask if it wasn't important," Florian assured him.

Pejus collapsed the tool and rested it on a rib. He walked the center keep stepping over the joints of the support beams to reach a ladder. There, the engineer climbed to a platform. After walking the boards to a spot just below the Sergeant, he put his fists on his hips and glared up at the NCO.

"I am here," the engineer announced as if the NCO hadn't watched him the entire way.

Florian dropped to a knee and leaned forward.

"Centurion Sisera has been arrested," Florian informed the engineer. "And a Century from Tribune Subausterus has moved into Stifone."

"That's excellent. Subausterus should be pleased with our progress," Pejus declared. "Perhaps we should arrange a sacrifice and prepare a feast to honor the Tribune."

"Master Monilis, Centurion Sisera has been taken into custody," the Sergeant said again, this time slowly. "And the Century is going to burn the trireme."

Pejus' mouth fell open and gurgling sounds came from his throat. Finally, he closed his eyes and mouth, breathed in through his nose before opening his eyes.

"They are going to burn this magnificent ship-of-war?" he commented. "What madness it this?"

"The kind played by rich and powerful men," Florian replied. "The kind who would crush a junior infantry officer and eliminate witnesses, because his plans were upset."

"What are we going to do?" Pejus inquired. "Flee?"

"No, master engineer," Florian informed him. "You are going to warn Master Pous not to go to Stifone. And I am going to speak with the laborers. Then, we're accelerating the schedule."

"If we leave now, we can be at Fort Orte before moon rise," Pejus suggested.

"Then run again when Nardi Cocceia comes after us demanding revenge," the Legion NCO described. "No. We have a plan and we will work the plan."

"We have a plan?" Pejus questioned.

"We do," the Sergeant assured him.

***

As soon as Optio Florian reached the top of the stairs, seven men separated from the laborers' camps and clustered around him.

"Sergeant. What's the plan?" one inquired.

"Who has hunted boar?" Florian queried the militiamen.

Five of the Umbrians raised their hands.

"Who liked it?"

Only four hands remained in the air.

"You four will go and meet with Lieutenant Roscini," Florian informed the ones who enjoyed hunting animals with man-killing tusks. "He's on the ridge above Stifone. Use the animal trail and avoid Stifone. And take rations and wine for Tite as well as an animal skin blanket. Make that two blankets."

"What do we do?" one of the three remaining militiamen questioned.

"Two of you need to go around and quietly identify twenty-five Umbrians who are loyal to Administrator

157

Nardi Cocceia," Florian instructed. "Have them meet me here before dusk."

"And me?" the last unassigned militiaman asked.

"You are going to scour the shipyard for poles," the Optio directed. "We need twenty-five of the longest poles you can find. Fifteen feet or longer is best."

"I'm sensing a correlation between the number of supporters for Administrator Cocceia and the number of poles," the Umbrian suggested.

"Here's another connection for you," Florian remarked. "You'll dump the poles inside the trireme's hull."

***

By the lunar zenith, the craftsmen and apprentices had settled down from the evening's hobbies. In Stifone, the villagers and most of the infantrymen slept. There were exceptions. Sentries walking posts yawned while waiting to be relieved. They wouldn't have to wait long as the high in the sky moon triggered a rustling of activities among the squads. The men assigned to third watch washed sleep from their eyes and prepared to come on duty. In the boatyard area, three militiamen and twenty-five chosen laborers tramped through the worker's camps to the edge of the shelf and made their way down the stairs.

A few craftsmen raised their heads, noted the night passage of men, and lay back. Each planned to send Humi a message in the morning about the nocturnal movement.

Fifteen of the loyal Umbrians reached the trireme, walked up the ramps, stepped over the hull, and onto the

158

inner ring of the platform. The other ten, and the militiamen, slipped into the thin woods to wait.

In Stifone, the guards changed at the Centurion's quarters, the Century supply tent, the pack animal pen, the ten contubernium areas, and at one additional post.

The single Legionary at the fourteenth guard position squatted beside a campfire next to a pair of doors set in a hillside. It was the most isolated post of all. Unlike the others, with interlocking views, the Private at the root cellar could only see an outline of a supply tent in the light of the full moon, the flames of the campfire, and the other sentry by silhouette.

Beneath the doors and underground, Alerio Sisera took another squirt from the wineskin and tightened the blanket around his shoulders. The drink, one of many, was to ward off the chill he told himself and not so much to dull his senses against the situation. He hoped Optio Florian received his message and had spirited Cata Pous and Pejus Monilis away from the Stifone area. He drank again and saluted Lieutenant Tite Roscini. The young farmer had done a good job of running security during the building process. He wasn't worried about the militiamen. They could go home and while they might have to answer questions from their tribal leaders, they couldn't be blamed for the loss of the trireme.

Alerio took a bite of bread and cheese which called for another drink to wash down the food. It was as good an excuse to drink as he could think of with his senses dulled. He was grateful for the altered state because for the first time in a long while, Centurion Alerio Sisera did not have a plan. But he did have a wineskin, so he squirted another stream of vino into his mouth.

After the guards settled into their posts and the off-duty Legionaries were wrapped in the arms of Hypnos, four blankets in first squad's area got tossed back. Rising from their bedding, four thugs, playing at being Legionaries, headed down the terraces to the sand bar. Their orders directed them to cut the throats of the Greek boat builder, the Latian engineer, and the Legion Optio.

Their mission was an additional reason Sergeant Florian hadn't seen Legionaries guarding the boatyard. None of the command staff from First Century Subausterus wanted their Legionaries to witness, let alone be aware of, the bloody work of the assassins.

Chapter 21 - Overconfidence for the Loss

The four killers walked in single file and rolled their booted feet to keep the noise down as they snuck along the sand and gravel. Just before the sandbar ended, the lead man mounted the earthen dike. One by one, the others climbed and dropped down the far side. With soft leaves and pine needles under foot, they increased their pace.

Master Humi had instructed them if Cata Pous and Pejus Monilis weren't at the rented house in Stifone, they would be sleeping near the ship. Although Florian was missing from the village, Humi assured them the Legion NCO would be found with the engineer and boat builder.

In the Capital, the four were known to be reliable and cheaper than assassins from the Golden Valley Trading House. For this, there was no need for finesse. These killings were butchers' work.

160

They broke the single file formation and spread out in a line. Knives were pulled in preparation of eliminating anyone they crossed on the way to complete the contract. With bare blades, the four stalked towards the shipyard and the sleeping victims.

***

"Four Legionaries armed with knives are crossing the sandbar," a militiaman whispered. "Not armored."

"Get back to your sections and wait for my signal," Florian instructed.

The three men from the militia went off in different directions leaving the Sergeant standing with four woodsmen. Florian touched his side where his gladius should be hanging. But his shield, armor, helmet, and gladius were in his room in Stifone. He touched the Legion pugio in its sheath and drummed his fingers on the hilt of the heavy iron sword in his hand.

"An inelegant weapon," he muttered.

"What's that Optio?" one of the woodsmen standing with him asked.

"Nothing. When I say attack, do not give the Legionaries a chance to set their guard," he warned. "Strike them hard and often. Hit them even when they go down."

"When will we know they've had enough?" one questioned.

"I'll let you know when to stop," Florian informed the Umbrian.

The ten Umbrians loyal to Nardi Cocceia were divided up and clustered in groups around the NCO and the three militiamen. Florian feared Subausterus' infantry officer would send an armored squad. If a combat contubernium had entered the woods, his orders would be very different. Kind of in the vein of, run for your lives. But four unarmored killers, boosted his spirits and gave the Legion NCO hope for the success of his plan.

***

Tite Roscini and his four militiamen sat on the ridge. Between the tree branches they watched the sentry's fire and sometimes the man when he walked around to stay alert. Tite wished the Legionary would just fall asleep and make it easier.

The militia Lieutenant searched the sky, located the full moon, and waited for it to move four fingers beyond the zenith. When it reached the proper position, he tapped his two strongest men and sent them downhill. He and the last two followed close behind.

There was no hesitation or delay. The two boar hunters struck the Legionary's midsection with their shoulders. He was lifted into the air before they drove him into the ground. The only sounds were his armor hitting the soil and the breath exploding from his lungs. Then a pair of fists hammered the sides of his helmet and the Legionary lay still.

"Get dressed," Tite ordered one of the militiamen racing downhill beside him.

While the man pulled on the Legion helmet, slipped the infantry shield on his arm, and rested the javelin on his shoulder, Tite and the other three crouched in a semicircle. They waited to see if the takedown had drawn the attention of any Legionaries. Or if the shadowed outline of his man dressed as the sentry fooled the other guard.

"Walk around," Tite urged when the fake Legionary ambled over for inspection. "Let us know if anyone comes calling. One blanket on the door. Use the other to shield us."

With a blanket blocking any light from the root cellar and another hiding the maneuver, Tite removed the cross beam and opened one of the doors. Peering down, he saw a lantern and Centurion Sisera wrapped in a blanket.

"The bastards," he said. Sisera lay on the steps in what had to be an uncomfortable position. Assuming the Legionaries had beat the Centurion before tossing him down the steps, Tite descended the treads, knelt, and began to feel for broken bones.

"Lieutenant Roscini. I thought you would have had the good sense to run," Alerio slurred. "Please tell me Optio Florian made his escape."

Tite smelled the wine on Sisera's breath and he relaxed. They might have to support him but, thankfully, the Centurion did not require carrying.

"The Sergeant is expecting us, sir," Tite replied. "And we really need to get going. Can you run?"

"Most people ask about walking before going directly to the hard stuff," Alerio suggested while attempting to stand. He sagged, missed the step, and almost fell over. "You know, hard, like standing up."

"Lean on me," Tite insisted. "I'm got two of my best to help you."

They stumbled up the steps. At the top, Tite let Alerio sink to the grass.

"Take the Centurion up the ridge," the militia Lieutenant instructed. "Walk him fast. He needs to be running by the time we catch up."

163

"There you go again, Roscini," Alerio whispered. "Going right for the hard stuff."

Two of the militiamen grabbed Alerio, jerked him to his feet, then walked off with his feet dancing in the air as he tried to touch the ground.

"Put the sentry in the root cellar," Tite directed. "Throw his Legion gear down with him and let's get out of here."

They caught up with a still confused Centurion Sisera and his two minders at the end of the ridge. All five dropped down to the road and quick walked. Alerio's feet were just starting to keep pace with the others, although his strides were unsteady.

"Optio Florian is always bragging about Legionaries running," Tite commented.

"Running is required," Alerio informed him. "But I'm not sure my head or body is ready."

"In that case, Centurion Sisera," Tite remarked. "I'm sorry about this. Militia, double-time, march."

With an Umbrian on each arm, Centurion Sisera joined the run. Head wobbling from side to side and his knees trembling, he resembled a sack of onions more than a veteran infantryman. It would take a mile and a half before the infantry officer hardened, shifted to the Legion shuffle, and carried his own weight. Although he hid it from the others, it would take two more painful miles before his headache subsided and he could think clearly.

***

Sergeant Florian allowed the four killers to clear the trees. In the moonlight, they stood out clearly from the trunks and branches. The positioning was necessary.

Most of his troops lacked training. Fighting among the trees in the shadows of the moonlight would be a disaster.

"I am Optio Florian," he announced while standing up. "Can I help you?"

"Where are Cata Pous and Pejus Monilis?" one of the slayers demanded.

The four angled towards the Legion NCO while attempting to hide their knives beside their legs. Their posturing was the sign he needed.

"Attack," Florian shouted. He reached down and picked up the heavy iron sword. "Attack."

As directed, his team of woodsmen stood and formed a wedge behind the Legion NCO. The assassins scanned the loose formation and realized it was amateurish and weak. They increased their pace.

Florian swung the heavy blade back and forth forcing the killers to split apart. Moving around the heavy sword, they figured on dispatching the woodsmen behind the Optio. Then, they could focus on the Sergeant. The four murders were two body lengths from the woodsmen and the Sergeant when they sensed movement behind them.

The three militiamen, backed up by the final six craftsmen, charged. They all carried long clubs that crashed down and through the quick guards thrown up by the assassins. As directed, the beating didn't stop. The four professional murders resembled hogs that had been savaged by a pack of wolves before the Optio called a stop to the pounding.

"Halt. Halt. Hold off," Florian shouted. "I think they're down."

"One moved," a craftsman told him.

Florian leaned down and studied the body.

"That was a flap of skin from his skull falling over his face," the NCO announced. He nudged the body with the toe of his boot. "I declare, the battle of Stifone is a total victory for the Umbrians of Nardi Cocceia."

A cheer went up from the craftsmen and they started repeating the declaration.

"The battle of Stifone is a total victory for the Umbrians of Nardi Cocceia."

"The battle of Stifone is a total victory for the Umbrians of Nardi Cocceia."

"Enough. Those fatuus thugs will be missed," Florian informed them. "Simpletons or not, the Century will want revenge. Umbrians, it is time to leave."

The thirteen walked away from the dead bodies. While Optio Florian marched towards the trireme, the craftsmen moved to the stairs and the laborers sleeping in the camps.

***

"Corporal of the Guard, there is something strange going on," the sentry from Eight Squad called up to the Century's command post. "You should see this."

"Is it an imminent attack?" Tesserarius Maurilius shouted back.

He rolled out of his blanket and sat up. Too much vino and venison at the feast for Master Humi made him sluggish.

"No. It doesn't seem to be," the Legionary admitted.

The NCO shook his head and pushed off the ground.

"Then why are you shouting, Private?" Maurilius demanded.

166

"Because there are about a hundred or so people coming up the sandbar and crossing the river," The Legionary told him.

The Corporal jogged down the terraces until he reached the second level. The moon reflecting off the river illuminated men with tool bags and boxes balanced on their heads splashing into the Nera.

"Lance Corporal. Get your squad down there and find out what's going on," he ordered.

The Decanus kicked the sleeping members of his contubernium awake. As in any unit, some men can sleep through anything. Limiting them to javelins and shields, the squad leader quickly had his men assembled. He marched the nine Legionaries down the steps to the edge of the crowd.

"Umbrians, what is going on?" the Lance Corporal inquired.

"Is this a tribal migration?" one of his Legionaries suggested.

"Keep your mouth closed, Private," the squad leader ordered. "Umbrians. Where are you going?"

"We're going home," one craftsman said. He shifted the tool bag balanced on his shoulder to a more comfortable position. "The contract has been cancelled and we're leaving."

"Corporal. They say their work is done and they're heading home," the squad leader informed the NCO. "What do you want to do?"

"Let them go," Maurilius advised. "Pull your people back but keep an eye on the migration."

The laughter from the squad puzzled him but he ignored it. While climbing the stairs to the command post, the NCO debated informing the Centurion and Master Humi about the craftsmen leaving. A quick check of the sky showed him the moon was only partially to the horizon, meaning sunrise was a little way off. Figuring he could get some sleep before morning, Corporal Maurilius decided to report the event when the Century woke.

***

Alerio recognized the turn off. When he first came to Stifone, he and his horse and mule had left the road to take a direct trail to the village. In hindsight, he was wrong to leave the road but it did show him the sandbar.

Centurion Sisera shook off the hands of the militiamen and picked up the pace.

"We can reach the shipyard by that trail," he announced.

"That's not where we're going, sir," Tite informed him. "Optio Florian gave specific instructions for the meeting place."

"Did he and the master engineer and builder already leave?" Alerio questioned.

Tite glanced over his shoulder at the moon to judge the lateness of the night.

"I don't believe they have left yet," Tite told Alerio. "But we do need to be early."

"And where are we meeting him?"

"A spot four and a half miles from here," Tite said. "Do you need a break?"

"No, but I could use a drink of water," Alerio reported.

A militiaman handed him a waterskin. Alerio drank on the run and handed back the skin.

"What's four and a half miles from here, Lieutenant Roscini?" Alerio asked.

"It's where the road bends towards the riverbank before drifting southeast," Tite replied.

"So, Florian, Pous, and Monilis are coming on horseback?" Alerio guessed.

"No, sir," Tite said. "You are not even close."

***

Two men waiting in the woods watched as the last of the craftsmen vanished in the dark. If the Century sent squads, their job was to warn the Sergeant. So far, the expected investigation of the four missing Legionaries had not developed. Except for the night sounds of animals and insects, the woods grew quiet after the exodus.

On the eastern end of the shipyard, four men stood in the bottom of the channel. A pair of lanterns cast light on their tools and their location. Mallets rested on their shoulders. Behind them the bow of the trireme rose and vanished against the dark sky. And, to their front, the cofferdam stretched from one side of the construction trench to the other. Beyond the dam, the waters of the Nera flowed downstream. They listened to the river splash against the iron and wood barrier, eyed the braces holding up the dam, and waited for a signal from the warship.

On the incomplete aft deck of the trireme, Master Pous gripped the hands of men holding long poles.

"During the initial surge," Cata Pous explained while shoving backwards. "Push us away from the rear wall of the trench. The ship will balance once the channel is full."

On the port side, Optio Florian walked men with long poles up and down the rail platform mimicking pushing off against the shore with the poles. Across the width of the warship, Pejus Monilis walked men and poles along the starboard side explaining the same procedure.

"Master Pous, if we are going to do this, now would be better than later," Florian suggested. "That Century is bound to come calling at dawn."

"But the crew, as they are, require more training," Cata informed the Optio. "Much more."

"What's the issue, master ship builder," Pejus Monilis challenged. "Do you fear your boat will flip over and not float like a proper ship-of-war?"

"This trireme is sturdy and constructed to survive war and Poseidon's fury," Cata declared. "If you doubt me, sound the signal and free my warship."

"As you wish, Master Pous. But I prefer the Latian Neptune's fury," Florian acknowledged. He squeezed around the polemen and walked the planks to the bow. At the very front of the ship, he leaned over and looked down at the four men, the cofferdam, and the dark water beyond. Then casually, he ordered. "Release the river."

In response to the Optio's words, the four men pulled the mallets off their shoulders. After spreading apart and centering themselves on bracing struts, they lifted the hammers above their heads and paused.

"May the God Clitumnus not take you for a plaything," one of the labors prayed.

"If the river god wants me, I'm here for the taking," another boasted. "Let's get on with it."

"Release the river," the first man shouted.

From overhead, the mallets arched downward and struck the heel blocks holding four of the braces. After knocking out one group, the men shifted away from the center. The dam held but the structure stretched and tightened from the weight of the water.

Again, the men lined up on struts and the mallets descended. Four more blocks shot away making it a total of eight unsupported braces. It was enough freedom for the cofferdam to flex. River water poured over the center as if it was a spout on a pitcher.

The men sloshed to new positions and lifted their hammers. Another set of heel-blocks flew from impacts and the pressure along the dam exceeded the strength of the iron and wood barrier. Resembling a wave curling along the beach, river water folded the cofferdam in sections, slamming each to the bottom of the trench.

The channel filled with torrid and rushing water, rolling everything in its path downward and crushing it against the stone bottom. Three of the laborers clung to the sides of the trench. The fourth had fulfilled his own prophecy and became a plaything for Clitumnus, the Umbria river god.

***

Cata Pous heard sloshing as if someone had pitched water from a bucket onto a tile floor. But rather than fading, the sound grew to a roar. Then he stopped paying attention to noises, grabbed a post, and fought to keep his balance and stay on the warship.

The bow of the trireme elevated on the surge of water. In response, the aft section squatted and the platform planks inclined so sharply, the crew fell and slid down the boards. Everyone grabbed on for their lives, except four men on the stern.

In pairs, they held long poles against the rock face at the back of the channel. Using the poles, they walked up the steep deck attempting to keep the rear keel from smashing against the rock. Standing almost parallel to the ground, they looked down at the dark rising water, and screamed as their muscles strained to hold the ship steady against the flow. When it seemed their strength and nerve would run out, the front of the trireme slammed down, popping the tail section up and momentarily out of the water.

The poles were ripped from their hands and the four men vaulted into the air. As they flew, the warship settled under them. From the height of three men, they fell. Two landed on the aft planks and crumbled into painful heaps. The other two missed the incomplete decking. From above the deck, they continued to fall an additional thirteen feet to the uneven surfaces of the ship's ribs. Neither moved once they bounced off the beams.

"Poles, grab your poles," Optio Florian commanded.

Scrambling around, a few men located poles, swung them over the sides, and pushed against the ground. When five on both sides of the boat had purchase, the trireme glided forward and out of the channel. To Cata Pous' delight, the warship floated upright as it entered the flow of the Nera river and began to float downstream.

Act 6

172

Chapter 22 - Not Paddles

Shoots of color stretched across the sky announcing the start of a new day. While the stars faded in the light from the rising sun, the ground and Nera river were deeply shadowed.

"Look there," a militiaman urged. "Up river."

From the gloom, the tall bow of a trireme emerged. Unlike the ones Alerio had seen at sea with one hundred and seventy oars stroking in unison, this one had twenty sticks haphazardly slapping the water. Despite the shortage of rowers and the lack of proper oars, the ship angled towards the shoreline.

"It's headed this way," Tite observed. "I don't know anything about warships. But it seems to be traveling at a high rate. Maybe as fast as a trotting horse. Is that normal for taking on passengers?"

"It is not," Alerio informed him.

The trireme slid almost into the riverbank and only frantic poking with long poles kept the ship from running up on the dirt.

Optio Florian jogged to the bow area, cupped his hands around his mouth, and shouted, "We can't slow. Grab a rope."

Six men ran to positions along the one hundred and thirty feet of hull. Once braced, they began twirling ropes as they prepared to throw the lines.

"Run," Alerio shouted.

He turned to face downstream, kicked off hard, and sprinted along the riverbank. While he ran, a section of the hull caught up and began to pass him. A sideways glance showed an Umbrian on the ship increasing the spin as he readied to toss the rope.

"Throw it," Alerio shouted while lifting a hand.

The line sailed from the ship, hung over Alerio's head for a heartbeat, before falling into his outstretched hand. Two steps towards the river while gathering in excess rope and he jumped.

Swinging on the line, his arms and face collided with the oak boards while his feet plunged into the river. As if dragged from a racing horse across rough ground, Alerio's legs sank into the water and bounced out in a jarring pattern.

He attempted to lift his body higher but the jerking caused his hands to slip and he dipped deeper. Then, he turned his face and caught sight of Tite Roscini.

The militia Lieutenant had his legs lifted to waist level and his feet pressed against the hull. He seemed to be resting. Alerio, rather than trying to climb, mimicked Tite by bending and lifting his knees. Two attempts later, the Legion officer had his feet, flat on the side planks. Following Tite's lead, Alerio began to pull on the rope and walk his feet up the hull.

Alerio reached the top where hands grabbed him and pulled him onto the trireme. He fell onto the platform breathing hard.

"Good morning, sir," Florian greeted him. "We seem to have stolen a warship. I'm hoping you know what to do with it."

"I do, Optio," Alerio assured him. "First, we need to stop at Fort Orte."

"Stopping and steering are issues, sir," Florian explained.

"I noticed,'" Alerio said. He climbed to his feet and looked at the twenty Umbrians craftsmen splashing water with long poles. "We need to fix that if we are going to arrive at the Capital in good order."

"I thought we would leave the ship at a Legion post along the Tiber," Florian suggested. "Now, we're taking it to Rome?"

"We must," Alerio informed the NCO. "It's where the senate is."

"I thought this was a Legion naval vessel," the Optio questioned. "What reason would the senate have to care about a single warship."

"One million eighty-eight thousand and one hundred seventy-three reasons," Alerio explained. "But first Sergeant, we stop at Fort Orte."

***

One fact of boating on a river, in order to steer, the ship must travel faster than the water. Splashing and beating the surface with round poles would not propel the vessel faster than the current.

"No speed, no steer," Alerio stated. "Pull the sticks out of the water and cut flat surfaces near the ends."

"That won't make them paddles," Pejus Monilis offered.

"Paddles are for taking your girl for a spin around the local pond. What we want are oars to control a warship," Alerio corrected the engineer. "Hopefully, the adjusted poles will get us across the Tiber to a beach on the far shore."

A little over two miles later, the brown water of the Nera flowed into the yellow-whitish water of the Tiber. And as smoke does in the wind, the brown water was

175

swept downstream where it dissipated. The trireme reacted to the power of the bigger river and the bow was pushed towards the near bank.

"Stroke. Stroke," Alerio shouted from the aft platform. He worked one of the two rear oars back and forth while directing the inexperienced oarsmen. "Starboard side, ship oars. Port side, stroke, stroke, stroke."

The bow angled away from the bank and the warship nosed into the center of the Tiber. With the current pressing on the right side and only the oars on the left in motion, they managed to nudge the warship diagonally across the river.

"Starboard side, dip oars and stroke, stroke," Alerio commanded. The trireme now drifted in the direction of the high, rocky riverbank. "Don't let up. Stroke, stroke."

With the increased flow of the river, Alerio needed to get as much speed out of his rowers as they could deliver. Finally, Optio Florian, standing in the fore section, raised both arms and waved at the shore.

"Just a few more strokes. Stroke, stroke," Alerio promised the oarsmen. He attempted to see the beach that Florian indicated but it was too far in front of him. Finally, after several more rounds of rowing, the low section of the shoreline came into view. "Starboard side, ship oars. Port stroke, stroke. Ship oars."

The twenty poles hovered over the water and the ship drifted. Alerio and one of the big militiamen shoved their rear oars to the side and the warship partially spun. This time the current worked in their favor by pushing the trireme up and onto the beach.

"Everybody, over the side," Optio Florian directed. "Get us as far out of the water as possible. If this ship floats away, I'll have the lot of you swimming after it."

Thirty-four men jumped to the beach. They pushed and pulled the ship halfway out of the current. Four ropes were tied together and the long line used to secure the ship to a tree.

"Optio Florian, you're with me," Alerio ordered. "We need to get to Fort Orte as soon as possible."

The two Legionaries marched northward following the Tiber. Their fast walk quickly ate into the two miles distance to the Legion fort. But it wasn't fast enough for Centurion Sisera. He indicated a change in pace before breaking into a Legion shuffle. Florian required a short sprint to catch up.

"Why the rush, sir?" the NCO inquired.

"Century Subausterus has horses and can send a troop to the fort," Alerio informed the NCO. "I don't know how long it will take them to reach and cross the Tiber. But I don't want to force Senior Centurion Baccharis into making a judgement call about who has the rights to the trireme. So, we're in and away quickly. That's the plan."

"I'm still not sure what we need here," the NCO questioned.

"What else do you find at a legion post?" Alerio replied. Then he answered his own question. "What we need are equipment and Legionaries."

When the Centurion and Optio marched away, Cata Pous and Pejus Monilis crawled under the hull. They ran their hands over the birch pitch seeking bulges. Any raised area could be a crack in the keel or hull. After the

177

violent launch, they wouldn't be surprised to find damage.

***

The sentry on the main gate of Fort Orte called for the Sergeant of the Guard.

"Optio. Two men approaching fast," he called towards a window in the duty office. "They look to be Latian but don't have travel baggage."

The door opened and an Optio stepped onto the narrow porch. He strolled to the guard post.

"Do you think they were robbed?" the Private questioned.

"I hope not," the Sergeant replied. "Organizing a chase and tracking bandits is not a great way to start the day."

They watched as the two men reached the bottom of the hill and began running up the road.

"One has a pugio and is wearing leather hunting clothing," the Optio observed. "The other is unarmed and wearing a short sleeved red tunic."

"Like we wear under our armor," the sentry said.

The strangers reached the crest of the hill and broke stride as they approached the gate.

"Centurion Alerio Sisera and Optio Florian. Take us to Centurion Baccharis," Alerio directed. "And send for Centurion Decalcavi."

"Sir, it's early," the Sergeant of the Guard pointed out.

"Optio Florian, how much sleep did you get last night," Alerio quizzed his NCO.

"None, sir," Florian answered. "I've been up all night."

"See there," Alerio informed the duty NCO. "We're not early but late. Too late to stand at a Legion gate having the position of the sun pointed out to me by a Sergeant of the Guard. Understand?"

"Yes, sir," the SOG acknowledged. "Follow me."

***

They waited in the fort's administration office until Senior Centurion Baccharis and junior Centurion Decalcavi pushed through the doorway.

"Just once when you enter my command," Baccharis confronted Alerio. "I would like to see you in proper Legion attire."

"Senior Centurion, I also would enjoy seeing you in situations other than those I find myself in," Alerio replied. "But, as the fates would have it, I must beg your forgiveness while asking for favors."

"More than one favor?" Baccharis questioned. "How many exactly and to what degree?"

"I need Lance Corporal Ippazio and his contubernium to accompany me to the Capital," Alerio told the post commander.

"When do I get my Second Squad back?" Decalcavi asked.

"That depends on the senate," Alerio stated. "If they want a trial or not."

"A trial for my Second Squad?" Decalcavi inquired. "What trial and why?"

"Lance Corporal Ippazio gave the mail from Stifone to a third party," Alerio reported. "It's caused a conflict over who owns the warship we built."

"That's Legion business," Baccharis commented. "We can handle that internally on the punishment post."

179

"Unfortunately, Senior Centurion, there are large sums of coins involved," Alerio informed him. "Big enough that only the senate can settle the disagreement."

"Well, it sounds like you only need the Decanus."

"I also need his nine Legionaries," Alerio said. "To guard and row the ship. Which leads me to the other favors."

"You are just an early in the morning joy, Centurion Sisera," Baccharis remarked. "A gift that keeps on giving. What do you need?"

***

Cata Pous and Pejus Monilis noted the guarded wagons coming from the north.

"Do you think Sisera got everything he wanted?" Cata asked.

"Seeing as he failed to inform me of his requirements," Pejus replied. "I haven't the foggiest notion."

The wagons pulled up beside the warship and a squad of Legionaries and the drivers began to unload pieces of oars.

"Those are broken," Cata pointed out to Alerio when he arrived.

"And they are too short to use on a trireme," Alerio told him.

"Then what good are they," Pejus remarked. "Or did the Legion cheat you?"

"Have the craftsmen split the ends of our poles and insert the blades from the broken oars in the groove," Alerio directed. "There's leather pieces and rope to secure the spliced segments."

"The oars will be too frail for heavy rowing," Pejus offered.

"As someone recently accused me of being," Alerio commented. "You, Master Monilis, are a joy in the morning."

"We just have to be faster than the current," Cata stated. "Those temporary oars will work for our needs."

"That's correct, master ship builder," Alerio agreed. "If the God Sors grants us luck and Tiber allows us uneventful days of rowing."

"May the gods smile on our voyage," Pejus prayed.

Chapter 23 - Seventy Miles to Rome

Although the trireme had a long snout, the forward keel beam was sans the heavy bronze battering ram. Without the weight, the warship tended to favor its aft section. The elevated bow had aided in the run up the beach. Relaunching the hull from the shoreline, with only forty-two men proved difficult.

"They usually row these things in aft first," Cata advised.

"They usually have a full crew of oarsmen," Pejus shouted back. "to move the beast afterward."

Both the master ship builder and the master engineer were covered in mud from pushing, slipping, and falling onto the pulverized soil. Their appearance matched the other forty men attempting to move the ship-of-war.

Disgusted at the procedure, Pejus Monilis stomped ten feet away before spinning and glaring at the stuck warship. Then his eyes shifted to the wagons and the mule teams.

"You and you, bring down some ropes," Pejus ordered a couple of Legionaries.

"We don't know where the ropes are stored," one responded.

"Young man, the hull is empty," the master engineer informed the Private. "Just use your eyes and you'll find the ropes."

The Legionaries scrambled up the raised keel and vanished over the side. They were gone for so long, the engineer thought about climbing up to see if they were injured. Before he acted, the Legionaries appeared on the hull and, with a yell, the two tossed the reserve hypozomata over the side.

Three hundred feet of triple woven line unrolled before smacking into the churned-up soil. Centurion Sisera, Optio Florian, Cata Pous, and Pejus Monilis gasped as the pristine fibers soaked up moisture as the reserve hypozomata sank into the mud.

"We found it, Master Monilis," one of the Legionaries shouted. "There's another one if you need it. But it'll take us a little work to untie it."

"No young man," Pejus responded quickly. "You've done enough already."

"Come down," Alerio directed. Then he mouthed, so they couldn't hear. "You've done enough damage."

"You ordered the rope, Master Monilis," Cata informed the engineer. "What are you going to do with it?"

Pejus Monilis' mouth fell open at the sight and for a heartbeat he appeared to be a defeated man. Then his face lit up and a smile broke through. He ran to the teamsters and exchanged words with them. In response, they unhooked the mule teams from the wagons and walked a pair to either side of the warship. Then Pejus organized groups of men to untangle the hypozomata. Once the triple-strand line was unknotted, he stretched the rope across the raised fore keel and tied it to the mules.

"This ship is going into the river," Pejus Monilis announced. "Get on now or you'll miss the boat."

Every man climbed the hull, then stood on the platform looking down at the mule teams. The master engineer walked to the fore section and posed with his arms reaching to the sky.

"Teamsters, lead them forward," Pejus declared with a wave of his arms.

The mules moved, the hypozomata stretched then tightened, and the trireme slid backward into the Tiber. With water only knee high on the animals' legs, the ship bobbed in the river free of land.

A teamster called from the shore, "What about this huge rope?"

"Keep it," Pejus replied. "As a gift from master engineer Monilis."

"You are generous with the ship's supplies," Cata noted.

"We're floating, aren't we?" Pejus scoffed. "If you want the line that bad, jump in, and swim back."

They were both flung to the side and forced to lean forward and grip the top of the hull.

"Oars, oars," they heard Centurion Sisera command.

The ship had caught the current, dipped sideways, and then righted itself. But they had a problem. No one was sure how much stress and abuse the spliced oars could handle. And the Trireme was drifting uncontrolled into a bend on the Tiber river, backwards.

A well-trained crew could dip their oars deep, put their backs and legs into a few hard strokes, and carve a half circle in the water. The crew on the trireme was barely cognizant of the rowing commands and their oars were questionably serviceable.

***

Sixty-eight miles from the docks at Rome, the Tiber went from a gentle curve to a sharp left-hand turn. Engineers designed roads to bend like the river to avoid obstacles or to respect property lines. The powerful Tiber cared little for either reason. What did influence the flow was granite. A jagged rock wall lurked under the water at the turn. On the surface, an aft heavy out of control ship-of-war traveled towards the wall.

"Port side, hold water," Alerio bellowed. The eighteen rowers on the left placed their oars in the water and held them steady. "Starboard side, stroke, stroke, stroke."

The fore section began to come around the left side. Unfortunately, the movement placed the hull broadside to the current.

"Give me three Port side Legionaries to repel the riverbank," Alerio directed when he realized the maneuver was too late to avoid the rocks.

One benefit to adding the Legion squad to the crew, the Legionaries were trained in rowing and boat handling. Three flipped their oars, putting the butt ends forward while rushing to the front of the ship. As the trireme's nose swung around on a collision course with the stone embankment, they placed the poles on the

184

bank, braced their feet, and fought to keep the keel from smashing into the granite wall. The Gods Sors and Tiber noticed the near tragedy and allowed the bow to swing downstream undamaged.

However, as the gods are known to do, they hadn't finished mocking the mortals. Twenty-four hundred feet from the first bend, the mighty river smacked another wall of stone and made another left-hand turn. Compounding the navigation, silt and gravel deposited when the current slowed after the first turn, creating a sandbar on the right side of the river.

"Starboard side, stroke, stroke, stroke" Alerio ordered. "Port side, hold water. Hold…"

The right side of the hull scraped the silt and sand, vibrating the warship. Finally, the bow angled away and the ship reached midstream.

"Hold, hold. Now, all stroke, stroke, stroke."

Alerio and the man on the other rear oar shoved to the right forcing their blades to the left. The Trireme rowed around the next bend staying in the center of the river. They entered a long-curved section of water and the rowers relaxed.

Three miles later, they fought another twisting section of the river. With only thirty-six oarsmen rowing the sides, two men on the rear steering oars, and a handful of extra bodies, the crew was exhausted when the ship emerged from the turns, having avoided the rocks and the sandbars.

At forty-eight miles from the Capital, Centurion Sisera called it a day. They entered a broad section of the river and located lowland. This time, the swung the aft around and backed the ship down until the keel was beached.

"Everybody, over the side," Optio Florian directed. "Get us as far out of the water as possible. If this ship floats away, I'll have the lot of you swimming after it."

***

In the morning, the trireme made twelve twisting miles under low threatening skies. Before the rain started, Tite Roscini handed his oar to a relief rower and worked his way to the aft platform.

"Centurion Sisera," the farmer turned militia officer advised. "We should find shelter."

"If you're afraid of getting wet, I'd give you an oiled skin if I had one," Alerio replied. "We have to reach the Capital before any messengers get there."

"I realize the need for haste," Tite replied. "But the clouds are coming in from the northeast."

Fat, cold rain drops splattered on the deck. A few struck Tite, sending strands of his hair flying. But other drops soon plastered the wild hairs down. The militia Lieutenant didn't move when water ran into his eyes as if to show he wasn't afraid of getting wet.

"You've proved your point, Tite," Alerio acknowledged.

"Getting wet wasn't my issue," Roscini informed the Centurion. "Getting this vessel off the river before we are swamped, is the problem."

Thunder cracked across the sky and small explosions of water followed each drop that impacted on the deck. Almost as if the deck was attempting to shoot the beads back at the sky, the rain drops jumped to ankle height.

186

"What exactly is your issue?" Alerio shouted to be heard over the downpour. "We are safer in the center of the river then trying to land in this weather."

"It's not this," Tite said while leaning forward and pointing at the heavens. "The clouds came from the mountains to the northeast. They have dumped rain up there all night. That water has to go somewhere."

Alerio glanced over the side. The river's surface was dimpled as if a thousand slingers were pelting the water with rocks. A bad memory of being ensnared in a flash flood zipped through Alerio's mind. In that instance, he was caught walking up a sandbar and nearly drowned in the wave of turbulent water.

Designed to handle sea swells and crashes into troughs between waves, the trireme had the buoyancy to survive. But that included a full crew of veteran rowers and an open ocean. This situation had neither.

"Take Florian to the bow and find us a way off the Tiber," Alerio ordered.

"Yes, sir," Tite confirmed.

The Umbrian walked the side platform, tapped the Optio on the shoulder, and both men moved to the front of the ship. Immediately, Alerio had a problem. He could only see a gray outline of the men. From one hundred and thirty feet away, their arm movements were lost in the sheets of rain.

Imagined or not, Alerio felt the deck under his feet lift and panic tighten his chest. A wave of water could easily propel the warship off the river. It would splinter against a grove of trees, ending his life and leaving a legacy of Alerio Sisera as a thief and a swindler.

"Master Pous. Master Monilis," Alerio instructed after fighting off the despondency. "I need you to form a relay from the fore section."

The two masters spread apart until one could see Florian and Roscini, the other had a view of Alerio and both could see each other. Then they waited for a signal while Alerio waited for a massive wave and the arms of Nenia Dea.

***

Sixteen and a half miles from where they had bivouacked the night before, Florian patted his butt then pointed to the left. Cata Pous repeated the movements for Pejus and, in return, the engineer demonstrated the actions to Alerio.

Trust was hard in stressful situations. Most people would hesitate and require confirmation. But Centurion Sisera was a combat veteran. Life and death decisions made by the wave of a hand or a warning transmitted by the jerk of a shoulder were as clear to a Legion infantry officer as a written set of orders. And as in those situations, there was no time to read or even think.

"Starboard side, hold water," he commanded. The eighteen blades stopped in the water, acting as brakes for the right side. "Port side, stroke, stroke."

To help the vessel turn, the two rear oarsmen pulled their oars to the left which pushed the blades to the right. The trireme pivoted sharply.

Alerio peered over his shoulder to see a stream with low banks in the distance. Florian and Roscini had located a creek fed backwater off the main river.

"Back it down," Alerio instructed. "Back it down."

Again, having the trained Legionaries as examples helped the rowers to propel the warship to the rear and into the backwater. After a few more reverse strokes, the hull rose up onto the creek bed.

"You are already wet," Optio Florian announced. "Over the side with you all."

It brought a smile to the experienced Sergeant's face when most of the crew finished the speech for him, "If the ship floats away, I'll throw you in and have you swim after it."

"Exactly, so move your cūlī," Florian declared while walking back to see Alerio. "Sir, why are we beached up a creek?"

"Because Lieutenant Roscini is expecting a flash flood," Alerio reported. "He is an Umbrian and they are a mountain people."

"Next thing you know, Centurion," the Optio informed Alerio. "You'll be telling me they are skilled hunters."

"Aren't they?"

It rained continuously and the crew of Legionaries, masters, and craftsmen spent a damp cold night huddled in wet clothing. Before dawn, a rumble shook them awake. Most had no idea what was causing the commotion. The Umbrians and Alerio recognized the source. When the warship lifted and floated further up the creek, everyone realized the sound was a wall of water flushing the Tiber.

At dawn, they nudged the trireme from the swollen creek. Alerio called for strokes as the two rear oars angled the vessel to nose it downstream. They were thirty-one miles from the docks at the Capital.

189

Thirty-one miles of winding river in an underpowered warship equated to almost a day of rowing. Conversely, on horseback, the distance from that area of the Tiber to the Capital measured twenty-five miles. Adding to the riders' advantage, once on the Northern Legion's road system, the messengers could use way stations to change mounts. When the trireme launched in the morning, only one mile away, two horses left the Legion stables.

On land, the messengers, dry and rested with full bellies, let their fresh mounts set their own pace. On the water, the crew worked the oars to warm up and generate enough body heat to dry their clothes. Plus, they were hungry as their rations were gone.

It wasn't a race to a finish line. Both voyaging entities were on course to a flashpoint. An embattled crossroads where other parties, much, much higher in society, would clash over riches, power, and influence. Unfortunately, their proxies would suffer burns from the flash. One was thirty-one miles from the docks, and the other twenty-five miles from the walls of Rome. And both were moving towards their fate.

Chapter 24 - Millstone of Power

The last three and a half miles, Alerio yelled, snapped, and talked to keep the rowers' attention. None of the Umbrians had seen a city of one hundred thousand people. Or brick buildings so tall, walls as massive, and the handful of majestic temples constructed from granite.

They stumbled, forgot to row, bumped into the oarsman in front, and fouled their oars.

After snaking through giant coils of river, the trireme rowed into a long sweeping curve. It wrapped around until the crew had a view of Quirinal Hill rising from behind the defensive wall. A small island in the distance marked the beginning of the docks and, in his elation at finishing the trip, Alerio neglected to pay attention. The heights of Capitoline Hill slid by too quickly.

Before passing the docks and coming parallel to Palatine Hill, Alerio called out, "Hold water."

The oars stopped moving but, as instructed, the blades remained in the water. Unfortunately, the current continued and carried the warship dangerously close to the island.

"Starboard side, stroke, stroke," he said directing all of the power to the right side so the vessel turned left. "Port side, blades up."

The oars on the left rose into the air as the hull slid along an open section of the city's dock.

"Starboard side, hold water," Alerio ordered.

The oar blades, acting as brakes, slowed the trireme while Legionaries jumped to the dock hauling lines. Once on shore, they looped the ropes around piers and pulled. The ship came to a gentle stop when the ropes went taut.

"Starboard side, blades up," Alerio instructed then added. "Good work everyone and thank you."

The men on the wharf took in the slack from the mooring lines. In response, the warship moved backward for a couple of feet before stopping against the dock. They tied off the lines and stood looking at the Centurion for directions.

"Orders, sir," Sergeant Florian inquired.

Alerio scanned the port. To his disappointment, a squad of city guardsmen marched by the warehouses, scattering laborers carrying bundles and causing carts to swerve off to the side. The guard unit ignored the protests of the harbor's work force and continued on a direct path to the trireme.

"Optio Florian. Arm the squad and defend the ship," he replied. "This is your post until relieved by Fleet Praetor Sudoris or me. Understood?"

"Yes, Centurion. If I may ask, where will you be?" the Sergeant questioned.

"Getting everyone something to eat," Alerio informed the Optio. "Afterward, I'll state my case to important people. Then I'll try to stay out from under the millstone of the senate."

"I've never heard the workings of the senate described like that," Florian commented. "What does it mean?"

"It means, Sergeant, if I'm not careful, rough grains like me can easily be crushed by the political machinery," Alerio answered. "The Legion's navy and I are depending on you. Carry on."

While Optio Florian and Decanus Ippazio helped the squad of Legionaries pull their war gear from inside the hull, Alerio collected Cata Pous and Pejus Monilis.

"I need a screen," he explained while stripping off his clothing. The borrowed shirt, and trousers were wrapped around Alerio's boots and folded into a bundle. "I would appreciate it if you'd have the craftsmen block the view. And if one of you would toss this down to me."

Unseen by the dock laborers and the approaching city guard squad, Alerio slipped over the side and hung for a moment from the top boards of the hull. Then he released and dropped into the Tiber. All Legionaries are required to be proficient swimmers in order to qualify as heavy infantrymen. And Alerio was an excellent swimmer. He came to the surface, used scissor kicks to keep his arms and shoulders out of the water while reaching up.

Pejus dropped the clothing over the side then turned away. Yelling from the dock drew his attention. He didn't wait to see if Centurion Sisera caught the bundle.

***

Garrison contuberniums are composed of nine men plus their Decanus and an Optio or Tesserarius if more authority is required. The northern Legion squad had an Optio in command while the city guard squad brought a Centurion. An officer usually beats an NCO, unless the Sergeant has a standing order not to relinquish his post.

"Optio, stand down and step aside. I'm here to take Alerio Sisera into custody," the guard officer informed Florian. "and to secure the boat."

"I can't do that, sir," the Sergeant replied.

"And why not?" demanded the Centurion.

"Because Centurion Sisera is not here to release me from my orders nor is Praetor Sudoris," Florian explained. "Until one of them arrives, I will guard this naval vessel."

Nine armed Legionaries climbed from inside the trireme, hopped over the side and lined the dock. Now, nine guardsmen stood braced, shield to shield facing an equal number of heavy infantrymen. Behind the lines, their squad leaders stood beside their commanders waiting for instructions.

"Decanus. As the dock officer, I order you to remove your squad," the Centurion said shifting his threats to the Legion Lance Corporal. "Not complying will go hard on you and your contubernium."

"Sir, I am Decanus Ippazio of Second Squad, Fort Orte, Northern Legion," Ippazio reported. "My infantry officer is Centurion Decalcavi and he isn't here. In light of that, my orders are to follow the directions of Optio Florian, sir."

The guard officer puffed up and his face darkened. Then he glanced up and down the lines of armed men and realized they were very close to clashing and drawing blood. At the thought of being responsible for a skirmish in the harbor, he calmed and turned to his NCO.

"Lance Corporal. Back off five paces while I sort this out," he instructed the guard squad leader. "I'm going to get clarification. Nobody leaves that ship."

"Yes, sir," the squad leader said while hiding his relief.

He could tell by the appearance and self-assured stance of the Northern Legion squad that they were accustomed to fighting. His contubernium would be better at breaking up drunken brawls, crowd control and, collecting taxes. The skill sets didn't favor his men and with enthusiasm he ordered his squad to back up.

"Guard squad, five paces to the rear, march."

"Squad, stand easy," Ippazio directed his contubernium. Then he asked. "What now, Optio Florian?"

"We wait, Lance Corporal," the Sergeant remarked. "For what or how long, I have no idea."

***

The porters at the warehouse paid little attention to the naked man when he climbed out of the Tiber and scrambled up the riverbank. Baths were available but some citizens enjoyed the exercise of swimming while cleaning their bodies. The nude man, as demonstrated by his physique, obviously fell into that category. When he slipped on a shirt of good quality wool with hand woven designs, they knew he favored the exotic such as a swim in the river to end his day.

Alerio tugged the shirt down over hips and slipped on the trousers. He felt the fine fabric and was thankful to the Umbria craftsman who loaned him the clothing. After his hobnailed boots were strapped on, he broke into a run heading southeast out of the harbor area.

He passed the Golden Valley Trading House, crossed the boulevard, and took the road into the commercial district. After a number of turns, Alerio trotted by Zacchaeus the cloth merchant's establishment and increased his speed as he approached the intersection. One of the cross streets ended at the property line for an inn. Alerio mounted the steps to the porch of the Chronicles Humanum Inn, crossed the tiles, pushed open the front door, and entered the great room.

***

"Master Harricus," Alerio greeted the proprietor. "Good afternoon to you."

"Alerio Sisera, dressed in workmen's clothing, barging through my front door without baggage or transportation, means one thing," Thomasious Harricus

195

stated. "But don't hold me in suspense, lad. Who have you offended? And what do you want?"

"I believe a segment of the senate opposed to building warships," Alerio offered. He held up three fingers. Then, reached up and collapsed one of the digests ticking off an item. "I need food and drink for forty-one men. No, wait. Make that fifty-one because the city guard is there."

Alerio pushed down a second finger as he counted off the answers to Harricus' questions. In response, the inn keeper waved him to a chair and indicated to a serving girl to bring food to the table.

"You don't want much do you?" Harricus challenged. "What else?"

"I need a Centurion's armor and helmet before I visit Senator Maximus," Alerio said finishing the list. "My rank should help with my defense."

"That is a lot of baggage. Go back to the anti-warship faction," Harricus instructed. "That's interesting as the senate has debated the issue and reached compromises. Tell me about your troubles."

A clay bowl of soup landed in front of Alerio along with a wedge of cheese and half a loaf of bread. He ate some of all three before continuing.

"Stifone sits up north in Umbria territory and Tribune Subausterus is trying to discredit it," Alerio told the inn keeper. Then remembering Thomasious Harricus' alter ego, he warned. "But the Clay Ear can't gossip about or mention Stifone. It's a secret ship building location. At least it should be, if the staff officer doesn't ruin it."

"Should be? Ruin?" Harricus remarked. "I know the Subausterus family. Big on horses in the Capital. But their largest land holdings are in the east."

"Well, the Tribune doesn't want any ships built in Stifone," Alerio commented. "And he has managed to hang the expenses of building one on me."

"Building warships is expensive," Harricus observed. "But if you have a product to show for the coins, you should be fine."

"That's why I need food sent to the craftsmen on board and the Legionaries defending the trireme," Alerio stated. "The warship is at the city docks."

"You built a warship up north and rowed it to the Capital?" the inn keeper questioned.

"I had to. Subausterus' Century was going to burn it," Alerio assured Harricus. "And murder Cata Pous, Pejus Monilis, and Optio Florian so they couldn't testify at my trial."

"Oh, but the Goddess Muta is a cruel mistress," Thomasious Harricus cried after Alerio explained who the people were. "Here is a story for my scrolls that would bring me coins by the purse full. Yet, the Clay Ear must not write the tale. But I have to see this wonder of a vessel."

Thomasious Harricus jumped up and ran to the doors leading to the back hallway.

"Erebus. Harness up the wagon," the inn keeper called to his barbarian assistant. "We are going shopping for cheese and bread. Then, we will go to see a trireme. I can say no more but hurry."

"Thank you, Master Harricus," Alerio acknowledged. "Those men worked hard for me."

"You owe me, Centurion Sisera," the inn keeper chided Alerio. "Not for feeding your crew. But for bringing the Clay Ear a story that he can't publish."

***

Blocks from the inn, Alerio rapped on the door to the Historia Fae. A glance at the sky showed the sun was low and the end of the daylight coming on fast.

A small square of iron opened in the door and an eye peered out.

"Decent people are at supper," Tomas Kellerian, the armorer to the gods, stated. "Upright citizens are resting after a hard day of work."

"I am not decent or upright," Alerio informed him. "I'm an infantry officer in the Legion. I haven't done a hard day's work since they attached the rooster comb to the top of my helmet."

"At least you're honest," Kellerian acknowledged.

An iron bar squealed as it was removed and the hinges squeaked when the door opened. Alerio walked over the threshold and the sounds of tortured iron accompanied the closing and bolting of the door.

"Looking at your Umbrian clothing, I don't know where to begin," Tomas Kellerian admitted. "Just tell me why you have interrupted my extravagant meal."

Alerio scanned the room. A bowl of stew resting on a workbench was the only thing in sight qualifying as nourishment.

"I need armor, under clothing, a gladius belt, a gladius to go with it, and a Centurion helmet," Alerio informed him. "And I need it right away, Master Kellerian."

"Someday, you will enter my shop and respect my time," Tomas challenged. "Until that day arrives, come with me."

In short order, Alerio marched out of the armor to the gods' establishment wearing Centurion gear. Alerio located a carriage and climbed to the seat.

"Senator Spurius Maximus' Villa," he instructed the driver.

As a rule, Alerio preferred walking and taking in the sights and sounds of the Capital. But today, with the city guard hunting him, riding was the better idea. He pulled the curtain closed and sat back as the carriage lurched and bounced while it crossed the city.

***

The finely carved statue of the winged Goddess Bia glowed golden in the afternoon sun. Alerio paused to offer a silent prayer to the goddess of force and might after stepping down from the carriage. Once he thanked her for the strength of his body, he moved to the front door of Villa Maximus and knocked.

The peephole cover slid back and a stranger wearing a helmet appeared in the opening. Besides the helmet, the man wore aged leather chest and shoulder armor.

"What do you want?" the man-at-arms inquired.

Alerio knew most of the Senator's home guards. They were all veteran infantrymen and he had interacted with them on occasion. But he didn't recognize this one.

"Centurion Sisera to see Senator Maximus," Alerio replied to the house guard. "Or Belen, if the Senator is unavailable."

"Master Spurius Maximus and his secretary are at the Senator's country estate," the man-at-arms informed Alerio. "They're expected back next week."

The peephole slid closed and Alerio stood staring at the door. He didn't know who else to contact about his dilemma. He remained on the front porch, thinking with his back to the street.

Besides processing a list of potential allies, one thought tugged at Alerio's mind. All of the Senator's personal guards referred to Spurius Maximus as Senator or General. None called him Master.

Not that it would have made a difference how long Alerio lingered on the stoop. The ten city guardsmen and their officer came on him fast.

At the sounds of boot leather on pavers, Alerio spun to challenge them. His hand was on the hilt of his gladius when a cloud passed over the face of the sun. In that moment, Alerio happened to glance at the statue of Bia. The golden light faded and, in the shadow that took its place, the granite turned as grey as the pale of death. Taking it as a warning from the goddess, Alerio lifted his hand from his weapon.

"Alerio Sisera?" the guard officer demanded.

"I'm Centurion Sisera."

"You're under arrest," the guard officer charged. "For the crime of treason against the Republic."

The door to Villa Maximus swung open and the man-at-arms from the peephole and three others, also dressed in aged leather armor, strutted through the doorway.

"I told you it would work," the man bragged to the guard officer.

"There's no reward," the officer responded.

"It's already been paid," the mercenary assured the guard Centurion. Then to a man standing behind the line of guardsmen, he instructed. "We're off for vino. Let's go."

The five mercenaries strutted away and Alerio glanced over his shoulder. They had left the front door open.

"What about checking and securing the General's villa?" Alerio questioned. "And where is the household staff?"

"Don't you worry about the villa," the Centurion stated. "One of my guardsmen will close the door. Now, move, traitor."

Chapter 25 - Somewhat Involved

Surrounded by armed guards, Alerio was marched down backstreets to the city guard headquarters and barracks. Inside the walls, they guided him to a row of holding cells constructed of brick and mud.

"I have orders that no one can be near the prisoner," an NCO stated while stepping in front of the detachment escorting Alerio. "Our main holding room is standing room only and the individual cells are full."

"What are you saying, Sergeant?" the officer asked.

"We need to clear cells to isolate him," the Optio explained. "But I'm not sure which ones to...?"

"I'll make it easy on you," the Centurion told him. "Clear the first three and put the prisoner in the center one. There, it's done. Now make it happen."

"But sir...," the NCO began to protest when the officer pointed two accusing fingers at him.

"Clear the cells. I do not want to say it again," the guard officer directed. "Or you can think about your disrespect on the punishment post."

"Clear the cells," the Optio directed his two-man team of Privates.

The locking beams were lifted from the brackets, set aside, and the doors opened.

"Get out," the NCO bellowed at the cells. "Consider yourselves lucky. The Centurion has interceded on your behalf with the Praetor and your court day has been cancelled. You would be well advised to stay out of trouble. And to make an offering to the God Sors for your luck."

The Guard officer and the NCO glared at each man as the freed detainees left their cells, collected their possessions, and headed for the main gate.

A man stinking of urine and animal dung stumbled from the first cell. Even through the sun rested behind the defensive wall, he jerked up his forearm to protect his eyes from the brightness. After picking up a herding club and a pouch from a table, he staggered towards the gate.

The man's hangover would really hit him later when the vino left his system. Unless the stockyard worker replenished his thirst for Bacchus' blessing. Then the chances were, the drunk would be back in the care of the city guard before dawn, the Optio decided.

Next, a man dressed in a quality linen toga and a blue robe ducked through the low doorway. He placed a hat on his head and cocked it at an angle while straightening and stretching his back. The petasos hid his eyes but the brim didn't cover his bright white teeth and overly friendly smile.

"Centurion, I congratulate you on the fine facility you have here in the Capital," he exclaimed while bowing to the Guard officer. He selected a purse and a scroll from the table before adding. "Hopefully, there will be no more misinterpretations of my business practices."

"Cheating old people by charging interest rates they can't afford is not business. You'll be back," the NCO assured him. "And the next time, we'll gather witnesses and you'll stand trial for usury."

Even though the smile never left the man's face, the officer knew the Optio hit a nerve. The description of his crimes had the loan offender increasing his pace. The Centurion figured, maybe not tomorrow but, within the week, the fraudster would be back in custody.

The third internee appeared in the doorway and paused. Before leaving the sanctuary of the cell, he scanned the yard. Only after checking the location of the guardsmen, the officer, and the Guard Sergeant, did he walk out into the open.

Alerio recognized Civi Affatus and the veteran's practical awareness. As a Legionary, the NCO had been in Spurius Maximus' First Century. After years in the Legion protecting the General, he joined Senator Maximus' household guard.

The former Sergeant plucked his gladius belt from the table without breaking stride. Not pausing to strap it on, he slung the belt over a shoulder and marched directly for the main gate.

Although Civi's eyes took in every person and every item in the drill yard, former Optio Affatus did not acknowledge Centurion Sisera. Until he exited the main gate and turned left. Then, before the gate frame and defensive wall blocked Alerio's view, Civi Affatus hammered a fist into his breast in a cross-chest salute. Alerio smiled at the stealth sign of recognition.

Civi was sure to report seeing Alerio in the custody of the city guard. At least Senator Maximus would know of Alerio's arrest if not his fate. It was a small comfort, Alerio thought as a guardsman shoved him into a cell. The door closed and Alerio realized he was in the cell recently occupied by the stockyard man.

***

Civi Affatus fumed at the situation. Then he tried to calm himself and figure out a logical reason for his arrest. Earlier in the day, a note requesting his presence at the city guard barracks arrived at the villa. Thinking it concerned the General, he went. As soon as he announced himself, five guardsmen disarmed him and tossed him in a cell. Now, again for no reason or explanation, he had been released.

Seeing the General's protégé in custody made him think Alerio Sisera was somehow involved. Putting aside the questions, Civi began to walk faster. After years of running and marching with a full load, he couldn't sprint or shuffle on his weak knees. But he still had the heart so he pushed through the pain and hurried back to check on villa Maximus.

***

Returning to the property, only added to his list of questions.

"They came in right after you left," the cook complained. "Locked me and the gardeners and the housemen in the stables. And you were nowhere to be found."

204

"I was locked up as well," Civi said in his defense. "What was taken?"

"Nothing. Well, five food platters and five mugs of vino were used," the cook offered. "But nothing else was taken."

"It seems to be a pretty elaborate plan just to allow five people to have lunch in the Senator's house," Civi observed. "There had to be another purpose."

"Master Affatus?" a small voice from behind the cook asked.

"And who are you, lad?" Civi inquired

A small boy peered around the cook's legs.

"Orsus, sir," the lad replied. "I am the cook's helper."

"By next year, he'll be grown enough to start as an apprentice," the cook explained. "He was away when we were penned in. What did you see Orsus?"

The little lad stepped around the cook, held up two fists, then extended a finger from each.

"Not only saw," Orsus bragged while waving one finger. He stopped the movement and switched to rocking the other finger. "But I heard the men and city guards talking."

"Bright lad," Civi commented. "What did they say?"

"The five men talked about a reward while they ate," Orsus stated. "When a carriage pulled up, one of the men ran out the side door. I followed him and hid in the bushes. He came back with the guardsmen. What does traitor mean, Master Affatus?"

"Traitor?" Civi repeated. "Who said traitor?"

"The officer of the guard," Orsus informed the former Sergeant. "He said it to the man they arrested."

From the statement, Civi knew that seeing Alerio Sisera was more than a coincidence. His being released after the capture indicated that the entire operation revolved around the ambush of Centurion Sisera. Three opposing duties were obvious to Civi. The General would want him to investigate Alerio's trouble and at the same time, guard the villa.

The closest reinforcements were from the house guards at Villa Duilius. While Senator Gaius Duilius and Maximus disagreed on many issues, they socialized because they respected each other. And their villas were a block apart.

"I'll be right back," Civi said.

"Where are you going, Civi?" the cook demanded.

"To prevent anyone else from invading the villa," Civi replied as he rushed through the doorway.

***

A block away, with his knees swelling and hurting, he located the head of Senator Duilius' security. After the former Centurion heard the report, the infantry officer sent a pair of armed men to protect Villa Maximus. Then to Civi's surprise, the Legion officer motioned for Civi to follow him. They entered Villa Duilius and found the Senator in his office.

"Sir. There have been some strange activities today," the Centurion reported. "I think you should be aware. Optio Civi Affatus can tell you more."

Civi informed the Senator about the subterfuge, his detention and release. The five men who stayed at the villa, and about the arrest of Centurion Sisera. And finally, about two of his duties as a household sentinel.

"I was a cosigner of Sisera's warrant to Centurion," Gaius Duilius responded. "My guards will see that Spurius' villa is guarded. That will free you up to handle the other two things you must do."

"Two other things, sir?" Civi inquired. He had only mentioned two obligations.

"Of course, you will find out what Sisera is doing in the Capital and why he was arrested. After you report your finding to me, you'll be free," Gaius Duilius remarked. "I hear you were an Optio for the General's First Century. I can only imagine how eager you are to find the men who invaded the Senator's home. And gently explain to them the error of their ways."

"Yes, sir. Thank you," Civi Affatus said as he and the commander of the house guard backed out of the Senator's office.

As they walked the hallway towards the exit, the Centurion turned to the Optio.

"Tall orders, Civi," the infantry officer suggested. "Where will you start?"

"Centurion Sisera stays at the Chronicles Humanum Inn when he's in the Capital," Civi answered. "I'll start there."

***

The borrowed horse stopped at the crossroads and Civi Affatus dismounted. Riding was easier on his knees than walking and he offered a silent thanks to the Centurion. Once the reigns were tied to a post, Civi walked the stairs to the porch.

"I'm looking for Master Harricus," he informed the serving lass.

"He's not around," she answered. "He and Erebus took vino and the wagon to the docks."

"Is that normal?" Civi questioned.

"Is anything ever normal around here?" she shot back. "Are you eating or drinking or leaving?"

"I'm heading for the dock," he replied.

"Then be off with you," the woman ordered. And she winked and added. "Maybe next time you'll stay for a while."

"I might do that," he stammered while backing out of doorway.

He crossed the porch and walked the stairs without once thinking about his sore knees.

***

It might have been the most civilized standoff Optio Affatus had ever encountered. At the edge of the docks, Legionaries in the armor and helmets of the Northern Legion squatted beside their infantry shields sat eating bread, cheese, and meat. Between bites, they passed around wineskins.

Across from the contubernium, a squad of city guardsmen also dined. Behind both lines, Lance Corporals eyed each other while watching their men.

Thomasious Harricus and his barbarian man, Erebus, walked off a trireme carrying empty cloth bags. Behind them, civilians stood or sat on platforms chewing on food.

"Master Harricus, a word if you please," Civi called as he dismounted.

"You're not Umbrian or Legion or city guard," Thomasious Harricus commented. "Who are you?"

"I'm from Villa Maximus, sir," Civi replied.

"I can see by your gladius that you aren't a stableman or a gardener," Thomasious remarked. "What can I do for one of Senator Maximus' personal guards?"

"Centurion Sisera has been arrested," Civi informed the inn keeper. "I've been sent to discover why he was in the city. And if possible, why he was detained?"

Thomasious Harricus pointed to the warship.

"There's your answer to both," Thomasious replied. "A warship that should not exist. Bought but not paid for."

"I'm not sure I understand," Civi admitted.

"What do you call a trireme that hasn't been delivered to the navy?"

"I don't know, Master Harricus."

"A floating bonfire," Thomasious answered.

The former Legion NCO bit his lip while attempting to decipher meaning. Then he put the concepts together.

"Someone wants to burn the ship," Civi ventured. He thought for a few heartbeats before adding. "And Centurion Sisera owes someone for it?"

"You said it not me," Thomasious explained. "If he's been arrested, it appears someone other than the navy is laying claim to the trireme."

"Senator Duilius should be able to find out who that is," Civi said as he climbed onto his mount.

Civi Affatus jerked the animal's head around to face the street and dug his heels into the horse's flanks.

"Senator Gaius Duilius. He's involved in this?" Thomasious Harricus cried as Civi trotted out of the harbor area. "I am without fail cursed by Muta."

***

Alerio sat in the dark and smelly room with the low ceiling. It took a long while of standing with his head bent to the side before the knot in his neck forced him to sit on the frame of the bed. While he could now hold his head up, he couldn't bring himself to lay on the dirty straw bedding.

Outside the room, the door rattled as the beam was lifted off the brackets.

"Step away from the door," a voice ordered.

Alerio chuckled. The room was not only lacking in height, but the depth was just a little longer than the door was width. The thought of standing stooped over while pressed against the wall and arm's length from the door tickled him. But he moved as far from the door as the small cell allowed.

"What's funny," a guardsman inquired.

Two lanterns behind the man made him an outline in the doorframe. Then delicious aromas drifted to Alerio.

"Just giddy from lack of food," Alerio lied. "Is that for me?"

"Strew, bread, and one lantern," the guard replied.

He placed a tray on the floor and after taking the lantern from the man behind him, he set it near the tray.

"Aren't you afraid of fire in the cell?" Alerio questioned.

"Not at all, Centurion," the guardsman admitted. "If there's a fire and you burn, it'll save us the trouble of transporting you to the Temple of Jupiter Capitolinus in the morning."

"Why am I going to the Temple?" Alerio demanded.

"For the same reason all prisoners go there," the guard replied while backing out of the cell. "To stand trial."

Then he closed the door. Alerio was still sitting on the bed when the beam dropped into the brackets.

Chapter 26 - Momus, The God of Mockery

Trials were public affairs with over one hundred citizens in attendance and they were held in the forum. A pair of Praetors, in white robes to identify their purity of thought, presided over the legal arguments before rendering a final judgement. And a scribe jotted down every aspect on parchments to record the trial for the public archives. In that case, Alerio could tell his side of the story and plead his case to the citizens.

Unless the trial was a tribunal convened in a temple. Then, the laws of Rome as written on the Twelve Tables intermingled with the edicts of the Gods as deciphered by Priests. Bile rose in Alerio's throat and his appetite fled from the lingering stink of the stockyard man.

Alerio eventually sank to the floor, scooted over to the tray, and ate. But he didn't remember the taste. His mind traveled over the months in Stifone and Amelia and he worked all night to recall every detail of his negotiations with Nardi Cocceia. The lantern had long ago burned out when the locking beam scraped while being removed and the door opened.

"Let's go," a guardsman ordered.

Alerio peered over the man's shoulder at the dark yard.

"Awful early," he commented.

"Move," the man insisted.

Ducking under the doorframe, Alerio came upright outside the cell then stopped. The man, rather than a city guardsman, was a temple guard. Plus, in the torchlight, Alerio saw robed figures standing at the back of a covered cart. The Priests weren't the problem, nor were the armed temple guards. It was the ominous covered cart and the fact that none of the city guard commanders cared to watch the prisoner transfer.

During his trip to the temple, Alerio would be blind and unobservable to any citizen. For all purposes that mattered, Alerio Sisera's fate was already sealed.

"Get in the cart," the temple guard ordered.

Resigning himself to the gods, Alerio climbed in the cart and settled on the bench. The goatskin cover closed, a voice encouraged the mule with the crack of a whip, and the cart began to roll.

***

The cart crossed the city and, other than jerking from side to side, the road felt flat. Then, Alerio sensed the incline as the cart started up Capitoline Hill. Back and forth on the winding road, Centurion Sisera visualized the way. Based on hiking tours of the city, he knew the twisting street topped out above the Tarpeian Rock. A half mile beyond the deadly drop, the Temple of Jupiter occupied the apex of the hill.

It didn't escape Alerio's notice that the tribunal was being held in the temple closest to the deadly cliff. A place notorious for not only the execution of people convicted of capital crimes but, the undignified and humiliating legacy of shame suffered by people thrown from the cliff over the Tarpeian Rock. Yet, he might have been reading more into the location than his situation warranted.

Two things belayed his worry. Jupiter was the patron of good faith and Tribune Subausterus was certainly acting in bad faith. The temple seemed a fitting place to reveal the truth. And, those sentenced to be thrown from Capitoline Hill were fed a solid, heavy meal before the execution. Seeing as Alerio hadn't even been provided a light breakfast, he set his concerns aside. Instead, he concentrated on forming his best arguments.

***

The sounds from the wheels told the tale of transitioning from stone pavers to fired clay tiles. When the cart stopped, the cover parted, and Alerio stepped down onto the tiles of a courtyard.

The main temple of Jupiter towered over lower buildings that created the sides and back of the enclosure. Columns lined covered walkways that connected offices, where the temple's business was conducted and where the Priests lived.

While the cart drove away, the entourage remain. A guard directed Alerio in the direction of a door. As they moved, most of the Priests and guards walked away. By the time Alerio reached the entrance, his escorts were reduced to a Priest and two temple guards.

"You'll find light refreshments to break your nightly fast," the last Priest explained. He pulled off his cloak, revealing a yellow robe and added. "Plus, you'll find a dark colored tunic. You will face the Praetor as a citizen of the Republic and not as one of her defenders. Leave the Centurion armor and helmet in the room."

"The officer gear is borrowed," Alerio informed him. "After this is over, I'll need them back."

"Or you won't care," the Celebrant of Jupiter advised. "Change clothing and eat. I'll be back to get you when all the parties are assembled."

Alerio cast a look at a small platter of bread, cheese, olives, and a pitcher of vino. A peak into the carafe showed him the vino was diluted with an excess of water.

"I've had better," Alerio remarked. "And I've had much worse. Thank you."

The Priest didn't comment, he simply closed the door. Along with candles, the other light in the room came from high slits in the walls. Not as large as windows, but more substantial than cracks, they were open enough to allow the first rays of the rising sun into the room. As if painted on, the strip of light clung to the ceiling.

Alerio pulled off the helmet, placed it beside the food, then began unstrapping his armor.

***

Another yellow robed Cleric and a different pair of temple guards came to collect Alerio. He checked to see how far down the wall the sunlight had traveled. His only sense of time was the band of light pouring through the slits. The strip of light hit the bricks a hands width below the ceiling. It was still early.

"In the Legion, if we started anything this late in the day," Alerio suggested to the Priest of Jupiter. "the Senior Centurion would accuse us of sleeping in. I guess living in a temple gives you an altered sense of life."

"The Temple of Jupiter is available day and night for those seeking guidance," the Priest stated while waving an open hand at the door. "All is prepared."

Alerio straightened the grey tunic and marched out of the room. One guard led them down the covered porch while the other guard and the Cleric fell in behind. Where the colonnade continued at the end of a long building, they turned into an alley. At the far end, the four entered a small amphitheater.

A table with ink and parchment on the surface rested off to the side of the orchestra circle. In the center, a highbacked chair sat facing the tiers of granite benches. Placed between the chair and the bottom row were two tables. One on the left and the other on the right.

"Tiny but convenient for your entertainment needs," Alerio mentioned to the Priest. "A little intimate, but serviceable. Seen any good plays here lately?"

"Never. This is a teaching auditorium," the Priest corrected. "And a venue for serious issues."

Up the center aisle and behind the top row of benches, another Priest raised a knife overhead. He stood by a small altar, spouting invocations. His words flowed in a rhythm but in a cadence so rapid, Alerio couldn't understand the words.

"Opening the day with prayers," Alerio said. "Always a good idea."

"The morning prayers were given at sunrise," the Priest advised.

Then from behind the altar, a second yellow robed Cleric brought a sheep to the one holding the knife.

"Sky Father, Jupiter, patron of good faith, we offer this sacrifice," all three Priests boomed as if the volume

215

would travel beyond the clouds and reach the God of Thunder. "We ask only for your blessing of these proceedings."

The blade plunged into the sheep's neck. Bleating in pain, the animal quivered before the steel cut deep enough to silence it. Blood spewed onto the ground and, when the sheep fell on the altar, all three Priests dropped to their knees. With their arms raised to the sky, they prayed.

"The life given this day, is given to you with no petition," the Celebrants of Jupiter intoned. "It is only to make you aware of our activities."

For a temple as wealthy and popular as the Temple of Jupiter, sacrificing a sheep wasn't a financial burden. For a household of the average citizen or a craftsman's shop it was a very generous offering. But it seemed stingy for such a big complex.

"I expected a larger turn out for the morning sacrifice," Alerio remarked.

Alerio's mother taught him to be respectful. To honor her, he decided to keep his opinion of the value of the offering to himself.

"Two bulls were sacrificed to Jupiter at sunrise," the Priest explained while dusting off the dirt clinging to his robe.

"Then why the sheep?" Alerio inquired.

"To bless the events unfolding in the amphitheater," the Cleric replied while placing a hand on Alerio's arm and propelling him to a seat at the table on the left.

"I assume then my hearing will be quick," Alerio proposed. "To clear us out before the big event."

From a screen behind the orchestra area, a man in a plain tunic entered and walked quickly to the chair and desk. Behind him, a man in a pure white robe entered majestically as if the gods were analyzing his every step. He walked to the highbacked chair and sat, resting his hands on the arms of the chair. Then a shiver ran down Alerio's spine as a Fetial Priest glided onto the floor of the theater.

The ecclesiastic brother moved to the center of the bottom row. Although he was a Celebrant of Jupiter, the Fetial Consors wore a blue robe with red trim. And to highlight his duties, he wore a red cloth belt with a dagger. Not for fighting, but to remind the Senators who consulted with the order that Jupiter's judgement could advise war or peace.

The Fetial Priests were God's spokespersons on foreign affairs and international treaties. Considering Alerio was charged with breaking the trust of a treaty, his worry about Priests, especially Fetiales, inserting the Gods' opinion into the law was well founded.

Just as the brother sat, another man scurried into view. He carried a pouch with the ends of scrolls sticking out of the top. The man selected a place on the bench between Alerio and the Fetial brother.

Next, a pair walked from around the theaters backdrop and Centurion Sisera came off the bench. He was two steps towards them and would have attacked Ludovicus Humi and Lucius Trioboli, if the Priest and the temple guards hadn't restrained him. With Alerio held in check, the former Corporal and the Centurion of Subausterus' Century selected seats on the bench as far from Alerio as possible.

"There's my answer," Alerio exclaimed to the Priest. "With those pieces of merda here, we should be able to finish quickly. And the temple can get on with the major event."

"Centurion Sisera," the Cleric stated. "There are no other activities scheduled for the venue today."

Alerio dropped onto the bench. It appeared he was the defendant in a secret tribunal with international ramifications. And, they hadn't provided him with an Orator or a Jurist advocate.

Almost as if the God Momus descended into Jupiter's temple to mock Alerio, Jurists Master Imprecari strolled from around the backdrop and entered the orchestra area. The thin lawyer with the bushy hair eyed the meager audience and his face showed disappointment. Obviously, he expected a larger audience for his presentations. He shook off the disappointment and faced the highbacked chair.

"Magistrate, in light of the overwhelming evidence against Alerio Sisera," Imprecari declared to the judge in the white robe. "the Republic moves to forgo the trial and go directly to sentencing."

"Orator Imprecari. Save your speech for when we get started," the judge advised. "Is the defendant's advocate here?"

Alerio watched the stage backdrop for his legal team. None walked in but the Priest in the yellow robe beside him stood.

"If it pleases the court," the Celebrant announced. "I will serve as the advocate for Alerio Sisera."

"Excellent. We seem to have all parties represented. I am Praetor Valerius Seubus and I will be deciding this case," the magistrate proclaimed. He pointed to a man at the table who was writing down every word. "Our scribe is Master Convelli. Let's get started. Now you can start Orator Imprecari."

"Judge, in light of the overwhelming evidence against Alerio Sisera. The Republic moves to forgo the trial and go directly to the sentencing."

"Denied. State your case and call your first witness," Praetor Seubus instructed.

Imprecari walked to the table on the other side of the small stadium and began laying out stacks of parchment. Alerio recognized the lawyer from a trip to the east coast and knew him to be a political sycophant. They had clashed during a trial and there was no affection between the infantry officer and the lawyer. Character deficiencies aside, Imprecari was a law scholar and a quality advocate. Which wasn't good for Alerio.

"Tell me, Priest, that you are a student of law," Alerio begged. Then he got specific. "Are you blessed of the God Mercury with a quick wit and a tongue that ties adversaries in knots of logic?"

"I am not a man who has spent time studying the Twelve Tablets. Nor am I a whip sharp debater," the Celebrant admitted. "I am a man of passion who believes in Jupiter's promise of good faith in all agreements."

The Fetial glanced over and nodded his approval at the words. Alerio allowed his head to hang and decided he was in deep trouble.

"Do you have a name?" Alerio inquired.

"You may call me Pastor Pamphilus," the Cleric replied. "Trust in the sky father, young man."

Alerio felt like pulling the Golden Valley dagger and stabbing everyone in the amphitheater before cutting his own throat. Instead, he folded his arms and waited for Orator Imprecari to state the charges. Then, at least, Alerio would know how bad this trial was going to get.

***

"Some months ago, Alerio Sisera was sent to Amelia in the Umbria region," Advocate for the Republic Imprecari said in a voice too loud for the tiny theater. "His job was that of military adviser to Master Ludovicus Humi."

Alerio gripped Pamphilus' robe and jerked on the yellow fabric.

"That's not right," he insisted.

"Be silent, my son," the Priest instructed. "You do not want to incur the wrath of the judge."

Simmering, Alerio released the fabric while muttering, "Nenia Dea, grant me patience." Then Alerio sat back to listen.

Pastor Pamphilus shifted his eyes and watched to see if Sisera blasphemed a Goddess or prayed in a serious manner. The stoic posture told the Priest Alerio was serious when he mentioned the goddess of death.

"The village of Amelia is an idealistic farming community with a headman named Nardi Cocceia," Imprecari described. "But Master Cocceia is simply the patriarch of the largest family and so assumes the title of mayor. Now that we have the location and the circumstances, I call as the Republic's first witness, Master Ludovicus Humi."

The former Corporal stood and dipped his head to show his humility to the court.

220

"Tell us why you were in Amelia?" Imprecari questioned.

"I was sent to make an assessment of the viability of the Umbria region as a construction base for warships," Humi stated. "I found it unacceptable."

"And why is that?" Imprecari probed.

"The Umbria craftsmen had neither the skills nor the will to build ships," Humi said. "Plus, the location is too far up the Tiber river. After weeks of talks, I was about to return to the Capital to make my report…"

Alerio leaned over to Pamphilus and whispered, "He wasn't in charge."

Orator Imprecari heard the comment.

"Were you in charge of the fact-finding mission?" the Orator asked.

"No, sir. There was a Tribune but he left after the assessment," Humi answered.

"Let the records show that the staff officer is not part of this case," Imprecari informed the judge. "The Tribune left before the events occurred that we will discuss. Out of respect for the nobleman, we ask that his name not be included in the records."

"The court agrees," Praetor Seubus said accepting the request.

"What happened after the Tribune left?" Imprecari inquired.

"I was preparing to follow the staff officer when Master Sisera assaulted Nardi Cocceia," Humi testified. "In full armor, he pushed his way through the farmers petitioning Master Cocceia and attacked the mayor."

"He was guarded by Umbria warriors," Alerio blurted out.

"So, you admit to assailing the Umbrian headman?" Imprecari charged.

"It was the only way to get an appointment," Alerio offered.

"Judge, I asked that this aside be included in the records," Imprecari requested. "Specifically, where the accused admits to assaulting Nardi Cocceia."

"I will allow it," the Praetor instructed.

"Tell us Master Humi, what happened after Master Sisera's uncivilized behavior?"

"He ordered me to remain in Stifone and physically kept me from meeting with the mayor or returning to the Capital," Humi lied. "And well he should have, because I could have stopped what happened next."

Alerio jumped to his feet and pointed a finger at Humi.

"You are a murder and a saboteur," Alerio shouted. "It's you who should be on trial."

"Guards. If the accused continues his outburst," Praetor Seubus advised. "You will tie him to the chair and gag him. Do you understand Master Sisera?"

"It's Centurion Sisera," Alerio corrected. "I am a Legion infantry officer and everything said so far had been twisted beyond recognition."

"I asked you a question, Master Sisera," the Praetor reminded him. "Do you understand me?"

Pamphilus gripped Alerio's arm and pulled him down into the chair.

"Yes, sir. I understand," Alerio confirmed.

"Master Humi. What did happen next?" Orator Imprecari prompted the witness.

"Sisera threatened Nardi Cocceia into supplying workers and coins," Humi explained. "In return, Sisera promised Nardi vast rewards including citizenship in the Republic."

"Let the records show that a carrot and stick approach was used to force a provincial into Sisera's criminal enterprise," Imprecari summed up the testimony. "And what did the Umbrians have to say about this travesty?"

"They couldn't say anything. Sisera hired local thugs to keep the workers in line," Humi replied. "In one case, a craftsman and his young helper sneaked out trying to reach Amelia and warn Nardi Cocceia."

"What happened to the Umbrian?"

"He was found on the side of the trail shot to death by arrows," Humi testified. "No one would say it. But we all figured it had to be Sisera who hunted and killed the carpenter and his apprentice."

"Judge. Here sits a man who held craftsmen from an allied nation prisoner and, defrauded an entire village of the Umbria people," Imprecari recapped. "Through the abuse of his authority as an officer of the Legion and his use of terrorist tactics, Alerio Sisera declared himself a barbarian warlord. I have no more questions for this witness."

Pastor Pamphilus rose from his seat and stared at Humi.

"Are you an honorable man who respects the gods?" the Priest inquired.

"I honor the Republic, my fellow citizens, and my family," Humi vowed. "And I make daily sacrifices each day at dawn to my family's and my personal god."

"I have no more questions," Pamphilus stated as he sat.

"That is a tremendous defense you're mounting," Alerio whined. "Are you sure you aren't a Tribune?"

"I am positive," Pamphilus replied, missing the sarcasm in Alerio's question.

***

"You have an idea of the crimes," Imprecari stated. "And, now Judge, I want you to know the scope of Alerio Sisera's treachery. I call on Lucius Trioboli to supply the details. Centurion, please introduce yourself."

Trioboli hadn't worn a tunic with identifiable military patches. Although he had allowed the advocate to use his Legion officer's title. The disparity confused Alerio until Trioboli began his testimony.

"I am Lucius Trioboli, a Centurion with the Northern Legion," Trioboli stated.

Alerio leaped to his feet and yelled, "You lie. You were never with the Northern Legion. You were with 1st Century Subausterus, an unassigned unit."

Judge, Praetor Seubus, raised a fist in the air and ordered, "Guards. Muzzle that beast. I will not have these proceeding interrupted again."

Alerio didn't notice the smug look on Humi's face or the satisfied gleam in Trioboli's eyes. Centurion Sisera was too busy being thrown to the ground. Once down, the guards tightened a cloth around his head that cut into his mouth. When both wrists were tied together, he was lifted and dropped onto his chair. By then, Humi got control, and put a neutral expression on his face.

"Please continue," Orator Imprecari urged.

"We received word from Master Humi about the troubles in Stifone," Trioboli described. "We always tread carefully in Umbria territory. They are allies of the Republic. We arrived late in the day and Master Humi asked my opinion of a ship under construction. I'm a supply officer by training and have experience with construction projects."

"And what did you find?" Imprecari questioned.

"From what I could tell in the afternoon light, it was a quality mockup of a trireme," Trioboli responded. "Fearing Sisera would destroy the fake ship-of-war, I posted four Legionaries to guard it overnight. That was a mistake, I'll live with for the rest of my life."

Trioboli sagged, squeezed the bridge of his nose and, closed his eyes.

"Take a moment to compose yourself," Imprecari counselled. "Then tell the court why you are so emotionally distraught."

Alerio gnawed on the gag but resisted pounding his hands on the table. Finally, Trioboli exhaled and squared his shoulders.

"In the morning, I found all four Legionaries dead. Sometime in the night, they had been brutally clubbed to death," Trioboli stammered, his emotions almost getting the better of him. "They were good lads from good families. I blame myself for their deaths."

"No Centurion Trioboli, it isn't you who murdered the Legionaries," Imprecari assured him. The Orator spun in the direction of the defendant's table, raised an arm, and pointed at Alerio. "The responsibility for the deaths of four, fine young men, falls on that rogue, Alerio

Sisera. But, back up Centurion Trioboli. Where was the accused when you arrived that morning?"

"Under cover of night, Sisera and his confederates launched the replica ship," Trioboli informed the court. "Clearly, he took the trireme to prevent me from documenting the irregularities in construction."

"Thank you Centurion Trioboli, I have no more questions," Imprecari said.

Pamphilus half stood while leaning with his arms pressing on the tabletop.

"Master Trioboli, what's the first act when you receive a shipment of vino," the Priest asked.

"You count and record the number of amphorae," Trioboli responded.

"Thank you," Pamphilus said before sitting down.

"An interesting line of questioning," Orator Imprecari suggested. Then he turned to the man with the pouch full of scrolls. "Pease stand and state your name."

"I am Libitus Belivum, a Quaestor for the city of Rome," he answered.

The Quaestor's were the basic level of magistrates. They oversaw the Republic's treasury and conducted audits of companies and estates owing the government taxes or payments. If a Legion Tesserarius collecting road taxes and keeping a Century's books was at the bottom, a Quaestor sat at the top of the accounting ladder.

"You have heard the proceedings," Imprecari stated. "Tell us the amount, in coins, of damage done to the Republic by Sisera's activities."

"I have reviewed the bills of laden," Belivum reported. "They total one million, eighty-eight thousand, one hundred seventy-three silver coins owed to the Umbrian, Nardi Cocceia."

"Is there a slave worth that?" Imprecari inquired. "Or a set of armor, or a Centurions pay that could be docked to repay that enormous figure?"

Behind the gag, Alerio swallowed. He knew the point being made by the Orator.

"Of course not," Quaestor Belivum assured him. "You're talking about a capital expenditure. That sum would be used for building villas and ships, bridges, miles of roadway and aqueducts."

"Thank you, Quaestor," Imprecari said with a slight bow at the waist. Before sitting, he added. "I have no further questions."

Pastor Pamphilus didn't bother to stand. From his chair, he asked Quaestor Libitus Belivum, "Do you have plans for the future? Ones that include being elected to the position of Praetor or maybe even Senator?"

"I do," Belivum replied.

"I have no more questions," Pamphilus said.

Imprecari raised slowly while elevating his arms. By the time he was erect, his hands were high overhead.

"I feel as if I am drowning in corruption," he announced. "From murder, to theft, to broken trusts, to the destruction of treaties. And trade agreements ground under the hobnailed bootheel of one man."

Lowering his arms, the Orator turned his back to Alerio.

"A trusted Centurion sent to give military advice sees an opportunity," Imprecari bellowed. "A chance for ill-gotten gains, a prospect honorable men would ignore but, a lure that Alerio Sisera could not resist. The monster grabbed coins and supplies with both greedy hands until he had stolen a fortune. And, left a border in crisis and near war. But what does the death of good men mean to such an animal? Nothing. And so, I ask in the name of the Republic, for a sentence of death. The Republic rests its case."

Imprecari sat slowly as if exhausted while Pamphilus shot to his feet as if excited.

"Master Humi. You said you sacrifice to your god and your family's every morning. But you didn't this morning. And yet, you failed to call on your personal god for forgiveness for missing the day," Pamphilus informed him. "Are you normally given to lying in a court set in a temple. Or is it just in the case of Alerio Sisera?"

"I don't know what you are talking about," Humi stammered. "Why would I lie? Why?"

"I don't know but I suggest you consult a temple priest for guidance," Pamphilus offered before nodding in Trioboli's direction. "Centurion. When queried, you stated the first thing a supply man does when receiving a shipment of vino is count the amphorae. In fact, the first thing every supply man does is check the quality of the items to be sure he is receiving what was ordered. Are you incompetent or given to flights of imagination when telling untruths?"

"I don't have to reply to that," Trioboli countered.

"Of course, you don't," Pamphilus acknowledged. "Just as you didn't have to tell the court what really happened in Stifone. Judge, I submit that the witnesses lied for unknown reasons. You need to hear from Alerio Sisera in order to balance the testimony."

228

Alerio was impressed by the Priest's common-sense approach to the law. He waited for the gag to come off so he could tell his side of the story.

"Request denied. Take the prisoner out," the Judge declared. He looked away from Alerio and focused on the Fetial Priest. "Brother Azeglio, I require your consultation."

The guards plucked Alerio out of the chair. They pulled the gag and untied his hands then, before he could voice a protest, quick marched him from the amphitheater. They retraced their steps through the alleyway and turned at the colonnade. Just before the trio reached the holding room, Alerio caught a glimpse of a familiar figure. Tribune Subausterus ducked out of sight between columns on the other side of the temple's quad.

"Not fast enough," Alerio said with a laugh.

He pledged when this was over, he would find a way to get revenge on the nobleman. Then the door opened and a wave of aromas rolled over him. As he stepped into the room, the sight of a feast greeted his eyes while the delicious smells made his mouth waters.

Unfortunately, it was all solid, heavy food.

Chapter 27 - The Fatal Half Mile

People uninitiated in the ways of war or those more sensitive to their fate might be sick to their stomachs. Mentally crushed by the circumstances, they would find it impossible to eat.

For an infantryman, the meal before a battle always tasted like hope. As if the ritual of eating extended the day, pushing the conflict further away. And the flavor of

229

each bite was relished as it heightened the thrill of being alive in the moment. Not as important, or as sought after, as the meal after a battle that confirmed the Legionary survived. But, enjoying a meal prior to facing death always seemed to leave an opening for a future.

Alerio, as an infantryman, poured a mug of vino and circled the spread of dishes. Despite the ominous meaning of the banquet, Centurion Sisera exclaimed, "Bless me, Bacchus. This feast will not go to waste."

The banquet offered slices of roast and beef in sauces; slices of ham and pork in sauces; and slices of chicken and fowl in sauces. Absent were greenery, fruits, vegetables or anything light. Conversely, the temple provided breads made from a variety of grains, plus pies, and honey cakes. The pitcher of dark red, un-watered, vino confirmed this solid, heavy meal was a last supper.

Alerio sipped, filled a platter, and carried the drink and food to a sofa. With the platter on a side table, he reclined and began to eat. It tasted like hope.

The strip of morning sunlight came through the east slit and splashed color across the floor tiles on the west side of the room.

***

Alerio napped, woke, refilled the platter and the mug, and sat consuming more of the feast. The idea of a plan half formed in his mind. Then, filled with vino, delicious food, and hope, Alerio Sisera drifted off.

The two guards were smashed to the ground and the Priest shoved aside. Alerio apologized to the holy man as he ran from the room. Although he didn't know the temple complex, as a bold outlaw, Alerio sprinted, jumped, and knocked a passing visitor from his mount. Then, sitting astride the stolen horse, he rode at a breakneck pace down to the Strait of Messina. After braving the dangerous currents of the strait, Alerio presented himself in the town of Messina. There, he claimed his title as a Captain in the Sons of Mars. His prior life forgotten, Alerio flourished as the dashing commander of a pirate vessel.

The strip of light vanished while the sun transitioned across the sky. Later in the day, the sunlight entered from the west slit and reflected off the tiles on the east wall of the room.

***

"Alerio Sisera, prepare yourself," Pastor Pamphilus stated while opening the door.

Still half asleep, Alerio reached to the small of his back and touched the Golden Valley dagger.

Six temple guards flowed in from behind the Priest and Alerio's hand stopped. The guards spread out and leveled their spears.

"Your days of fighting are over, Centurion," Pamphilus offered. "Use the rest of your life to make peace with your personal god."

"Goddess," Alerio said softly, letting his hand drop from the small of his back. He stood and straightened the tunic. "My personal deity is a Goddess."

"Usually, I think of Legionaries as being closer to Gods," Pamphilus admitted. "But I understand. I will make a sacrifice for you at dusk. Which Goddess is it? Athena for war, Bia for bodily strength, Pietas for duty, Spes for hope, or Victoria for success?"

"You are a good man, Pastor Pamphilus," Alerio told him. "Make the sacrifice a worthy one Priest, for it is offered to Nenia, the Goddess of death. You can chant to her if you like. She enjoys that."

231

Pamphilus cringed and his power of speech fled. Not because Alerio named the goddess who lifted souls from bodies near death, but from the man's casual familiarity with the shadowy Nenia.

"I haven't the voice for chanting," Pamphilus admitted after recovering. "But the sacrifice will be adequate."

"Make it exceptional," Alerio instructed while handing a small purse of coins to the Priest. Then he cuffed and pulled the dagger from the small of his back. "This needs to be returned to the Golden Valley trading house."

Holding the blade under his wrist and out of sight of the guards, Alerio slipped the dagger into Pamphilus' hands.

"That is not a donation to the Temple of Jupiter," Alerio warned. "The blade has a death curse on it. Only by returning it to the Golden Valley can one avoid dying violently."

"For one so young," Pamphilus observed. "you seem to have a strong affiliation with death."

"Ever since my actions at a terribly sad pub in a backwater grain collection town," Alerio replied. "Death has been my companion. I'm ready."

Three guards filed out of the room, followed by Alerio and Pamphilus, and finally the last three temple guards. The sentries formed a moving diamond formation around the convicted and the priest.

"You would think a man could get a ride to his fate," Alerio commented. He rotated his face feeling the warmth of the late afternoon sun.

"It's only a half mile to the Tarpeian Rock," Pamphilus remarked. "I thought you would enjoy the walk. If you like, I'll call for the cart."

"No, I was thinking of a stallion," Alerio teased. "It's not the half mile walk. It's the last eighty feet down to the rock that interests me."

"You do have an odd association with death," Pamphilus said.

"Yes, I do, Priest," Alerio confirmed.

***

Praetor Valerius Seubus and Scribe Convelli stood near, but not too close, to the edge of the cliff. In a cluster facing the Judge were the witnesses to the execution.

The Quaestor, Libitus Belivum, and the Fetial brother, Azeglio, maintained serious expressions and kept their own counsel with their heads held high. That ran counter to Humi and Trioboli. Their heads were down and they whispered excitedly to each other.

When the condemned and the priest appeared on the road from the temple, the official and the witnesses turned to face the procession. But Alerio and Pamphilus' nonchalant stroll took so long that when they reached the area of the cliff, the witnesses were shuffling their feet and Humi yawned.

"The choreographed death of a man, no matter his crime, is a serious matter," Praetor Seubus explained. "I will maintain the dignity of these proceedings to the extent of ordering arrests."

Real or faked, the four observers stopped shuffling and straightened their backs to demonstrate their concern for the execution. But Alerio didn't stop to listen to the Judge, he continued past the gathering. Thinking the prisoner was attempting an escape, the temple guards quickly formed a semicircle. Hemmed in with no exit, everyone watched to see what Alerio would do.

Centurion Sisera marched to the very edge of the cliff and peered down at the Tarpeian Rock.

"Whether you grant me eighty years, Nenia Dea, or eighty feet more of life," Alerio prayed. He turned his back to the cliff and, with his heals hanging over the edge of the clifftop, raised his arms to the sky. "The end will be the same. You will lift my soul from a wretched body. For once, I offer no choice. My battle this day is not contested against a foe I can submit for your consideration."

Alerio slammed his fist into his breast in a cross-chest salute. For a heartbeat, he lamented the lack of armor that would have made the salute boom over the gathering.

"Praetor Valerius Seubus. Centurion Alerio Sisera requests permission to be relieved of duty, sir," Alerio stated.

Valerius Seubus' lips quivered in surprise and he appeared at a loss for words. Convelli, the court scribe, reached up, gathered a handful of the white cloth, and pulled the Praetor down to his level. The scribe, knowing Praetor Seubus had no military training or understanding of Legion ethos, whispered into the Judge's ear.

"Alerio Sisera, you are convicted of treason against the Republic and are sentenced to death on Tarpeian Rock. Most people condemned to death put up a fight," the Praetor commented then stopped to consider the makeup of a man who would voluntarily jump. After a pause, he declared. "This is highly unusual but, permission…"

Act 7

Chapter 28 - Praetor's Authority

Big, massively muscular animals, whipped and driven up a steep twisting road, snorted and huffed, filling the air with a physical manifestation of their breaths. Adding to that, their hoofs thundered on the stone pavers. The wall of sound rolled up Capitoline Hill, broke on the crest as if an ocean wave, and crashed over the execution party.

The first rider to reach the top was bent over the horse's neck. He drove his heels into his mount's flanks urging the exhausted stallion forward. Behind him, ten mounted Legionaries, their cavalry armor weighing down their horses, struggled to reach the top.

Pulling back on the reigns, caused the lead horse to rear up, his hind legs hopping while the animal attempted to stop. With the stallion still in motion, the man slid off and ran forward to keep his balance.

"Centurion Sisera, remove yourself from the clifftop," Praetor Zelare Sudoris ordered as he jogged to a stop. "Before you fall and get yourself killed."

The ten cavalrymen, in not so dramatic a manner, reigned in their horses and dismounted.

"Sir, I believe that my death is the object of this exercise," Alerio advised the commander of the Republic's Navy. "Or else someone wasted a really nice feast."

"Praetor Sudoris. You are interfering with my decision as the Judge in this case," Praetor Valerius

Seubus stated. "You may witness the throwing of the convicted but you may not interfere."

"I don't see anybody throwing or pushing. It looked to me like one of my best junior officers was about to jump," Naval Commander Sudoris challenged. "Who here is the Jurist?"

"I am, Praetor," Imprecari replied with a respectable nod of his head. "Do you require an opinion on a matter of the law?"

Alerio took three steps off the clifftop. Wide eyed and confused, he repeated Zelare Sudoris' words, "One of my best junior officers."

"I do have a legal question, specifically, about rigged tribunals," Zelare Sudoris questioned. "What are the limits to the veto power of a Praetor?"

"Roman law states that a Praetor of equal or higher rank can veto the decision of an equal or lesser Praetor," Imprecari said quoting the law. "In the case of a court's judgement, another Praetor can reject a decision made by a single Judge if he qualifies as previously stipulated. In the case of two Judges, the refuting Praetor would not have a strong enough standing to refute the ruling unless he held the rank of Consul."

"That's what I thought," Zelare Sudoris confirmed. "As the senior Praetor, I proclaim this court vetoed."

"You of course mean, the sentence is overturned," Imprecari suggested.

"No Advocate. I mean the entire court is vetoed," Praetor Zelare Sudoris declared. "Legionaries, arrest everyone here."

Cavalry shields were lifted from the sides of horses, strapped to arms, and gladii swooshed from sheaths.

Then the ten Legionaries began herding the witnesses together. Two of the temple guards leveled their spears.

"Any reason to let them live, sir," the cavalry officer asked.

"This would be easier if they all died," Praetor Sudoris suggested. "But I don't think I could explain that many bodies to the senate. Unless, they attack first."

Hearing the cold-blooded discussion, the temple guards threw their weapons to the ground and fell in with the others. When Praetor Valerius Seubus and Convelli the scribe failed to move, Praetor Sudoris lifted his arm and pointed in the direction of the temple.

"Please go to the small stadium," he instructed. "Failure to follow orders will result in your deaths. And trust me, I won't have much to explain to the senate."

Valerius Seubus and Convelli fell in behind the Legionaries.

***

"Sisera, you too," Praetor Sudoris called. "Move it or I'll throw you off the cliff myself."

Alerio was so taken by the surprise interruption of his death that he stood still afraid of moving and breaking the spell. The sky never looked so beautiful and the gardens on Capitoline Hill drew his eyes from one colorful blossom to another. At the sound of the Navy commander's voice, he snapped out of the trance and trotted to the Praetor's side.

"I'm not sure what happened here, sir," Alerio stammered. "I was sentenced to death for treason."

"What happened here, I don't know about," Praetor Sudoris told him. "What I do know is I was finishing dinner last night with several of my Centurions. The main topic of our conversation was the shortage of warships. Suddenly, a retired Optio barged in and informed me, I had a trireme docked at the city pier."

"Civi Affatus, sir?" Alerio guessed.

"One of your patron's household guards," the Navy commander confirmed. "I dispatched a cavalry troop to investigate. I had turned in for the night when my Senior Centurion walked in with news that indeed there was a trireme at the dock in the Capital."

"Yes, sir. We rowed it down from Stifone," Alerio informed him.

"Don't say that. Don't even think the name," Praetor Sudoris scolded. "Before dawn, I took a Century of cavalrymen and rode for the Capital. We arrived and, as I'd been warned, there were city guardsmen preventing anyone from boarding the ship or leaving it."

"I jumped over the side before…"

"I spoke with an engineer and a Greek ship builder," the Praetor of the Navy described. "And then a Centurion from the guard informed me. Me, the Praetor of the Republic's Navy, that the ship was being taken. It seemed a consortium had purchased the ship to satisfy bills acquired while the warship was being built."

"What did you do, sir?" Alerio inquired.

"Did I mention I brought a Century of cavalry with me?"

"Yes sir. There is a problem and a large sum owned to an Umbrian, up north," Alerio said being careful not to say Stifone. "It, apparently, is the cause of a treaty violation triggered by my traitorous actions."

"Centurion Sisera, the sum is not large," the Praetor stated. "Up north is the only location that has produced a

239

warship so far. And according to your ship builder and engineer, the territory can build everything we need. I'm going to get a fleet out of the Umbria. Squadrons of triremes and quinqueremes to go ram to ram against the Empire. And the Qart Hadasht will never know where we are building the warships. You think the bill you ran up is large? I'm going to pour one hundred times that amount into the area."

"Sir, I'll be proud to work on the fleet," Alerio remarked.

"No, you will not," commander Zelare Sudoris responded. "I need trained and aggressive officers for the new ships. You won't be working on the fleet. You'll be working in the fleet."

"Wherever the Legion needs me sir," Alerio assured him. "I'd like to serve on Neptune's Fury."

"The name the ship builder gave the trireme," Praetor Sudoris said. "No. I need you elsewhere."

***

They arrived at the amphitheater and the Praetor sent Legionaries around the venue to prevent anyone from approaching the area.

"You will strip the name of Stifone from any records," Zelare Sudoris instructed. "And you will never mention the name of the town again. If you do, you will find yourself on the clifftop at midnight. And early rising citizens will find your body on The Tarpeian Rock at dawn. We are at war with the Empire. They have fleets on every ocean and the Republic has twenty triremes. That will change and I swear, Qart Hadasht will never see us coming. Questions?"

Alerio was standing off to the side listening when the Legion cavalry officer approached him.

"There's a fresh horse in the quad for you," the Centurion informed Alerio. "The Praetor wants you away from any burning embers until this political firestorm burns itself out. Ride to Ostia and report to the Furor's Face trireme. The ship's senior Centurion is Dilato Invitus."

"Furor's Face. The God of mad rage has a warship named after him?" Alerio inquired.

"And once it was a face to be feared," the officer replied.

"And now?" Alerio asked.

"The Praetor wants you out of the Capital before dark," the cavalry officer directed. "Better get moving."

Alerio backed out of the theater, located the alleyway, and made his way to the holding room. After retrieving his armor, Centurion Sisera marched to the Legionary with the horse. Once mounted, he rode from the temple grounds and, a half mile later, Alerio passed the place where he should have died.

Chapter 29 - The Face of Mad Rage

The stars burned holes in the early morning sky.

After crossing the Capital and riding through the southern gate in the Servian Wall, Alerio exchanged the temple's mount at the first posthouse. Without delay, he started off on the road to the coast. Caution in the dark night forced him to allow the sturdy Legion horse to walk the ten miles. Although he could usually sleep anywhere, the animal's jerking gait kept him awake. Due

241

to the rough ride, Alerio arrived at the next posthouse stiff and exhausted.

Following a short nap in a pile of hay, Alerio led the fresh mount a few steps while admiring the stars. Then he hopped onto the horse's back and, with a tug of the reigns, guided the animal through a break in the stable's fence. On the road towards Ostia, he kneed the horse to urge the animal to pick up its pace.

Seven miles to the Navy port wasn't far but, Alerio wanted to reach Ostia by daybreak. From the horse's back, he shifted his attention, alternating from peering at the dark road ahead to admiring the million points of light overhead.

***

The beach gently elevated from the water's edge to a line of sheds. Tall and long but narrow, the five buildings rested on land not too high above the surface of the ocean. Yet the buildings were far enough back from the shoreline, they were safe from the highest of tides or the fiercest of storm surges.

Following general directions from the stableman, Alerio ambled around until he located the five trireme sheds. Then, after recognizing three figures standing beside the second structure, he lengthened his stride.

They didn't notice Alerio approach. Their focus was on a Priest standing on a ladder painting an eye on the side of the hull. Two buckets of paint hung from the top rung and the Celebrant selected brushes as he put the finishing touches on the artwork.

"Neptune, see what we offer you. Use these eyes to avoid obstacles. Use these eyes to find safe harbors," the Priest prayed while leaning back to admire his work.

"Use these eyes to frighten off monsters from the deep. And use these eyes to guide the ship to safety before the storm. Neptune, King of the sea, bring luck to this vessel, your namesake, Neptune's Fury."

At the conclusion of the chant, the Priest pulled up his buckets and began climbing down.

"I see, Master Pous, they kept the name you gave the trireme," Alerio said to the boat builder.

Cata Pous, Pejus Monilis, and Optio Adamo Florian spun around. Wide eyed and with mouths open, they gawked at Alerio.

"Is something wrong?" he questioned the three.

"Master Monilis had suggested they might sell you into slavery to pay the bills," Adamo Florian remarked. "You are still a freedman, aren't you, sir?"

"Yes, and still a Centurion," Alerio assured the NCO.

"That is a relief as Pejus was very persuasive in his argument for debtor slavery," Cata told him. "Will you be commanding Poseidon's, no excuse me, Neptune's Fury once the benches are constructed? Or will you be accompanying us to, I mean, up north?"

"I've heard the speech about the nameless place," Alerio informed them. "I'm afraid neither is an option. I've been assigned to Furor's Face."

"Can't you get out of that assignment?" the engineer inquired. "It's not good, not good at all."

"At least the Centurion has an assignment," Sergeant Florian complained. "I've got to make my way to the Capital and ask about an opening for an Optio."

Alerio ignored the NCO and studied Pejus for several long moments. Finally, he asked, "Master Monilis. Why is it you are positive, energetic, and filled with ideas when things go wrong? Yet so negative when the situation is going smoothly?"

"I am an engineer. Finding solutions is my training and my nature," Pejus answered. "In chaos, I'm solving problems which brings me joy. In good times, I am anticipating the worst so I'm prepared."

"That does explain some of your comments," Alerio acknowledged. Then he inquired. "What are your plans?"

The engineer and the ship builder were excited to return to Stifone and get started on enlarging the ship building facility. While Adamo Florian, as he mentioned, worried about securing a place with a Legion. There was only one Optio in each Century and a majority of the time, the Centurion picked his own NCOs.

The four men talked for a while then Alerio excused himself. With promises to meet later for a meal, he left to find ship's senior Centurion Dilato Invitus and the Furor's Face.

***

The warship wasn't in the next three sheds. But on the far side of the last building, beyond several patrol boats, and sitting off by itself, was an old trireme. As Alerio got closer, he noticed the eye on the starboard side of the hull. Cracked paint over hull planks ranging from slightly aged to weathered to bent and curled gave the ship's eye the appearance of being crazy. It fit the name of the warship, if this was the Furor's Face. Having no other options, Alerio walked towards it.

An old man sitting on a stool dabbed the corner of a cloth into a bowl, scooped up a little paste, and rubbed it on the trireme's bronze ram. Alerio passed under the raised keel of the ship and stooped to admire the ancient one's work.

"Good job on the bronze," Alerio said about the glistening blades on the ram. "What's your secret?"

"Vinegar and salt," the man replied. He indicated the bowl without looking away from his task. Then, he added. "plus, hard non-stop rubbing. I mean put your shoulder into it polishing. That's how you make the business end of a warship shine."

"I can't argue with those results," Alerio admitted. "Tell me old timer, where I can find senior Centurion Invitus?"

Looking up, the man's face took Alerio by surprise. The ancient man had only one good eye. A scar running diagonally across the eye, gave testimony to the blade strike that took half his vision. Plus, the round face was deeply lines and pock marked. Like the eye painted over the ravaged side of the vessel, the man's ragged face was the embodiment of insane. Both matched the name of the warship.

"The Centurion is around," the old man replied

With a dismissive wave of an arm, he returned to polishing the bronze ram. Alerio had to chuckle at the disparity between the glowing ram and the loose seams of the hull boards. They were so bowed and gapped, a line of thirty laborers worked at caulking the spaces.

Alerio strolled behind the men. He watched them take rods, dip them into bags of hemp fibers, lift out a fistful of strands, then plunge the hemp into a kettle of hot tar. After spreading the mixture along a seam, the laborers took mallets, and by tapping on the end of the rods, they pushed the sealant deep into the cavity. All of them, except one.

Alerio stopped. He hadn't realized the broad age range of the workmen. From youths barely old enough to effectively hold a gladius to old men who may have been too old to lift a blade, they seem to be a strange mix.

"You tap the hemp and tar into the gaps just enough to fully fill them. Too deep and you'll push it into the ship," Alerio instructed. "If you do a poor job of caulking, you'll be bailing water more than you'll be rowing."

"Yes, Centurion," the lad responded.

Then Alerio noticed what age group was missing. Anyone in their prime between the teens and the old men was absent.

"Are you part of the crew?" Alerio asked.

"Yes sir. Forward rowing section," the teen replied.

"Carry on and watch your sealing technique," Alerio advised while walking around the aft of the warship.

On the port side, he found another group of too young and too old applying hemp and tar to the spaces between the hull boards.

"Has anybody seen Senior Centurion Invitus?" he inquired.

Several hands pointed towards the front of the ship. Following their lead, Alerio finished circling the trireme and he arrived back at the bronze ram.

"Dilato Invitus?" Alerio questioned.

The old man lifted his face and flashed a crooked grim.

"That's me, former cavalry officer and now senior Centurion of Furor's Face," the man polishing the ram replied. "And who are you?"

***

Alerio and Dilato crawled out of the bilge by placing their knees on the benches used by the lower oarsmen. Then they crawled to the center of the trireme and placed their other feet on the rower's walk.

"The leaking is why we only patrol up and down the coast. Never traveling far from Ostia," Invitus explained with a grunt and a hesitation while he pushed up and stood on the lower walkway. "And why we don't have a shed? Praetor Sudoris wants the Empire to see the Republic's Navy as being made up of aging warships."

"No offense, sir," Alerio remarked. "But from the look of your hull, it is an aging warship."

"It's a winter vessel, Sisera," Invitus remarked.

"Because it's in the twilight years of its life?" Alerio questioned. "Like winter marks the end of a year?"

"No. Because the Furor's Face only lasts for a short day," Dilato Invitus replied. "and needs a long night to recover."

"Perhaps we could sacrifice to the Goddess Angerona," Alerio suggested. "Maybe she can help."

"Sisera. It'll take more than the goddess who helps men get through the dull days of winter. A lot more to heal these old bones," Centurion Invitus said. Alerio wasn't sure if the ship's Centurion was speaking about himself or the trireme as being old. "The best we could hope from the goddess would be her breaking up the vessel and burning the wood to keep warm."

"I don't believe Praetor Zelare Sudoris would appreciate that," Alerio commented.

Then, as if the commander of the Republic's Navy heard his name, a messenger arrived. Invitus left for a meeting with the Praetor and Alerio walked to the foredeck. Standing looking out at the beach and the horizon, he pondered what life would be like simply patrolling the same stretch of water, day after day.

Chapter 30 - Winter Vessel

Invitus came back from the meeting just before night fall. Even in the fading light, Alerio could tell something had the ship's Centurion excited. There was a spring in his steps while his arms swung in exaggerated arcs and, he had a manic smile plastered across his face.

"We're going to sea, Sisera," he informed Alerio while still climbing the ladder to the deck.

"I assumed we were, Centurion."

"Yes, yes we were after a week of maintenance," Invitus replied. Then, he brought his hands together and began clenching and unclenching them. "My other two deck officers and the ship's NCO are away. As are our most experience oarsmen. And we need supplies. And…"

"Centurion Invitus?" Alerio said interrupting the frantic officer. "When do we leave?"

"Praetor Sudoris wants, no, let me amend that. He needs us in Syracuse as soon as possible," Invitus answered.

"What positions do we need to fill before we row out?" Alerio inquired. Then he thought for a moment and clarified. "Every infantry officer wants a complete unit before he marches to war. But we know it's a rare case to fill every slot. Tell me your bare minimum."

"We have ninety-five, I'd like to have twenty-five more rowers," Invitus answered. A calm came over him when he realized he didn't have to do all the preparation for launching himself. Then the Senior Centurion's eye got glassy and he declared. "That'll leave us short about fifty. We can row with that, unless we come across an Empire quinquereme. Then we'll rake its side, destroying their sea worthiness, and snap their oars. It'll be glorious to send it to the bottom of the sea. Oh, where was I? That's right, I've got you as a deck officer so we'll stay with one deck Centurion but we do need an NCO."

"Why the rush, senior Centurion?" Alerio questioned. He realized neither the Furor's Face nor the naval post were equipped to rush a launch on short notice.

"The Qart Hadasht landed a second force at Agrigento," Invitus reported. "The Legions beat them back but not before they destroyed the main supply depot."

"We have allies on Sicilia," Alerio suggested. "I expect they'll send resupplies."

"King Hiero II of Syracuse has the grain but is afraid to send it over land," Invitus replied. "He's demanding escorts from the Republic for his grain transports. That's where we come in. The Furor's Face is part of a squadron being sent to Syracuse to shepherd the grain ships to Agrigento."

"I'm going to roam Ostia and try to find us personnel," Alerio informed his Senior Centurion. "If you'll procure our supplies and travel funds."

"Travel funds," Invitus cried. "I forgot about the ship's funds. How could I forget that?"

"You have a lot on your platter, sir," Alerio remarked. "It's understandable."

"Yes. Of course, I do," the ship's commander agreed. "Run along and get me people, Centurion Sisera."

"Yes sir," Alerio said.

He went to the ladder and climbed to the ground. Rather than go directly to the main part of the naval Post of Ostia, Alerio hooked around the back of the trireme. The Furor's Face needed oarsmen, and the best source of leads for them was from the ninety-five rowers camped on the port side.

As he rounded the aft section of the warship, a question occurred to Alerio. Was the compact patrol area usually ordered for the trireme based on the limitations of an old warship or because of the ship's senior Centurion? It was a mute inquiry. They would launch in the morning on a long journey and there was nothing a junior Centurion could do about it.

"We need oarsmen," Alerio announced as he walked into the rowers' camp. "Who can you get me by morning?"

***

A table rested in the shadow of the ship's hull. Its location had nothing to do with finding shade from the morning light. Being in the sunlight would be preferable, except for the stiff breeze blowing from the north. If unblocked the wind would scatter the stacks of parchment from the table.

"Keep the line in order," Sergeant Adamo Florian instructed the massed rowers. Then he reminded them. "These are your pay records. Don't get listed, and you don't get paid. Anyone here want to donate a few months for the glory of the Republic?"

He stood and eyed the groups of men. All of them held waterskins, bags of grain, and small bundles of personal gear. None of the rowers volunteered to forgo pay during the voyage.

"I didn't think so," Florian stated. "Form a line and keep it straight. Bending around to watch me work will not make the line move faster."

The NCO sat, picked up a quill with one hand and signaled a man to step up to the table with the other.

"Returning crewmember or new?" he asked.

"Returning," the next oarsman in line replied.

Florian' hand snatched the correct document and positioned it below the pen.

"Name."

On the other side of the hull, Alerio stood in the breeze, holding a wooden plank checking off supplies on a different set of documents.

"Sail lines, salted pork, two extra hypozomatas," he said while marking off items as porters wheeled carts from Ostia's supply depot to the Furor's Face.

The ten Legion sailors assigned to the trireme carried or hoisted the supplies to the upper deck of the warship. On the deck, the ship's quartermaster rechecked then sent the items off to be stored in every nook and unused space in the trireme.

251

While the rowers were signed on and the supplies loaded, Senior Centurion Dilato Invitus stood with his navigator and his helmsman.

"Twelve days to Messina," the navigator offered. "That's if we don't hit heavy seas or too much rain. It's another two days from Messina to Syracuse."

"The steerage along the route is not a problem," the helmsman added. "We'll trek along the coast virtually the entire way."

"Where is Sisera?" the ship's Centurion asked.

"Your First Principale is still checking in supplies," the navigator replied. "Do you want me to call him up?"

"No. I'm going to inspect the ship," Invitus announced. "We need to be off or we'll lose the day."

"Yes sir," both the navigator and the helmsmen responded.

***

Three days later, Invitus finished the morning prayer then signaled a sailor standing on the beach. One hundred of the trireme's oarsmen shoved the trireme off the beach. Alerio and two of the sailors stood on the foredeck and watched for obstacles. After the ram dipped and scraped the sea bed, it swung up to just below the surface of the water. As the Furor's Face leveled and floated into the narrow inlet of Procida Island, the rowers scrambled up the sides and onto the warship.

"Clear," Alerio shouted down to Sergeant Adamo Florian.

The Optio standing on the rowers walk, spun and called back to a sailor also on the lower level. "Clear."

That sailor called up to the aft deck to alert the ship's commander, "Clear."

"Run them out," Dilato Invitus ordered.

"Run them out," the sailor passed on the command to the Optio who in turn repeated the instructions for the oarsmen in the forward section.

In response only sixty of the one hundred and twenty oarsmen extended their oars through the oar holes, fixed the oarlocks to prevent the oars from falling completely through, and held the long poles with the blades above the water.

A sailor on the port side and another on the starboard side watched for late or fouled oars. Once all of them were hovering above the water, the sailors signaled to the commander.

"Dip oars and stroke," Invitus instructed. "Stroke, Stroke."

The message was passed to the rower's walk. Oars entered the water, stroked, and the trireme surged ahead, gliding out of the inlet.

"Musician, pipe us a medium rate," Invitus directed.

The ship's musician picked up his instrument and began playing.

Alerio turned around and studied the split top deck and the oars entering the water as far back as he could see.

'A winter vessel,' he thought.

Every morning the ship started out dry and responsive. Light enough they only needed half the oarsmen to row. This was important because the other half were soon busy bailing water from the bilge. The process wouldn't last long. Soon the old hull boards would swell and seal the leaks.

Shortly after launch, the sails were raised and wind power propelled the trireme across the waves. When the hull began to settle by early afternoon, rowers would be added to help maintain the speed of the ship-of-war.

As the ship settled lower in the sea from the old boards absorbing more water, all the rowers were required. That marked the end of the day. The sails got rolled and the navigator began looking for a place to beach.

Just as a winter's day, the old trireme was good for a short day, about forty miles, before needing a long night to dry out. Everyday mirrored the last and they were still nine days from Messina and twelve days from Syracuse.

***

Nine days into the trip, they launched before daylight from the beach at Tonicello. At about forty miles from Messina, they were entering contested waters. Qart Hadasht warships patrolled the strait and along either coasts. Hopefully the Furor's Face would reach the port of Messina without making contact. An early arrival was the reason for the early departure.

While Alerio and the crew dreaded coming across one of the enemy's quinqueremes, the ship's Senior Centurion felt differently.

"When I was leading my Century of cavalry," he announced while quick marching to the foredeck. "We didn't shy away from a fight. Right at them, I always told my Legionaries. Go right at them and your foe will break, every time. There's no reason to believe the same isn't true for warships."

Alerio stood watch at the bow, peering into the black before dawn, and listening to Invitus rant. If he thought it would do any good, Alerio would speak to the ship's Centurion about the reality of taking an aging trireme into combat. And the foolishness of fighting a quinquereme with Furor's Face. That would be the definition of mad rage.

When Invitus arrived, he scowled into the gloom as if he could will an enemy warship to emerge out of the darkness. But when the sun rose and no challenger appeared, the Senior Centurion made his way back to the steering platform.

At mid-day, the coastline split and the helmsmen threw the rear oar to the left and allowed the trireme to circle. Also tracing circles in the waters were two merchantmen waiting to enter the Strait of Messina.

"What's the situation?" the navigator shouted to one of the transports.

"There's still no driftwood or brown water along the shoreline," the merchantman called back. "It shouldn't be long."

While the ships circled, Centurion Dilato Invitus went to the rower's walk. There, he sat with each section of oarsmen. Alerio approved of a commander who cared about his men. It was commendable to interrupt his day to keep the crew motivated with compassionate words. Alerio couldn't hear the ship's commander until the Senior Centurion reached the forward gang of rowers.

"When we go at a quinquereme, it's all about the angle of attack and closing speed," Invitus described. "That means I need your backs and hearts into each stroke. Even if we sink afterward, it'll be worth it to take down one of their big warships."

'It's not very motivating to tell a man that he must row his heart out for the privilege of dying,' Alerio thought.

The ship's commander seemed oblivious to the sideways looks he received from the oarsmen when he walked back along the passageway.

The three ships rotated around an invisible axis until brown water, tree limbs, and leaves began to flow into view along the banks of the Messina strait. With the outer edges displaying the change to a northern flow, the transports and warship straightened and headed south. They would ride the center current, which now flowed in a southernly direction, into the strait.

While the transports definitely needed help, earlier in the day, the Furor's Face could have fought the current and rowed against the flow. But it was in the afternoon of a winter vessel's short day, and the warship required the current in the strait to travel the final ten miles to Messina harbor.

Chapter 31 - Ship Escorts

Fires flared to life on the beach. Most were for cooking with long tripods suspending pots high over the flames. A designated chef at each camp poured in grain and water or, the ingredients for stew. Several of the fires close to the hull had old, stained iron crocks on smaller stands. The bottoms of those pots hung just above the embers which allowed the black chunks dropped in by the sailors to be heated and melted. And unlike food, there was little fear of burning the tar sealant.

"We'll wait in Messina for a couple of days," Dilato Invitus informed Alerio. The ship's senior Centurion ran a hand over the hull boards as he walked. "Praetor Sudoris wants a show of force when we row into Syracuse. Said we should have at least three of our warships to display our resolve to King Hiero."

"Resolve for what?" Alerio inquired.

"That we have the determination and will to go against the Qart Hadasht," Invitus answered. "both on land and afloat."

"It'll give us time to pack in extra caulking," Alerio exclaimed. His mind turned over a question. One he pondered broaching since he reported to the Furor's Face. Deciding this wasn't the right conversation in which to bring it up, he offered instead. "Although three days or four days would be better for repairs."

The two Centurions strolled between the campfires while inspecting the ship. They had completed a circuit and stopped at the forward keel. The senior Centurion lifted a foot and rested it against the beam that supported the ram.

"I'm looking forward to facing the enemy," Invitus declared while looking towards the entrance to the harbor. He bent at the waist and patted the bronze ram as if it was a valued mount. "The Empire has quite the reputation. It'll be good to test myself against them."

And there was the opening Alerio needed.

"Senior Centurion, have you ever been in a battle at sea?" Alerio asked.

"I have, as yet, not had the privilege of going ram to ram with the Empire," Invitus replied. "I came close when three of their warships approached the mouth of the Tiber. At the time, my trireme was part of a blockade to stop them."

"But you have fought pirates?" Alerio asked hopefully.

"To my great disappointment," ship's officer Dilato Invitus answered. "There are few brigands along the coast flanking Ostia and the Tiber. Much to my dismay, I have not challenged bronze against bronze and delivered Republic justice to any pirates. Why do you ask?"

"Those are pirate ships," Alerio offered with a wave of his hand in the direction of beached biremes. "They belong to the Sons of Mars. Each carries one hundred and twenty oarsmen plus men-at-arms. On the east coast of Republic territory, our warships encounter Illyrians. Those pirates are sanctioned by their government. They row triremes and practice the same shock and awe tactics as our heavy infantry."

"Yes, yes, I've heard the tales," Invitus blustered. "Whatever is your point?"

"The Empire deploys neither biremes or triremes," Alerio told him. "They float quinqueremes. Expertly handled, towering four feet over us with bolt throwers, archers, infantrymen, and three hundred oarsmen. Senior Centurion, it is an entirely different class of warship."

"Are you telling me that you're afraid to engage with a larger ship?" Invitus demanded. "Maybe you should be less cautious, Centurion Sisera. As I often instructed my cavalry Century, go right at the enemy. No matter how big or numerous, go straight at them and the enemy will break."

Before Alerio had a chance to offer a comeback, a Legion patrol boat entered Massina harbor. The Legionaries at the oars were stripped to their waist, sweating, and digging their oars deep while staying in perfect timing.

"Impressive," Dilato Invitus noted.

***

All thirty oarsmen set their oars in the water before back stroking. The coastal patrol boat went from a high rate as it approached the beach to the keel gently touching the rocky soil of Messina harbor. It came to a halt with the aft of the boat resting on land next to the Furor's Face.

"How did they do that?" Invitus questioned. "We can barely get our oarsmen to stroke together in a straight line."

"Optio Martius, Southern Legion's rowing instructor," Alerio reported. "This boat crew is either showing off or on an urgent mission."

A Tesserarius hopped from the patrol boat and crunched gravel as he marched to them. He held a scroll in his hand.

"I'm looking for the commander of the trireme, sirs," he explained.

"That would be me," Invitus informed the NCO.

"Sir, you are invited to dine with Senior Centurion Patroclus of the Southern Legion," the Corporal announced. "This boat will take you to Fort Rhegium. And will await your pleasure as transportation back tomorrow."

"Who is the scroll for?" Alerio questioned.

"The scroll is for my notes of what you require to complete your mission," the Tesserarius stated. "I'm to meet with the First Principale and take notes before the patrol boat launches."

"I'm going to unpack an appropriate tunic," Dilato Invitus said excusing himself. Before leaving, he instructed. "Centurion Sisera. I can't think of anything except some salted pork and grain. If there's anything else, tell the Corporal."

Alerio scanned the coastal patrol boat and shifted his eyes to the midship of the trireme.

"Corporal. We need salted pork or fish. Plus, two officers who know sailing to serve as Principales for the escort mission," Alerio listed. Then he smiled before adding. "And some of Optio Martius' gentle training."

"Gentle, sir?" the NCO questioned. "I'm not sure anyone would call the rowing master's teaching techniques gentle."

"I guess you're right," Alerio remarked. "Just see what you can do. Be sure to tell him Lance Corporal Alerio Sisera made the request."

The NCO finished making notes and rolled the scroll just as the ship's Centurion climbed over the side. He had a bundle of clothes under his arm.

"I assume Rhegium has a bath?" Invitus commented.

"Yes, sir," the Corporal said as he indicated the patrol boat.

Alerio stood watching until the boat rowed around the hook of land that created the strait side of the harbor. After it vanished around the tip, he went to find the ship's sailors campsite. They had promised him a meal.

Later, when the sun was low and Alerio's belly full, two patrol boats appeared at the entrance to the harbor. Unlike the one earlier with the solid crew of oarsmen, these two were under powered. The ten rowers in each, while trained, were obviously infantrymen drafted into being oarsmen.

To confirm Alerio's observation, the patrol boats touched the beach and men vaulted to the land. Then armors, helmets, gladii, shields, javelins, and rations were tossed ashore. Shortly after landing, the twenty Legionaries marched towards Messina. Only two men remained with the boats.

"Lance Corporal Sisera?" one called to the campsites. "Alerio Sisera?"

Alerio and Optio Florian strolled to the water's edge and nodded to the boat handlers.

"Sir, we were told to speak with Lance Corporal Sisera," the other boat handler advised.

"Do you know him, Centurion?" Optio Florian questioned.

"No sir. Our rowing instructor told us to ask for him."

"What do you need?" Alerio questioned.

"Optio Martius said if you want your engine room tuned up," one replied. "Then they had best be on Rhegium beach before dawn. We're here to pick them up, sir."

"Stand by," Alerio ordered. Then he and the Sergeant walked to the crew's camp. "The forty middle oarsmen, get to the patrol boats."

"What's up, sir?" his biggest rower inquired.

261

"You and your beefy companions are going on a field trip," Alerio replied. Then he lied. "You'll have fun. And you'll get out of caulking duty."

After loading, the boats launched. As the two coastal patrol boats rowed for the entrance to the harbor, Optio Florian turned to face his Centurion.

"You have eighty jealous oarsmen," he remarked to Alerio. "Those left out are not happy. What should I tell them about missing out on a field trip?"

"Let them stew," Alerio instructed. "The grousing will only last until the rowers get back."

"How can you be sure of that, sir?" the NCO questioned.

"Bleeding blisters make people who missed the ordeal not so envious of the ones suffering," Alerio offered. "Keep on the crew. I want this vessel as water tight as we can make it in two days."

***

Later the next morning, a patrol boat appeared at the inlet's tip and rowed for Messina beach. As the crew did the day before, they cut a half circle and eased the boat back to shoreline.

Centurion Invitus jumped from the patrol boat, landed in ankle deep water and, rather than being upset, kicked the water in a playful manner. Behind him, two young officers stepped from the boat hauling personal gear.

"Sisera. Centurions Eosi Stratus and Bancus Nunzio. They have been forced upon me by Centurion Patroclus," Invitus announced with a chuckle. Then he went on to describe his meal. "Patroclus is the Senior Centurion for the entire Southern Legion. He's an infantry officer and a

262

fighter. We had a glorious discussion about tactics. Stratus and Nunzio joined us along with an interesting staff officer, Tribune Velius."

Something was off. The officer for Furor's Face was usually quiet. Although given to out bursts, between his bouts of enthusiasm, the Centurion was stoic. Now here he was prattling on like a school boy.

Invitus never asked how Alerio knew Optio Martius, the Southern Legion's rowing instructor. Thus, he had no idea that Alerio had been stationed with the Southern Legion. Not only did Alerio know the senior leadership of the Legion, he was an agent for the old spy master, Tribune Velius. That's why Invitus' next words hurt Alerio's pride.

"During dinner, I expressed my reservations about you and your timid approach to combat," Dilato Invitus confessed. "I had a lot of vino but you know what they say, *in vino veritas*."

"Yes, in wine lies the truth," Alerio said.

"I'm glad you realize that because the next thing I knew, both Patroclus and Velius insisted I take Stratus and Nunzio on as Principales," Invitus explained. "After talking with them, I realized they would make excellent deck officers."

"We had asked the supply Corporal for two more officers," Alerio reminded the ship's senior Centurion. "How did Senior Centurion Patroclus feel about letting two of his officers go."

"He seemed very keen about them going on the grain ship escort mission," Invitus replied. Then he got serious and added. "I hate to tell you but, bad news is best delivered quickly. Eosi Stratus is taking the position of

First Principale. After spending time with him, I believe he and I see eye-to-eye on combat tactics."

"And Bancus Nunzio?" Alerio inquired.

"Centurion Nunzio will assume the role of Second Principale and rowing officer," Invitus stated. "You've done a good job on the trip down the coast. But we are in enemy waters and I need a warrior as my second in command. And a rowing officer who will follow orders and not challenge them."

"Do Patroclus and Velius know about the assignments?" Alerio questioned.

He was watching the two young Centurions. His first unvoiced question was why they hadn't been assigned Centuries with the Southern Legion. And the second question, why did the Legion's Senior Centurion want to get rid of these two officers?

"Of course not," Invitus replied. "I am the ship's senior officer and I decide who serves where. Don't you agree, Third Principale Sisera."

"Absolutely, senior Centurion," Alerio replied. "With your permission, I'd like to go into Messina tonight."

"Yes, of course, you deserve a little recreation," Dilato Invitus agreed. "We have a full staff of deck officers. I can't imagine you'll be missed."

***

Milon Frigian stretched his leg, hooked a chair from a neighboring table with the toe of his boot, and slid it to his table.

"Sit, Captain Sisera," the pirate Captain instructed. He held a pitcher of wine and used it to indicate the chair. Then he poured a mug full and placed it in front of

264

the seat. "Now you can't refuse to drink with me. That would cut me deeply."

It wasn't that Alerio didn't want to sit and drink. It was the two big Sons of Mars oarsmen who were hugging the former Captain of the Messina Militia.

"And then he took our spears, swords and shields," one boomed so the entire room of pirates could hear his story. "I asked Captain Sisera what we were supposed to fight the perfututum Greek formation of hoplites with?"

"I said, with our mentulae?" the other giant Son added while he crushed Alerio in an embrace. "And do you know what this cold bastardis of a Captain replied?"

"Use your mentulae, if that's what it takes to keep their second line out of the fight."

They broke apart while laughing and Alerio managed to duck under their arms and reach the safety of Frigian's table.

"Do they still tell that tale?" Alerio asked while he dropped into the chair and snatched up the mug.

"It has, my friend, become a three-mug-myth," Frigian reported. "Every big man who fought off the Greek heavy infantry with just an oar stands and, after three drinks, tells the story. You showing up makes it that much better."

"They earned the bragging rights," Alerio acknowledged.

He raised his mug and saluted the big Sons. Cheering washed back over him, as the room of pirates hoisted mugs and returned the salute.

"Are you ready to join us?" Milon Frigian questioned.

"I really just came to drink with an old acquaintance," Alerio professed. "What makes you think I'd leave the Legion?"

"Come now, Sisera. We all saw the floating funeral pyre you rowed in on yesterday," Frigian replied. "You could dip that pile of soggy wood in a tar pit and water would still find a way through that hull. Thus, I figured, you've had enough and would come to join the Sons of Mars."

"No, just taking a night off and drinking," Alerio assured him.

"That is too bad, my friend," Frigian announced. He picked up the pitcher and refilled Alerio's mug. "We are about to become rich. And we could use another Captain."

"And just how are you going to earn this vast wealth?" Alerio inquired.

"It works this way," Frigian explained. "The Empire is pulling together fleets of warships. And the Republic is forming squadrons. Alright, it's lopsided but follow my logic. With Qart Hadasht and Rome massing their ships, there are none available to escort merchantmen. Except the Sons of Mars, we are available. And we won't even take their ships. We'll collect a fee then row to the next one and collect more gold."

"Gold?" Alerio asked.

"Sure, I said we weren't taking their transports," Captain Frigian informed Alerio. "I didn't say they would not pay me handsomely for the privilege of keeping their vessels."

Frigian had a point about shipping being endangered by a lack of warship protection. But the thing worrying

266

Centurion Sisera was the lopsided conflict. The Empire had hundreds of warships, most of them quinqueremes. While the Republic had only twenty warships, all of them triremes.

Chapter 32 - A Reminder of Violence

Furor's Face, Epiales' Veil, and two other triremes rowed from Messina harbor. Once out of the calm waters, they traveled south on the strait. Voices rose from the rowers in the center of Furor's Face and the forty oarsmen of the machine began to chant.

Furor is a blinder
Frenzy accepted
The nobility of frenzy
In the end is exposed as infamy
Night and day are frenzy and restraint
Too late to lodge a complaint after the taint
Frenzy builds a funeral pyre
not a fireplace
Frenzy has stolen your grace
Furor breaks a vase
Ignoring the craftsmanship
He urges not a snip
Preferring to chip and whip
Furor is a blinder
Frenzy accepted

From lackluster oarsmen accustomed to patrolling off the coast of the Republic, the newly sharpened oarsmen of the machine stroked in unison with enthusiasm.

Almost as if each side of the warship was competing with the other.

Furor is a brawler
Mad rage justified
The blade goes at cohorts
In mad rage as hard as at foes
Tactics are omitted in the fog of war's rage
But your sage guidance learned with age
Mad rage starts conflicts
Precision wins the battles
Mad is play and children's rattles
Furor is a weapon
To cleave or shatter
He silences chatter
All that matters is to batter
Furor is a brawler
Mad rage justified

Alerio recognized the sharp strokes and the aggressive nature. It was pure combat rowing as taught by Optio Martius, the rowing instructor. The challenge for the unified oarsmen, their commanders had no idea how to harness the new power.

Insanity embraced
Slurs slung before
The mind can control incivility
And swaps your tranquility for imbecility
Wine and insanity rule with the cost
of your sense of a mild mind
turns your inner eye blind
No calming breather
Furor values neither

Beauty nor mighty ugly
Only rant and rile
His blessing raises bile
Takes your guile and style
Furor is a trickster
Insanity embraced

If Alerio had another couple of days, he would have found a way to send Dilato Invitus and Eosi Stratus for lessons in combat leadership. But he didn't and his new position doomed him to standing on the forward deck, one hundred and thirty feet away from the warship's commanders.

***

Three days later, four Republic triremes rowed into Syracuse harbor. To the merchant ships at the docks, the laborers toting goods, the soldiers standing guard, and the Syracuse sailors waiting to launch or to sign onto a transport, the display of Republic naval power was impressive. The loading and unloading of ships bound for Egypt, the Greek city states, various islands, and the coast on either side of Qart Hadasht territory, stopped. The workers and Captains watched the ships-of-war cut sharply through the waters of the harbor.

Three of the warships cut neat half circles, reversed oar strokes, and powered backwards. With their sterns on the beach, one hundred rowers from those vessels left their posts, jumped over the sides, and manhandled the warships higher up onto the beach. The other warship over rotated and had to row farther out into the harbor. There, it adjusted the heading and came around for another approach.

Alerio, braced on the foredeck, called down to the rowing officer, "No obstacles."

Dutifully the Second Principale passed the word down the rower's deck to the ship's Optio who shouted, the obvious description, up to the stern steering deck. Frustratingly so, First Principale Stratus and the ship's Centurion Invitus could clearly see there were no obstacles in the section of the harbor.

"Confirmed, no obstacles," Stratus called back.

The short message flew downward, was passed along the rower's walk, and up to Alerio on the bow. Ever since Invitus discovered the new strength of his center oarsmen from the Legion training, he had been calling for power strikes. And just as you'd expect from a charioteer with a spirited but unfamiliar team, the vessel swerved off course.

Alerio had quickly learned why Senior Centurion Patroclus handed the two Centurions over for shipboard duty. Neither one would make a decision. Therefore, everything Invitus said, did, or suggested went unchallenged and was executed immediately by the First and Second Principales. Including power strokes on the starboard side when a little feathering of the oars would have done the job.

The Furor's Face backed down and the rear keel rode up on the beach.

"One hundred men," Alerio shouted. "Over the side."

He stood and did a quick count until he was sure enough oarsmen had gone. Then he climbed down to the beach to supervise the moving of the warship.

***

There were four transports loaded with grain, vegetables, and meat. Four treasures King Hiero II was wary of sending into Empire controlled waters just to reach Agrigento. Even if it saved Republic troops and their allies from starving. Not only were the ships valuable, the food stuff in the transports were as well.

"If you want our help, the King needs guarantees," the Syracuse Admiral informed the Legion officers. "A small deposit would go far in alleviating his concerns."

"We are ships' Centurions, not ambassadors," one officer stated. "We don't have funds to use as ransom."

"Such harsh words," the Admiral offered. "but alas, no coins, no food."

"But several units at Agrigento are Syracuse infantry and artillery," another Centurion pointed out.

"That is unfortunate," the Admiral acknowledged. "We will make sacrifices to the gods on the Altar of Hieron for them."

Each of the ship's officers was backed up by their three Principales. Yet, all they had accomplished since landing in Syracuse was for sixteen Legion officers to stand in a semi-circle being ineffectual.

"Admiral. Can I point out something you seem to have missed?" Alerio questioned.

Dilato Invitus and Eosi Stratus, the ship's senior Centurion and the First Principale spun on the Third deck officer.

"Sisera. If you haven't noticed," Invitus stated. "I have yet to say anything. Because I have nothing to add to the conversation. I suggest you do the same."

"Not add to the conversation or not say anything?" Alerio said with a glare. Focusing on the Admiral, he

271

asked. "When the two Consuls march their starving Legions back. What will you tell King Hiero?"

"I don't understand," the Admiral confessed.

"And neither do I," Invitus challenged. "I'm sure the Admiral has had enough of your inane questions."

"As you wish sir," Alerio agreed. "No more questions. Admiral, our breachers will cut through your walls and defenses like a knife through cheese. Our hungry Legionaries will feast and empty every storage building in Syracuse. The Republic will annex your city and all of her lands. Senator Otacilius Crassus hammered out the original treaty. He will be unhappy but will not veto the actions against an enemy that starved the Legions of Rome."

"That is extreme," Invitus scolded. "I think you should…"

The Centurion from Epiales' Veil placed a hand on Invitus' shoulder.

"Let's see what the Admiral has to say about the future," the other trireme's Centurion suggested.

"I'm not familiar," the Admiral questioned. "with the god you have named your warship after,"

"Epiales is the God of nightmares," the ship's officer reported.

The Syracusan Admiral swallowed hard, lowered his eyes for a moment before raising them.

"The transports row out at dawn," he instructed. "If that meets your approval."

***

Scrub trees sprouted from the brown dirt that ran right to the water's edge. Unavoidably, the soil absorbed the light rain making the dirt sticky underfoot. Adding to

272

the misery of being filthy, the sky was overcast threatening more rain.

Last night, the first wave of oarsmen over the sides churned the ground to mud. From then on, the brown clung to legs, bed rolls, clothing, and any flat surface. The crews and officers should have been in rotten moods. But they weren't.

The four warship Centurions and four transport Captain's debated whether to spend the day at Ciotta. They had fresh water from a stream and their vessels were sheltered from the sea and the weather. But the fishing village and the low shoreline were only eighteen miles from their destination. That accounted for the elevated mood and the discussion about launching and rowing out in the rain.

"In the worst case, we can be at Maddalusa by midday," one of the Centurions offered.

"We're three days out from Syracuse with no sighting of a Qart Hadasht quinquereme," the Centurion for Epiales' Veil explained. "I'd bet the Empire ships won't be sailing in this."

"The worst case is," Invitus corrected. "we don't find an Empire warship and all of this will be for nothing. For what good is a ship-of-war if not to match bronze against bronze?"

"They have at least five feet more of ram beam and weigh more with more oarsmen," another of the trireme officers informed the commander of Furor's Face. "A quinquereme can hold off a trireme while emptying barrels of arrows into your oarsmen and sailors."

Invitus blustered and seemed to want to argue but he held his comments.

"Our mission, despite what the Republic officer claims," a merchant Captain said. "is to deliver food for the men laying siege to Agrigento. If we can accomplish that without being sunk or captured, I'd consider that a successful journey."

"Can we get a consensus on the weather?" another Captain inquired. "Clearing or more rain?"

The eight ship commanders inspected the sky. After soaking their faces, they glanced around at each other and shrugged.

"I, for one, think we should remain here," Invitus declared. "Let us wait for better weather and a better chance to sink an Empire warship."

"If he says stay," the Centurion for Epiales' Veil advised. "Then I vote we launch."

They invoked the Goddess Tempestas and pleaded with her to remain calm and distance herself from the coast of Sicilia. Then someone produced an anemic chicken and they sacrificed it to the storm goddess.

"Not much of an offering," a Captain suggested.

"Best we have on short notice," another replied as the group separated to prepare their crews. "Besides, we only need her to hold back for half a day."

Tempestas must have appreciated the gesture because she drifted away from the southwest coast of the island. But the ship's officers neglected to call on the Greek God Boreas and sacrifice to him. As the gods are want to do, Boreas took offense at the absentmindedness of humans and rushed in from the north to show his displeasure.

Act 8

Chapter 33 - Eyes of the Archer

After launching from the muddy beach at Ciotta, the eight ships reached their assigned distance from shore and their spacing from the other ships. In formation, they rowed northward along the coasts.

The convoy placed the transports within line-of-sight of the shoreline. This allowed the warships to row farther off shore and use the cargo vessels as visual markers. Epiales' Veil rowed lead, tracking far off the port side of the first transport. Following the line of warships back, Furor's Face occupied the third slot with the final trireme lagging to the rear of the last merchantman.

Two things made the formation function. The placement of the merchant vessels prevented any Empire warships from attacking the convoy from the landward side. Being too close to shore and near water too shallow for an attack run, the escorts only needed to guard the port side. The second feature assuring good order was the interconnected views between ships. From stern to bow, crewmen on each Syracuse ship could see the transport ahead and the one behind. Although the triremes were too far apart for a solid visual on the other warships, each escort had a sideways view of at least one merchant vessel.

They rowed until traveling a fair distance. Independent of one another, the ship commanders sent crewmen to the masts. As the sails went up, the clouds lowered. The rain held off but the clouds continued to drop. The fog touched the top of the sea and the convoy sailed right into Boreas' curse.

***

Poor visibility closed in, isolating the ships.

"Sisera. Report," the Second Principale demanded from down on the rowers walk.

Alerio, until a heartbeat ago, had a view of two transports. Both were off to the right with one ahead and one behind the trireme. Then the god of fog came to visit.

"No view of either merchantman," he answered.

The response echoed back until it reached the steering platform. Alerio paused from peering into the fog to glancing down the length of the upper decks at the Centurion and the First Principale. Both men and the two rear oarsmen were faint outlines of gray ghosts. He caught sight of a group heading for the mast. Troubled by what he saw, Alerio called five sailors to the foredeck.

"I want five points of view," he directed. "Two to port and two on the starboard side facing forward. And one looking around the keel straight at our path."

The five men shifted to the assigned positions. Alerio scanned the fog bank one more time. Not seeing anything except the wall of clouds, he turned and, sprinted towards the steering deck.

***

"Centurion. Don't drop the sail," Alerio cautioned. "We'll slow down and we might lose the convoy."

"If we don't slow down," First Principale Stratus countered. "We might sail off to the west and lose the land."

"Afraid of getting lost at sea, Stratus?" Alerio inquired. Then to Invitus, he explained. "The convoy will

276

remain at the current pace. The fog will lift and we need to be there. Agrigento is contested. Not just the land but this area of the Mediterranean Sea, as well. I beg you, leave the sail up."

The ship's senior officer placed two fingers on his cheek. Then, the fingertips snaked up and rubbed the lid of the missing eye.

"Alright. First Principale, cancel the order to roll the sails," Invitus instructed. "We'll keep them for now. Sisera, return to your position."

"I'm on the way, Centurion," he said.

Alerio hopped off the steering platform. Four steps onto the upper deck, two of the sailors on watch at the bow cupped their hands over their mouths and screamed.

"Wreckage, starboard side," they announced.

Alerio changed direction, leaped the split dividing the upper decks, and ran to the right side. Leaning over, he saw wood in the waves.

Broken planks and boards rushed by the Furor's Face. Then, before the debris fell behind the speeding warship, a large section of broken hull rotated up from the depths. A painted eye on a smashed section of a Legion trireme stared at Alerio from under the surface. He jerked involuntarily.

Inhaling, he prepared to call a report to the steering platform. But his eyes caught the sailors at the mast attaching the sail lines. Thinking of the ship's morale, he closed his mouth and casually walked back to the steering platform.

"I thought you were ordered to return to your post, Third Principale?" Stratus reprimanded the third deck officer.

"What is it now, Sisera?" Invitus demanded.

Alerio leaned in close to the senior Centurion's ear.

"The wreck in the water was our lead trireme," Alerio whispered. "Or what was left of it."

"What?" Invitus exclaimed while spinning to the stern. He studied the water trying to pick the wreck out of the waves and fog. "I don't..."

"Not so loud," Alerio warned. "You'll frighten the crew."

"What will frighten the crew?" Stratus asked. Only he said it loudly, as if he was a child left out of a game. "What?"

"We need to go back and look for survivors," Invitus informed Alerio and the First Principale.

"Survivors?" Stratus inquired.

"No, we don't. Senior Centurion, we need to stay our course and find the transports," Alerio advised. "Protecting them is our mission."

Invitus clenched his teeth and stared at Alerio. His face darkened as if he was about to explode.

"Ship, port side," the cries came from a number of locations. While the first part of the message boomed clearly from different parts of the ship, the same multitude of voices garbled the second part.

Invitus, Stratus, and Alerio turned towards the front left of the trireme. There was nothing there except fog. Then the three of them caught a glimpse of a moving object out of the corners of their eyes. They spun to face the aft section.

A raised bow reached high above a deck that itself was twelve feet above the sea. Propelled by ninety churning oars on each side, the quinquereme shot out of the fog. It's speed so great, the ram on the front parted the water and threw wakes in the air. It was a ship killer at full speed seeking another hull to destroy.

Alerio jumped at the two men controlling the rear oars. With his shoulders, he slammed into both men driving them and the oars to the right. In response, the Republic trireme hooked to the port side.

The massive Qart Hadasht warship flew by. The deadly bronze ram missing the stern and rear oars by several feet. With Invitus and Stratus standing transfixed and Alerio on his knees beside the off balanced helmsmen, they gasped as the enemy hull blocked their view of the sea and fog.

***

In any encounter between a ship with three banks of oarsmen and a ship with five, by all that was lorded over by Mars the god of war, the Empire quinquereme should have stopped and unleashed barrages of arrows and bolts at the Republic warship. Except, the near miss and the quick turn placed the bow of the trireme parallel with the bigger ship's hull.

No one realized the positioning until oars began snapping. Before the Qart Hadasht Captain ordered a change in course, the Furor's Face cruised down the hull. Snapping the oars of the quinquereme's port side engine, the trireme forced the bigger ship to limp away. Until they could pull spare oars from storage, the quinquereme was at three quarters power.

"It resembles my little sister when she lost her baby teeth," Alerio remarked as he climbed to his feet. "That is a fine gap in the center of their oar display."

"Now is my chance," Invitus declared. "First Principale, roll…"

Alerio stepped between the first deck officer and the senior ship's officer.

"Don't do it, senior Centurion," Alerio warned. "I realize there is a crippled enemy ship escaping. But let me remind you. Our mission is to feed two starving Legions. I am begging you, stay and protect the transports."

"Killing that beast will protect the grain ships," Invitus barked. "I am so sick of your cowardly advice. When we return to Ostia, I want you off my ship."

"As you…"

"Wreckage, starboard side," the two sailors on watch at the bow sang out.

Invitus, Stratus, and Alerio sprinted to the right side of the warship. As before, there were boards and planks floating by but, this occurrence was different. They immediately identified the debris in the water as the remains of Epiales' Veil.

"Well?" Alerio questioned with a blank expression on his face.

Invitus chewed on his lip before admitting, "There's a second quinquereme out there."

"The Goddess Tyche smiles on you, senior Centurion," Alerio offered. "She sends you not one but two enemy ships for your ram."

"That's what you call fortune and luck?" Stratus muttered. "Two weapon's platforms?"

"Let's get those transports to Maddalusa," Invitus announced. "First Principale, dip a quarter of our oars. I need speed to run in and find our charges. And then get back onto our defensive track. Don't you worry, we'll go hunting later."

Stratus moaned before strolling to the top of the rower's walk to deliver the orders.

***

In the fog, the merchant ships had moved closer to shore. Without the protection of the triremes, they were contemplating running to the beach and returning to Syracuse in the morning.

The warship emerged from the fog and a deck officer, using his arm, indicated the merchant ship then signaled a northern direction.

"Grain ship," Alerio called out from the foredeck.

The words carried across the water and down to the rower's walk. While the second deck officer and the NCO passed the message back, Alerio continued directing the transport.

"Pick up your pace," he shouted from the swift warship. "Stay close and push on."

"We thought we lost you," the Captain of the transport shouted back.

The trireme glided by the sluggish grain ship.

"Pick up your pace," Alerio repeated.

The trireme moved ahead, searching for the next grain ship.

They located all four, confirmed that at least one Republic warship remained on station, then moved off to cut a track back and forth alongside the merchant vessels. It quickly became a comfortable relationship. Every so often, the warship appeared out of the fog, letting the grain ships know the Republic was still on guard. The cycle repeated for most of the morning.

Then, Boreas, the god of fog, grew tired of toying with the humans and vanished.

The shoreline became visible as well as the four Syracuse ships. Unfortunately, the single Republic trireme also materialized as the mist faded. This exposed the convoy to a pair of lurking Empire quinqueremes. With targets acquired, the Qart Hadasht warships dipped oars and headed for the grain ships.

***

"Sisera, signal our break," senior Centurion Invitus' command filtered up from the rowers walk.

Even as the message reached Third Principale Sisera, the trireme dipped its one hundred and twenty oars and cut a half circle in the waves. Once on a heading towards the first Empire warship, the under manned trireme surged forward.

A glance told Alerio the second quinquereme was moving around the port side. It would avoid the approaching collision and have an open lane to the transports. Furor's Face could do nothing about the second quinquereme.

If the trireme was an arrow and the ram the arrowhead, then ship's officer Invitus was a nearsighted archer. He drew the bow and roughly aimed his weapon via orders to the rowers and rear oarsmen. Yet he couldn't sight in on the sweet spot of his target. For that, he depended on the third deck officer.

The Third Principale's job had him standing above the point of impact, watching as the forward keel and bronze ram of the massive enemy warship came directly at him. Exposed on the foredeck, he would be the eyes of the archer and the most exposed man on the trireme. For this reason, he carried a shield and wore a helmet against enemy bowmen.

Alerio ground his teeth in frustration. He was an infantryman and had served with a Legion in Agrigento. To have come this far and nearly arriving with the food stuff, only to have the transports sunk, brought a scream to his lips.

Angry and seeking vengeance, Third Principale Sisera spread his feet on the foredeck, squared his shoulders and braced his legs. Then he lowered his hand and allowed the shield to slip from his arm. Next, he ripped off his helmet and dropped it beside the shield. Both restricted his vision and, for this mission, he wanted to be precise.

"Bring it," he shouted at the quinquereme.

It grew as the distance between the Empire's ram and the Republic's ram closed.

Then from the south, the fourth Roman trireme came over the horizon. Digging one hundred and seventy oars, the ship seemed to skim the surface of the ocean. Alerio wasn't the only one to see the warship.

Centurion Invitus waved it in the direction of the grain ships and the Captain of the second quinquereme broke off his attack run. He would need room and area to battle a second trireme.

For a few moments, the scene froze for Alerio. The four grain ships added their crews' oars to the sail power in order to get more speed out of the floating bowls. Behind them, the second enemy warship curved away from the transports while the fourth trireme raced in to assume sentry duty. It lasted only a breath before Alerio snapped back to the present.

***

As if a leviathan swam just beneath the surface, the ram plowed the ocean, throwing rooster tails up into the air. Before the twin sprays of water fell back into the sea, they were hammered into the quinquereme. The warship approached so quickly no splatters bounced off its hull.

Alerio raised both arms overhead until his thumbs and forefingers met. Almost as if he offered a target with the gesture, Qart Hadasht archers launched volleys of arrows at the exposed figure. Maintaining the position of his arms, Alerio leaned over to study the ram on the front of his ship.

In comparison, the rooster combs from the trireme rose half the height. And they splashed back into the ocean before the speeding hull reached the tail ends of the water features.

Third Principale Sisera shifted his eyes from the trireme's ram to the quinquereme's ram. Back and forth he mentally measured and tracked the distance between the converging warships. From his perch at about eight feet above the water, he studied the top deck of the enemy ship. Although only four feet higher, the quinquereme provided a more stable platform for archers. The things saving Alerio from collecting numerous arrowheads in his body were the jerking of the trireme between oar strokes and, the nose drop and rise suffered by the quinquereme from the power of its three hundred oarsmen.

Larger and faster with additional weapons besides a ram, the quinquereme was the more deadly warship. But Alerio didn't care, he stood and studied the ship as if it was an opponent in a sword fight. And like a duel with sharp steel, the first move would be the last.

***

Ram to ram, bronze against bronze were images favored by poets and land-based adventures. The issue with smashing rams together created two problems. Acting like fingers, the stacks of cutting edges in the faces of the rams would interlock. Much like interwoven fingers, the warships would be lodged together. Even after the battle was decided by the superior force, the victor would be trapped in a dual-hulled ship with two sterns and no bow.

The other argument preventing bronze against bronze contact was more germane to Alerio's situation. A behemoth of one hundred and eighty tons colliding with a fifty-ton mass could be equated to a single Billy goat butting heads with a bull. Not a good outcome for the goat or for the trireme.

In breaths and heartbeats, the quinquereme drew closer. So near in fact, Alerio could hear the Qart Hadasht drummers pounding out the stroke rhythm for their oarsmen. One good thing about his looming death. The archers couldn't lean far enough over to get a shot at the Third Principale. Their targets were now on the steering platform at the stern of the trireme.

***

On the platform, senior Centurion Invitus screamed, kicked the boards, and stomped his boots on the deck. Sisera was simply standing on the forward platform, transfixed by the approaching quinquereme. As the ship's senior officer paced, a sailor holding a shield shifted to keep the barrier in front of his commander. It had already picked up a few stray arrows.

Each of the men on the steering platform had a shadow with a shield. It wouldn't do to have the command crew of a warship swept from the platform in the middle of a battle.

But it wasn't the middle of a battle with ships angling for position. It was closer to a pair of bucks during rutting season preparing to buttheads. One hundred and thirty feet away, Alerio Sisera stood on the foredeck, stock still, with his arms over his head.

"If he is my eyes," Invitus mumbled coldly about his third deck officer. "We are already dead."

"Orders, Centurion?" First Principale Stratus questioned.

He, as well, could see the Empire warship growing taller and more menacing. And, his third deck officer carelessly watching, or maybe sleeping.

"We should begin maneuvering," Stratus suggested.

"No, we wait," Invitus directed. "Maybe the Qart Hadasht Captain will flinch."

Chapter 34 - A Lesson Passed On

After checking and dismissing the ineffective archers, Alerio peered down at the boiling water around the two rams. At this close a range, his eyes could take in both weapons. Heartbeats from impact, the Qart Hadasht Captain his showed his plan. He adjusted his ship.

The ram, ever so slightly, shifted to the left. It would take more travel for the weapon to come off center and the bronze blades to cut into the hull of the trireme and not strike the other ram. In that tiny move, Alerio's eyes perceived the change and the new heading. Just as Alerio would do in a gladius competition, he reacted.

Alerio's fingers separated when both arms arched over and pointed off to his right side. Holding the pose, he waited as the gap between the quinquereme and the trireme shrunk.

"Starboard side, five power strokes," he heard Bancus Nunzio from the rowers walk. "Port side, five and hold water."

The Furor's Face responded and swiveled around the strong center rowers' locations. Then after five lopsided strokes, oarsmen on both sides dug in and the nimble trireme shot out of the quinquereme's way.

Straight forward the bigger warship could easily outpace the smaller one. Out distance and overpower, plus carry infantry, bolt throwers, and archers that could overturn a trireme. But, spinning and twirling on the ocean's surface were the domain of the triremes.

***

The ram missed the stern and the trireme's rear cleared the front side of the quinquereme. To the First Principale and the helmsmen, they had averted a disaster and could breathe again. With a blessing from the Goddess Fortūna, they could now row closer to shore and avoid another confrontation with the enemy's ram. But the ship's senior officer had a different idea.

"Starboard side, power ten," Invitus ordered. "Port side, stroke three and pull oars."

287

At the instructions, five sailors yanked long poles from under the steering platform. Holding them in two hands, they raced to stations along the left side of the trireme.

The big warship may be powerful, but the trireme was agile. Furor's Face snapped to the left and its bronze ram dug into the hull of the quinquereme snapping oars as it advanced. Between momentum and the mad rowing from the right-side oarsmen, the ram gouged out a fifteen-foot gash below the water line. With the long poles set against the enemy's hull, the sailors pushed the trireme away from its victim.

When enough space opened between warships, senior officer Invitus ordered, "Port side, run them out and, stroke, stroke, stroke."

Optio Florian and Centurion Nunzio, one at each end of the rower's walk, passed the instructions to the oarsmen. After feeling the vibration of their ram eating hull and hearing the screams of tortured wood, the oarsmen were relieved to get the rowing directions.

Up on the steering platform, smiles and puffed out chests displayed the success of the command section.

"Well done, senior Centurion," Stratus gushed.

He reached out a hand, offering to grip wrists. Invitus, caught up in the thrill of his victory, turned to face the First Principale and extended his arm.

***

From his vantage point on the foredeck, Alerio marveled at the long and fat pieces of wood that splintered from the hull. As if watching sparks from a metalworker's grinding wheel, the ram flung fragments.

But rather than metal, they were showers of shredded oak.

Assisted by the sailors and their poles, the hulls separated. Once the gap opened between ships, the port side ran out their oars and joined the starboard side in powering the trireme away.

The damaged hull of the quinquereme tilted and its oak planks slid by. It was a rare occurrence to stand this close to a vanquished enemy ship and Alerio relished the victory. He turned to face forward and let the breeze wash over him. From the corner of his eyes, Alerio watched the Qart Hadasht's commanders issuing orders in an attempt to save their vessel.

"It was a good fight, Nenia Dea," Alerio prayed. "I picked up no scars and none of my people died."

The two warships slid by each other until Alerio could see around the stern of the Empire's vessel.

"Hard port," he shouted while jerking his arms to his left. The visual signal of the escape direction might give the Republic warship an out. It would be close, Alerio thought, if….

But the ship's senior Centurion stood sideways, gripping the First Principale's wrist. Invitus' blind eye was turned to Alerio when the second quinquereme plowed into their ship.

***

With almost four times the mass, the ram powered by the Qart Hadasht warship punched through the hull. The trireme tilted and skipped sideways as it was driven across the waves. As if launched from a ballista, Third Principale Sisera flew from the deck, sailed over the water, then plummeted to the sea. His chest armor and

289

hobnailed boots pulled him under. The next set of waves rolled by, erasing any sign of his plunge.

The ram reached deep into the trireme severing the legs of rowers in that section. Then, the beam holding the bronze weapon swept around destroying the internal beams and killing more oarsmen. When the Empire warship changed heading, the ram and beam popped out a long section of the hull as it reemerged.

Backstroking, the oarsmen stopped the quinquereme's forward progress. Bobbing alongside the fatally wounded Furor's Face, Qart Hadasht bowmen lined the rail. They notched arrows and targeted crewmen from the trireme. No one who crawled out survived and certainly none of the ones trapped in the sinking structure lived.

Senior Centurion Invitus died knowing he had killed a quinquereme. That might have been enough glory for the former cavalry officer. As for Optio Florian, Centurions Stratus and Nunzio, they were at the bottom of the sea and only Neptune was available to hear their comments.

***

The Legion required many trials before a man qualified as a Legionary. Over hundreds of years, the Republic's military picked up lessons from difficult situations. These skills were passed down from earlier generations and became core to the training. Among them were sprinting, jumping, and swimming. No man continued his Legionary training without first excelling in those skills.

Alerio sprinted three steps and jumped when the Qart Hadasht ram punched the trireme. Soaring off the deck, he snatched the Golden Valley dagger from the small of his back. He hacked at straps before splashing down.

The leather bindings were severed and the armor fell off. Even free of the weight, he sank. Franticly slicing on his boot wrappings, he plunged deeper.

It was black when he finally freed himself of the last heavy object. Pressure in his ears informed him how deep he had sunk. Then, he paused in the cold depths and apologized.

'Nenia Dea, I am humbled,' Alerio thought. 'If it is my time, I am ready."

Despite the fatalism in his prayer, Alerio kicked for the surface.

***

From black, to gray, to green water overhead, Alerio transitioned through the ocean layers as he swam upward. Lungs screaming for air, and his chest heaving, his body threatened to take in a breath. It became a contest between the urges of his lungs and the control of his mind. Then, the green filtered sunlight was blotted out. Given any spare air in his lungs, Alerio would have swum away. But the contest was in the final phase and his options were to surface or die.

He came up and used his hands to feel for the edge of the hull. Once clear, he allowed his face to break the surface and sweet air to fill his lungs. Realizing the shape of the Qart Hadasht's quinquereme hid him from those on the upper decks, he allowed his head to come out of the water. The low waves gave him no view of anything beyond the next wave.

With a kick, he rose higher above the surface and was sad he did. Farther out, arrows plucked the water or struck floating bodies. It didn't take a lot to deduce that he was the sole survivor of the Furor's Face.

Curious as to why the warship sat motionless, he inhaled deeply, ducked down, and swam under the keel. On the other side of the ship, he hugged the boards and allowed his head to bob under the waves. At the crest of one, he broke the surface.

Lines dropped to the water from the undamaged quinquereme. Men swam or used pieces of wood as floats and kicked their way from the sinking sister ship. At the hull, the faster swimmers climbed the ropes to safety.

"Come on man," a swimmer called to Alerio. "Climb up before the mob arrives."

With a mixture of joy, sadness, and trepidation, Alerio kicked away from the hull and swam to a rope. Treading water, he waited for an opening and the opportunity to scale the line.

Both Empire ships-of-war were out of the hunt for the grain transports. At least he could take comfort in completing the mission. Even with the loss of life from three triremes, the supplies would prevent thousands of Legionaries from starving to death. It was a difficult enough trade off, and now he was about to mingle with the enemy.

A space between swimmers gave Alerio access to the rope. He reached up grabbed tightly, kicked, rose out of the water, and grabbed higher with the other hand. Then he scrambled up to the crowded deck.

Chapter 35 - False Palisades

A quinquereme carried three hundred oarsmen. Plus, another one hundred souls composed of sailors, soldiers, and the ship's command staff. Adding three hundred and fifty survivors from the sunken ship-of-war created chaos on the already crowded vessel.

"Where are you from?" an Egyptian inquired.

"Messina," Alerio replied.

"Are you one of those Sons of Mars?" the rower questioned.

"You mean a pirate or a vicious fighter?" Alerio sneered. "Choose wisely before you answer. Right now, I can only prove one of those to you."

The man bristled and slinked away. He didn't go far, he couldn't. They were sitting on the rower's walk among a crush of bodies. By dissuading conversation with the Egyptian, Alerio managed to avoid discussing which ship he was assigned to and his duties. Two answers that might draw attention from people he was supposed to know.

It wasn't unusual after a disaster for people to seek self-contemplation or silent prayer. Many of the seven hundred and fifty men on board sat quietly with downcast eyes. Alerio mimicked them.

***

"Starboard half turn."

On either side of Alerio, oarsmen based on the quick order, rowed or held their oar handles still. The big vessel rocked from the extra weight of the survivors and from a sharp turn.

"Back it down," the rowing officers directed.

Three hundred oarsmen backstroked the one hundred and eighty oars. Alerio was amazed at the short orders and the complicated but precise responses. Glancing down the rowing deck, he saw skins of water hanging near the rowers. So packed in were the rowers and the waterskins, an archer could launch an arrow down the deck. The arrow would pass through so many waterskins, it would appear to be raining on the oarsmen. Even though they were in tight quarters, there was little talking between rowers. They appeared to be listening for the next order.

"Hold," the rowing deck officers called out.

All one hundred and eighty oars stopped with the handles held high. The blades on the other end of the oars rested deep in the water.

Alerio realized the oarsmen on the Empire warship had skills far superior to the Republic crews. It would take training and practice to approach the proficiency in ship handling of the Qart Hadasht mercenaries.

"Get up. Get off my ship," the officers on the rower's walk shouted.

The same order resounded from different sectors of the warship. Following shortly behind the order, Alerio heard the sounds of bodies splashing into the sea. He stood with the other survivors and followed the Egyptian to the upper deck.

***

Alerio expected to be up the coast and far away from the beach at Maddalusa. While he couldn't see the village, the shoreline, or the grain transports, he saw the taller structures at the Valley of Temples and the city of Agrigento higher up on the plateau. His view was from

294

the north not more than six miles or so away. Then a hand poked him in the back and he shuffled forward towards the edge of the deck.

The more bodies to drop off the quinquereme, the higher the warship rode in the water. Eventually, the water filled with people sloshing and wading ashore while others waited on the deck for a spot to clear in the water.

Another round of 'Get off my ship' came from the deck officers. To hasten the departure and further lighten the quinquereme, sailors began pushing the crowd from the rear. It seemed the Qart Hadasht Captain wanted to get his ship beached sooner, rather than later.

Alerio noticed an opening. Placing a foot on the edge of the deck, he launched himself. Windmilling his arms, the Legion officer managed to stay upright. After splashing down, he joined the throng moving to the beach.

When he reached shore, the military camps on the hills above the beach gave him an idea.

"Where are the Latian's camped?" he inquired.

His question, like his climbing on the enemy warship, was a calculated risk. The Qart Hadasht Empire used mercenaries. There was an excellent chance a unit of Latians would have hired on and joined the army. Alerio didn't plan on entering the camp of his tribesmen. But knowing its location gave him an answer to where he was coming from or going if questioned.

After getting a reply, he walked the trail twisting up through the campsites of an Empire army. Cavalry mounts penned in next to other livestock were separated from war elephants. Higher up and covering the hills, camps for infantry units, both heavy and light, spread from the saddles between hills up to the higher elevations.

Then bugles sounded and soldiers in the camps began pulling out armor, helmets, and weapons. It might have been in response to an attack. However, the NCOs and officers strolled around checking on the men and gear with no sign of alarm. Alerio decided it was a major call up and not a defensive response. He smiled and circled around behind the animal pens.

There were always places in disarray when an army mobilized. One in particular was ripe with abandoned clothing, wineskins, food stuffs, even swords and pieces of armor. Cavalrymen collected items while walking around only to realize they didn't want to encumber their mounts with the weight. The items, along with instructions to care for them, were given to the stablemen and grooms. Being rushed and in a slightly manic state, the animal handlers agreed. Then they tossed the excess gear into a pile, off to the side, and out of the way.

Alerio only cared about the food, a wineskin, and a robe. Coming in from the backside of the pile, he snatched what he needed, and faded back among the tents and campsites. The stablemen, busy rubbing down horses or checking hooves, missed the robbery. Unfortunately, the thief couldn't loiter to search for a pair of boots or sandals.

When a Company sized unit marched by, Alerio tossed the faded green cloak over his shoulders and pulled the hood over his head. With his non-descript appearance, he fell in behind the rear squad and he followed them into the hills.

The Company turned off the trail and moved into position while Alerio continued to the crest of a hill. From the heights, he finally had a view of the shoreline and the four Syracuse transports. Grain sacks were being carried off the ships and placed in wagons. Legionaries stood guard around the coastal village of Maddalusa protecting the valuable cargo.

As alert as the Centuries guarding the grain seemed, there was no other response to the activity in the Qart Hadasht encampment. Shifting his eyes to the palisades constructed in spots along the siege trench surrounding Agrigento, he marveled at the lack of movement there as well.

"Latian. Get your war gear," an officer in a tall conical helmet ordered. "Where is your Company?"

"I have camp guard duty," Alerio lied to the mercenary officer. He was tall, dark skinned, and not a native Latin speaker. Pointing to the Valley of the Temples, Alerio added. "I just wanted to see them from up here."

"After the breakout and rout, you'll have plenty of opportunities to visit the temples," the officer assured him.

"My Captain wanted to know if he could sacrifice before marching out," Alerio questioned. "Or do you need us right away?"

"The General wants everyone in position by dark. But really, we don't step off until dawn," the Empire officer replied. "My people don't relate to the Hellenistic gods as yours do. Nevertheless, tell your Captain to make his offering."

"Thank you, sir," Alerio said. He turned and backtracked to the camps.

As he hiked down the trail, Alerio ate, letting the cheese, bread and, a not too weak vino, fill his belly. With his appetite sated, Alerio dropped down to the beach. He needed a way out and didn't care for crossing a battle line and a no-man's-land to reach the Legion lines. Maybe an unguarded fishing boat would present itself or, a family of traders with a cart heading south.

***

There were no free boats or passing carts. Not that the beach was deserted. On the contrary, hundreds of campfires dotted the sand and rocky shoreline. In hindsight it made sense. Where else would the crews from the warships camp, except near their vessels.

Peering southward, Alerio noted the last group of campfires. With no other idea of how to reach the Legion, he began walking. Until he reached the final few fires and camps, no one had called out or challenged him.

"There's nothing down there except trouble," a man shouted from a camp.

Alerio turned to see an oarsman reclining by a fire. He was propped up on an elbow and had two companions. It would not go well for the rowers if they tried to stop the Legion officer.

"Don't bother with that one," the Egyptian from the warship cautioned. The oarsmen sat at an adjacent camp with a frown on his face. "He is decidedly anti-social."

The reclining oarsman waved a dismissive hand at Alerio.

"It's your funeral," he said with a yawn. "Don't say we didn't warn you."

298

A half mile from the last camp, Alerio broke into a Legion shuffle. Three miles later, a squad of Legionaries rushed onto the beach, linked their shields, and formed a defensive line. They thought it odd when the limping stranger coming from the north beamed a broad smile in their direction before saluting.

***

Colonel Gaius Claudius and Legion Senior Centurion Lembus sat in an office staring at Centurion Alerio Sisera. When he finished explaining about the dawn attack, they glanced at each other.

"I swear Sisera," battle commander Claudius offered while eyeing Alerio from head to his bare, bleeding feet. "You spend more time behind the enemy's line than you do here."

"It's not intentional, Colonel," Alerio assured the battle commander of Megellus Legion East. "that's where my ride ended up. What are you going to do about the attack, sir?"

"They caught us by surprise the first time," Senior Centurion Lembus stated. "We lost our storage depot and our grain. If they try that, we'll be waiting."

"Intelligence says General Hannibal Gisco has been sending smoke signals from Agrigento," Colonel Claudius remarked. "This could be a quick strike to free the Qart Hadasht General from the city."

"I don't believe so, sir," Alerio submitted. "They were bragging about taking and holding the Valley of the Temples."

"Grain storage, the city's gates, and the temple. That's three objectives to guard," Claudius commented. "How do we narrow them down? I don't have the

299

Centuries to cover three specific areas and, keep the palisades along the siege trench crewed."

"I don't mean to come across as a staff officer, Colonel," Alerio said defensively.

"Spit it out, Sisera. It appears, you're proclaiming your association with planning and strategies," Lembus suggested. "Talk to us."

"Pull Centuries from all but a few of the palisades, sir," Alerio recommended. "You don't need to defend a long trench in the daylight. Use some to defend the Valley of the Temples."

"You're suggesting we weaken our defense at the trench and protect the temples," Colonel Claudius summed up. "That's not much of a plan, Centurion Sisera. What about the city gates and the supply depot?"

"We have four empty transports beached at Maddalusa, Colonel," Alerio proposed. "A force hidden in the cargo spaces can come out to defend the depot. Or…"

"Or attack the rear of the Qart Hadasht mercenaries if they go for the gates of Agrigento or the temples," Senior Centurion Lembus broke in to finish the plan. "If we squeeze three Centuries into each transport, we can unchain a maniple of veterans."

"Sir, I'd be proud to fight in that maniple," Alerio offered.

"Never volunteer, Centurion Sisera," Colonel Claudius instructed. "And while I'd like to grant your wish, I need you on a horse and not on a battle line."

"I can ride, sir," Alerio informed the commander. "But I'm no cavalryman."

"I realize that. You aren't loud or rich enough," Claudius said. Alerio couldn't tell if the Colonel was teasing or not. "General Megellus wants King Hiero to have a first hand account of the sacrifice the Republic made to protect his transports."

"Five hundred and seventy men died, sir," Alerio reported. "to deliver the grain."

"No, Centurion Sisera. Five hundred and seventy Legionaries sacrificed themselves protecting the four Syracuse transports," Colonel Claudius informed him. "For this mission, I need you to set aside your infantry officer's attitude and access your diplomatic side. The King will be amazed by your recital. After your description of the ferocity of the Legion forces, he will go to bed each evening for the rest of his life fearing that if he hesitates in helping or, crosses the Republic in the future, the Legion will eat his heart. Is that clear?"

"Yes, sir," Alerio confirmed. "When do I leave."

"As soon as the Senior Centurion runs you through the armory," Claudius responded. "and finds you a pair of boots. But I don't want you in parade ground armor. Make sure he looks the part of a warrior, Senior Centurion."

"My quartermaster has a scroll dedicated to Centurion Sisera's bills," Lembus remarked. "He'll be pleased to note the war gear this time can be used and scarred. Come along Sisera, let's get you dressed and on the road."

Chapter 36 - A Promise Made

In the Capital, there were many roads. Most paved with large stones and engineered to run straight between roundabouts. If attacked, Legions could cross the city quickly. Hard, true roads, connecting one side of Rome to the other, gave defenders access to besieged sectors. Even with the civil engineering guidelines, there were a few streets covered in gravel and following the original contour of the land. One of them tracked up and down hills and wobbled from side to side along with an estates' defensive wall. Blocks of tradesmen compounds and shops occupied one side of the street. On the opposite side and over the defensive wall was an enormous estate. A property better suited to the country than an urban environment.

Close to a commercial district, the grand villa, offices, and stables on the private acreage seemed out of place. Most of the large villas clustered around the government building. But the value of the land, inflated by location and the limited availability, would have reduced the length of the riding trails. And if there was one thing the Subausterus family valued, it was room to ride their horses and race their chariots. Thus, they bought less desirable land and built a defensive wall around the entire estate.

Shortly after sundown, Scribe Ludovicus Humi left work through the side door of the office complex. It had been a long day and his shoulders slumped from exhaustion. Former Tesserarius Humi was looking forward to a meal and a mug of vino or several mugs. He crossed the porch, stepped between the marble columns, and strolled over the manicured lawn.

As he approached an exit, a bodyguard holding a lantern greeted him while a house guard opened the gate in the defensive wall. Humi's sandals and the guard's boots crunched on the gravel street as they headed for the scribe's favorite pub. Behind them, the crossbeam fell, locking the gate in the estate's defensive wall.

Twenty steps from the gate and in the direction of Humi's favorite pub, the bodyguard, partially blinded by the lantern, failed to see the shadowy figures rise up from behind a roadside bush. The man-at-arms was unprepared for the strike from a club. Then, it didn't matter. Another club swung and the scribe dropped unconscious to the gravel surface.

Humi lay oblivious to the horse and cart when they turned the corner from the commercial district. And remained unaware when the rig paused for a moment. Four hands lifted him from the street and tossed his body and two herding clubs into the bed of the cart.

The bodyguard was comatose, the lantern hissed, and the light flickered. Gravel crunched under the cart's wheels and the horse's hoofs while the cart rolled away from the street boarding the Subausterus estate.

***

Sputtering and coughing, Humi felt his hair yanked. In response, his head snapped up and out of the bucket of water.

"Good evening, Corporal," a voice greeted him.

At the sound of the voice, the scribe's stomach rebelled and he puked watery bile down his chest. After the initial blast, he coughed up mucus and attempted to spit it out.

"You had better watch yourself, Sisera," Humi warned.

The threat lost a lot of weight. Not only was spit hanging from the corner of his mouth but gobs of snot dangled from his nostrils.

"I apologize for the knot on your head," Alerio offered. "I was torn when I hit you."

While still gripping Humi's hair, Alerio dug the fingers of his other hand into the scribe's shoulder. Lifting, he pulled the man off his knees, swung him around, and shoved the scribe into a chair.

"You should have followed your conscience," Humi said when he realized he wasn't being flung to the stone floor. "and stayed far away from me and Master Subausterus."

"It wasn't that, Corporal," Alerio replied. "My impulse was to hit you harder, then beat you to death for treason. But that wasn't the promise."

"What promise?" Humi questioned.

"The one I made when you were sabotaging our work," Alerio reminded the scribe.

"The mad oath you made about taking my fingers," Humi said. Then slowly, he realized the significance of the statement. "But that was uttered in a moment of passion. Nobody takes that sort of promise seriously."

"True, but I do need something else," Alerio remarked. "Who was the mercenary in Senator Maximus' villa? And where do I find him and his friends?"

"I don't know what you're talking about," Humi vowed. "I know nothing about the Senator's house guard being arrested."

Alerio almost burst out laughing. To cover the expression of amusement, he walked to a corner, picked up a pitcher, and poured a mug of water. Humi wasn't as smart or sophisticated as Alerio thought. In one answer, Humi confirmed that he knew Civi Affatus had been arrested so the villa was unguarded. By extension, he must know who would be going there to wait.

"Tesserarius Humi. I wish it didn't have to be this way," Alerio said softly.

"What way...?" but the scribe didn't finish.

Alerio kicked him off the chair with enough force, Humi sailed for several feet before impacting then bouncing off the stone floor. When he settled, Centurion Sisera squatted on the scribe's chest and slammed a foot down on his hand.

"You transcribe with this hand, correct?" Alerio inquired.

"Yes. You wouldn't...?"

The dagger flashed. Its blade reflecting lantern light as it arced from shoulder height, down to where the steel scraped along the stone floor, then back up to shoulder level.

Humi shivered but remained still. His only reaction was a whimper and tears leaking from clenched eyes.

"Medic," Alerio said almost as an afterthought. "Fix this."

Footsteps came from a side room and walked to the scribe. He didn't want to look but when the footfalls stopped, Humi open his eyes. A pair of hobnailed boots rested several hands lengths away. Then the man reached down and Humi saw the red-hot poker.

He screamed and bucked as the stubs of two fingers were cauterized.

"I'll let you know when I need you again," Alerio manage to say while holding Humi down. "Best go and heat the iron. Now Corporal, I asked you a question."

"Abdicatus, he goes by Abdicatus," Humi cried. "Please. No more."

"That depends on you, Corporal," Alerio stated. "Where can I find this Abdicatus?"

"A tavern in the Firebreak District named the Unholy Fig," Humi explained. "I wish you had gone there first."

"And why should I have gone there first?" Alerio asked.

"Abdicatus has an enforcer. He is so fast with a blade, you'll be holding your guts in your hands and seeing your own merda, before you die," Humi described. "I'd pay to see Hircus kill you."

"I hate to break my promises but I only took your little finger and the tip of another," Alerio explained. "But that shouldn't be a problem."

"It isn't. I can still write without the small finger," Humi responded. "Now that you've had your fun. And gotten your answers. Let me up."

Alerio stood and walked away from the scribe before calling out, "Lieutenant Roscini. The prisoner is all yours."

Tite Roscini marched in followed by four of his militiamen.

"Ludovicus Humi. You are under arrest for the murder of an Umbri craftsman and his apprentice," Tite charged. "You are to be taken to Amelia where you will stand before Administrator Nardi Cocceia and be judged."

"You can't do this. I am a citizen of the Republic," Humi pleaded. "Tell them Centurion Sisera. Tell them they can't do this."

"Praetor Seubus is worried about the offenses visited on the Umbria. Now that we need Stifone and Administrator Cocceia to build our ships," Alerio replied. "the Praetor needed someone to offer up for all of the mistakes."

"I know things about Tribune Subausterus," Humi bragged. "He should be on trial."

"He is a nobleman and a staff officer. It will never happen without the backing of the senate," Alerio informed the former Corporal. "Lieutenant Roscini treat the prisoner well. But if it seems the judgement is anything except execution, please send me a message."

Tite understood as did Humi. The scribe walked out flanked by the Umbria militiamen. His shoulders stooped much lower than when he left his office.

Chapter 37 - A Man's Sanctuary

Early evening the next day found Alerio in the company of Civi Affatus and six armed men. They marched from the ordered roads of the Capital onto the dirt streets of Firebreak District. Two blocks in, the group walked an alleyway until it spilled out onto another street.

"We can take it from here," Civi Affatus said for the fifth time. "This isn't your fight, sir."

"As a musician," Alerio replied to the retired Optio. "you are merda."

Puzzled expressions appeared on the faces of Civi and the other six house guards.

"I don't understand, Centurion," Civi remarked. "I can't sing or play an instrument."

"And you shouldn't because you play the same tune over and over," Alerio teased. He draped the old green cloak across his shoulders and tugged the hood down over his face. "I, on the other hand, have a manly singing voice. Perhaps, I'll entertain you gentlemen someday. Right now, we have to pay homage to Nemesis."

"Yesterday, we made a sacrifice to the goddess of revenge," Civi informed Alerio. "Asking her to help us find the gang."

"Well, there you have it," Alerio announced.

"Have what, Centurion?" the house guard inquired.

"Divine approval of me taking the lead," Alerio stated. "You can't reject my help and go against the gods. That would be bad, Sergeant."

Alerio really didn't want to fight with a group of local mercenaries. But incensed by the home invasion, General Spurius Maximus' house guards were determined to teach the soldier of fortune and his crew a lesson.

Would Abdicatus and his men settle for a simple beatdown? Alerio doubted it. They were more likely to draw blades and blood. Although tough infantry veterans and able Legionaries, the house guards had lost half a heartbeat from their abilities. If Alerio was being generous. Plus, one of Abdicatus' crew was a swordsman. A few questions to some rough men and

Alerio gained intelligence on Hircus. Civi Affatus, even in his prime, couldn't go against a blade master. That fact alone, forced Alerio to get involved.

"Remember, give me time to set them up," Alerio instructed. Then he peered across at the tavern's sign. "The Unholy Fig. An inelegant name if I ever heard one. Give me time Optio Affatus but not too much. I don't want to die on the dirty floor boards of a rundown tavern."

Alerio crossed the street, stepped up on the porch, and shoved open the doors to the Unholy Fig.

***

Wood didn't care if it was old, new, used, weathered or fresh from the drying shed. While a variety of wood, oak, pine, fir and, cedar, had been crafted in some places and hammered into others to build the Unholy Fig, the customers in the tavern were generally of three types: hopeless and seeking a handout; mercenaries seeking employment; and shady middlemen who wealthy people contacted to hire swordsmen or muscle. None were interested in the artistry of the carpenters who built the place. But all sixteen people were interested in the man in the green cloak who walked in when the doors opened.

"Vino," the man ordered. He placed a coin on the tap manager's table then walked to an empty chair.

"This ain't no high-class gentlemen's club," the manager informed the man. He leaned against one of the huge wine casts and folded his arms. "We don't have a serving wench. Unless you count old Elianus there. But she hasn't moved for two days. If you want to wait for her next eruption, that's fine with me."

An aging, portly woman in the back of the room raised her arm, waved, and laughed. Alerio ignored her.

The manager unfolded an arm just long enough to drop Alerio's coin in his purse. He made no move to draw a mug of vino. During the exchange, Alerio located Abdicatus and his enforcer Hircus.

The two sat on either side of the other mercenaries as if they were herding dogs. This let Alerio know the three in the center were support bodies for the other two. While they might be dangerous in a formation, individually they weren't anything special. It was a good sign for Civi and the house guards.

"Then I'll have my silver coin back," Alerio stated while standing. "I'll take my business elsewhere."

"Silver? It was a copper," the tap manager insisted.

"I distinctly remember placing a silver on your table," Alerio maintained. "Let's test your claim. Tell me the number of silvers you have in your purse. Then empty it on the table and we'll see if you don't have an extra silver."

While talking, Alerio moved to the side of the manager's table. It felt awkward but Abdicatus and Hircus had to have a good view when the cloak moved.

"I will not empty my purse for you or anyone," the manager stated. He reached behind the table and pulled out a heavy iron bar with a wicked sharp and tapered point on one end.

Alerio fumbled with the edge of the cloak then paused. He dropped the corner of the cloak, almost tripped while he stepped back. Once his feet were properly set, after three tries, he flipped the cloak back to display the hilt of a sword.

Pearl handled with a pummel ringed with precious stones, the hilt flashed status and opulence. Adding to the aura of affluence, the sheath was covered in brushed fur with more stones.

The sword showed four inches of blade when Alerio halted the draw. As if he rethought going up against the iron bar, he slid the blade back, and raised his hands.

"Perhaps you are correct," Alerio said. "Return my copper and I'll be on my way."

Sensing the fear in the man with the green cloak, the tap manager laughed.

"I think I'll keep it as pay for my aggravation," the manager answered. He added a wiggle of the iron bar to reinforce his decision. "Now get out of my tavern."

Alerio hesitated as if not sure what to do. He was saved by Abdicatus.

"Nonsense. Please sir, join us," the mercenary captain offered. He added a smile to his face to show his sincerity. "We have vino and room at our table."

With a wave of his hand, the others in his crew moved to open a space and leave an empty chair. It might have been a neighborly gesture, except the chair placed Alerio next to Hircus.

Five against one happened to be bad combat odds. Especially when one of the six carried multiple blades. Now that he had them thinking about the fancy sword, Alerio needed to extract himself. And draw the mercenaries along in the process. For effect and to delay, he staggered and placed a hand on the manager's table to steady himself.

Some people are miserable humans. Their fun always comes at someone else's expense. And usually they are vindictive. The tip on the iron bar came up, slammed down, and pinned Alerio's right hand to the oak desktop.

Alerio screamed and the tap manager sneered, "I told you to get out of my tavern."

Abdicatus and Hircus glanced at each other across their table. In silent agreement, they stood and took a step towards the man spiked to the tabletop.

The door to the Unholy Fig opened and Civi Affatus rushed to Alerio.

"Sir, I've been searching for you..." his face fell. The script forgotten when he noticed the bleeding hand and the iron bar.

"I seem to be stuck," Alerio commented.

"Yes, sir," Civi acknowledged. He jumped around the table and hammered a fist onto the top of the tap manager's head. The man released the bar and sank to the floor. With his other hand, the retired Optio caught the iron spike. He yanked it out of the wood and Alerio's hand. "Pardon me, sir."

"I imagine this will be painful in the morning," Alerio lied while he examined the bleeding hole in his hand. "when the vino wears off."

"We should get you to a doctor," Civi declared. He pulled a cloth from his sword belt and wrapped the hand. After knotting it, the Optio hooked an arm around Alerio's waist and spun them both to face the doors.

With shuffling feet, the household guard guided the wounded man to the exit. As they opened the doors, Alerio sagged against him. Civi panicked and rethought the wisdom of seeking vengeance. Fighting and protecting your wounded created a different scenario than a straight forward attack.

312

They reached the porch and all Civi could think of was medical care for Centurion Sisera. On the street, the other house guards remained in position. Civi began to signal for them to break cover and follow.

"Hold on there," a man said from behind them. Civi and Alerio hobbled around to see Abdicatus, Hircus, and the other three mercenaries standing on the porch of the Unholy Fig. "I offered to buy him a drink. Nobody refuses to drink with me."

"Pardon, sir. But as you can see, my master is injured," Civi begged. "He requires medical attention."

"No. What your master needs is to give me that pretty sword," Abdicatus instructed while he and his crew stepped off the porch and onto the street.

"That took longer than I wanted," Alerio whispered while he straightened. Then he tossed back the hood and pointed the bandaged and bloody hand at Hircus. "I hear you're good with a blade."

***

Abdicatus rocked back when he recognized Alerio. "You're the one they took into custody at," he stopped before admitting to invading the senator's villa.

"And I'm Civi Affatus, house guard for Villa Maximus. You made a critical error. You entered the General's home without permission."

"No old man, you made the critical error," Abdicatus boasted. "This isn't the polite part of the Capital. To be honest, it's a neglected and hostile area."

A sword swiped the air making a whooshing sound as Hircus drew his long blade. Then he pulled a short sword with his left hand.

313

"I believe this is what you want," Alerio stated. He unhooked the fur sword belt and let it and the ornate sword fall to the street. "I started to bring two. But with this bandaged hand, I'll only use one sword. Fortunate, wouldn't you say."

"I'll take the sword and you two can leave," Abdicatus suggested.

Civi started to reply when a horrible sound came from Alerio's throat. Thinking the Centurion was in pain, he reached out to comfort him.

"Slurs slung before, the mind can control incivility," Alerio sang while pivoting away from the Optio.

A long sword with a heavy blade snapped into view from behind Alerio's back.

"And swaps your tranquility for imbecility"

His left arm crossed his chest while the Centurion finished the pivot. With the sword pulled back, Alerio offered his right shoulder to Hircus' blades.

"Wine and insanity rule"

Hircus displayed his contempt for a lesser swordsman. He accepted the shoulder for what it was. A blunder. His long blade slashed hard and sure, seeking to remove the arm at the shoulder.

"with the cost of your sense of a mild mind"

Alerio leaned to the side at the waist, then rocked back and continued rotating to the other side. Hircus' blade missed Alerio's shoulder by the width of two fingers.

"turns your inner eye blind"

Twisted from the hard swing, Hircus' long and short blades were slung off to one side.

"No calming breather. Furor values neither"

Alerio reached out with his steel and traced the tip up Hircus' side. Cloth and flesh parted from his thigh to midway up his ribs. The swordsman sagged.

"Beauty nor mighty ugly. Only rant and rile"

Alerio dropped to one knee and spun in a circle. Hircus' defensive swings were designed to back off his adversary by threatening the opponent's chest and neck.

"His blessing rises bile"

Alerio was bent at the waist and extended over his own thigh. Hircus' dual swords slashed over his head.

"Takes your guile and style"

Hircus grunted when Alerio's blade entered the side of the mercenary's stomach.

"Furor is a trickster. Insanity embraced"

The blade tilted with a snap of the wrist, ripping intestines from their internal moorings. Alerio's sword finished the turn then cut its way out of the man's belly.

Hircus' last dying act was to curl up around his gut before tumbling to the ground. Alerio glanced around to see if he was needed for the other fights. To his surprise, Civi and Abdicatus stood where he had last seen them. The three other soldiers of fortune also seemed glued in the same location as were the five house guards. They hadn't moved. Everyone was staring at him and the dead sword master.

"Carry on," Alerio ordered.

He fell back on his butt. From the street, he watched the house guards form a battle line. It was a little sloppy but just as effective as if they were young Legionaries. Then, his eyes closed and Centurion Sisera toppled over on his side.

***

315

In the morning, a man-at-arms appeared at the headquarters of the city guard. He explained that arriving staff had reported finding five bodies at a side gate. Additionally, he insisted the household guards had nothing to do with the killings.

Worried about the repercussions of dead men showing up at the gates of noblemen's' villas, the guard officer collected a squad and went to investigate.

"Those are dead men," the guard Sergeant confirmed. "I recognize one of them. His name is Abdicatus. He runs a crew of bodyguards for hire and does other dangerous work."

The guard Centurion's boots crunched on the gravel as he crossed the street.

"It appears the mercenary took on a job his crew couldn't handle," the officer suggested. "Do we know who he's worked for recently?"

The Optio glanced at the Subausterus house guards. Three stood next to the wall gate. One had a fresh bandage around his head.

After thinking for a moment, the Guard Sergeant replied, "I'll ask around, sir. But there's no telling who hired him."

***

Across town, Alerio Sisera waited in the Villa's great room. He had only finished half the mug of vino he'd been given when Belen beckoned him to follow. Down the hallway, the Senator's secretary took the mug before allowing Alerio to enter the office.

"Good morning, Centurion Sisera," Senator Spurius Maximus greeted him. Then he leaned over his desk and inquired. "Do you require medical attention?"

Alerio checked the wet bandage for leaks. The red remained in the center of the cloth and no blood escaped from the edges.

"I'm fine, sir," he replied to the former General. He placed the ornate sword down in front of Maximus and declared. "Mission accomplished. In the future, even the most desperate of men will think long and hard before invading your home."

"A man's villa is his sanctuary," Maximus declared. The General, as he liked to be called, indicated his war trophies on the wall by the door. "I fought many wars and political battles to earn my place. It riles me to think someone believed they could just walk in and threaten my staff."

Alerio glanced at the broken shields, spears, and swords mounted on the wall. All were keepsakes from the Samnite wars. And each item held memories for Spurius Maximus of glory, hard-fought battles, and long drawn out treaty and trade negotiations with tribal leaders.

"I understand, General," Alerio remarked after turning back to the Senator's desk. "A strong message has been delivered. I believe it will get the attention of the proper people."

"A strong message has been delivered," Spurius Maximus seemed to repeat Alerio's words. "You are dismissed Centurion Sisera with gratitude from me and my staff."

***

Two hundred miles by road from the Capital, ten Samnites woke in the deep forest. They weren't hunting or trapping or, even fishing in the mountain streams. Nor

317

were they migrating through on their way to another location. In fact, they traveled light with just their skinning knives for weapons, hatchets, and light packs with supplies.

All were fit young men known in their villages for their ability to run long distances. Other than that, they had nothing in common.

"I'm chilled," one stated. "I think a fire will warm my bones."

Without additional words, they banked sticks and started campfires. Once their salted venison was cooked, they ate. Then, one by one, they placed logs on the fires. Flames climbed to the height of a man, and yet they added more wood. They continued adding fuel until the flames touched the leaves of the highest branches.

With a wall of flames roaring, the ten Samnites jogged away. Behind them a forest fire burned. Then the flames jumped from one tree to another until individual fire storms raged in the forest. By then, the ten tribesmen were far away and high up on the mountain.

Unfortunately, the fire would hurt Tribune Subausterus financially and ruin his chances of landing a contract with the Republic to build warships. Indeed, a strong message had been delivered.

The End

A note from J. Clifton Slater

You have finished the 10th book in this series. Thank you for supporting the Clay Warrior Stories and for making Alerio's adventures a success.

Let's examine a few historical notes from Neptune's Fury. Stifone, Italy is alleged to have been a boatyard for the Roman navy. Unfortunately, there are only a few pictures of the wide deep cut in the granite. Many pictures on the internet of Stifone are mislabeled as the shipyard. The actual work channel is further downstream, overgrown, and sadly not a registered historical site. The boatyard existed and the lack of written records by the efficient and meticulous Roman's, hints that the base was a secret. The story told in Neptune's Fury about the start of the boatyard is purely fictional.

Research into the Agrigento siege presented several opportunities for stories but the events were spread out over a year. And as is the bane of historical adventure writers, other things were happening during that timeframe.

According to Cassius Dio (155 AD – 235 AD) a Roman Historian - the relief army led by Carthage Admiral Hanno Gisco attacked the Legions believing General Hannibal Gisco would sally forth from the besieged city of Agrigento. Together they would engage and defeat the Romans.

Somehow the leadership of the Legions learned of the attacks. Between ambushes from behind, and concentrated assaults, the Legions defeated Hanno Gisco's forces while keeping Hannibal Gisco penned in the city. Hannibal would eventually breakout. In a daring nighttime action, his mercenary troops filled a section of the siege trench with straw bales. They dashed across and escaped.

Looking back at Stifone and Agrigento, I could have named this book Deep Trenches.

If you have you have comments, please contact me. Email: GalacticCouncilRealm@gmail.com

To sig up for my mailing list and to read blogs about ancient Rome, go to me website.

www.JCliftonSlater.com

Alerio wishes you the blessing of Averruncus. May the ancient Roman God who Averts Calamity keep you safe. Until next time, I am wish you good health and happy reading.

I write military adventure both future and ancient.
Books by J. Clifton Slater

Historical Adventure – 'Clay Warrior Stories' series

#1 Clay Legionary	#2 Spilled Blood
#3 Bloody Water	#4 Reluctant Siege
#5 Brutal Diplomacy	#6 Fortune Reigns
#7 Fatal Obligation	#8 Infinite Courage
#9 Deceptive Valor	#10 Neptune's Fury
#11 Unjust Sacrifice	#12 Muted Implications
#13 Death Caller	#14 Rome's Tribune

Fantasy – 'Terror & Talons' series
#1 Hawks of the Sorcerer Queen
#2 Magic and the Rage of Intent

Military Science Fiction – 'Call Sign Warlock' series
#1 Op File Revenge   #2 Op File Treason
#3 Op File Sanction

Military Science Fiction – 'Galactic Council Realm' series
#1 On Station   #2 On Duty
#3 On Guard   #4 On Point

Manufactured by Amazon.ca
Bolton, ON

25947033R00179